WILD KINGDOMS

KATERINA HANSEBOURG was believed lost when her father's merchant caravan was attacked while crossing the vast wilderness beyond the Empire. Now word has come of a savage girl living alongside ogres in the craggy mountains of the east. For Florin d'Artaud and Lorenzo, this sounds like an easy way to earn some more gold. But ahead of them lies a dangerous journey into the unexplored Ogre Kingdoms, and no guarantee that their quest is anything more than a fool's errand.

A WARHAMMER NOVEL

WILD KINGDOMS

Robert Earl

A BLACK LIBRARY PUBLICATION

First published in Great Britain in 2004 by
BL Publishing,
Games Workshop Ltd.,
Willow Road, Nottingham,
NG7 2WS, UK

10 9 8 7 6 5 4 3 2 1

Cover illustration by Jon Hodgson
Map by Nuala Kennedy.

A CIP record for this book is available from the British Library

ISBN 1 84416 149 8

Distributed in the US by Simon & Schuster
1230 Avenue of the Americas, New York, NY 10020, US.

Printed and bound in Great Britain by
Bookmarque, Surrey, UK.

See the Black Library on the Internet at
www.blacklibrary.com

Find out more about Games Workshop
and the world of Warhammer at
www.games-workshop.com

THIS IS A DARK age, a bloody age, an age of daemons and of sorcery. It is an age of battle and death, and of the world's ending. Amidst all of the fire, flame and fury it is a time, too, of mighty heroes, of bold deeds and great courage.

AT THE HEART of the Old World sprawls the Empire, the largest and most powerful of the human realms. Known for its engineers, sorcerers, traders and soldiers, it is a land of great mountains, mighty rivers, dark forests and vast cities. And from his throne in Altdorf reigns the Emperor Karl-Franz, sacred descendent of the founder of these lands, Sigmar, and wielder of his magical warhammer.

BUT THESE ARE far from civilised times. Across the length and breadth of the Old World, from the knightly palaces of Bretonnia to ice-bound Kislev in the far north, come rumblings of war. In the towering World's Edge Mountains, the orc tribes are gathering for another assault. Bandits and renegades harry the wild southern lands of the Border Princes. There are rumours of rat-things, the skaven, emerging from the sewers and swamps across the land. And from the northern wilder-nesses there is the ever-present threat of Chaos, of daemons and beastmen corrupted by the foul powers of the Dark Gods. As the time of battle draws ever near, the Empire needs heroes like never before.

The Ogre Kingdoms

Chaos

Pass to the East

The Mountains of Mourn

The Plain of Zharr

Sky Castles

Firemouth Volcano

Ancient Giant Lands

To The Maw

Howling Wastes

The Silver Road

The Fallen City

Ivory Road

The Sentinels

Skabrand

To Far Cathay

Black Fortress

West to Worlds Edge Mountains Civilized Lands

Gnoblar Coutry

Spice Route

Celestial Dragon Monks

Pig Barter

Haunted Forest

Dragon Isles

Pour Clara
Mon Petite Coeur de Lionne

CHAPTER ONE

IT HAD TAKEN the merchants a fortnight to cross the World's Edge Mountains. A fortnight spent coaxing their oxen through passes of sparkling ice. A fortnight spent trying not to look down into the abysses that yawned open beneath them.

A fortnight spent shivering with nerves and chattering with cold.

It had been worth it, though. Well worth it. None of the men begrudged the coin that they had to pay at the toll gates. After all, since they had entered the dwarfs' realm they hadn't lost a single wagon.

Then they had descended into the plains below and things had become harder. According to their maps the land here was empty, as blank as new snow. In reality, the green wilderness teemed with sharp-toothed danger.

Even the weather had been roused by the merchants' intrusion. It had battered them with howling gales, dancing lightning and raindrops that were as hard as bullets. When that had failed to turn them back, it had baked them with months of white hot sun, bleaching their wagons to the colour of bones in Khemri.

The canvas that covered their wares grew as thin and stained as autumn leaves beneath this onslaught, but the merchants didn't care. They weren't dissuaded. Even as their clothes disintegrated off their malnourished shoulders they had kept their faith. They had had to.

And finally, like all true believers, their faith had been rewarded.

To others, the merchants' promised land may have been a disappointment. It was no realm of milk and honey, no nirvana of maidens and wine. In fact, the fabled town of Pig Barter was little more than a drab smear of hovels spread across an even drabber moorland.

Yet for all that, the sight of it filled the merchants with joy. Grinning through windswept beards they had rolled into the town, eager to begin work in the muddy streets of their paradise.

And what work it had been! They had sold dwarf-forged axe heads, blood-red Estalian wine, pewter cutlery, barrels of smoked herrings and bundles of dried herbs from the plains of Kislev.

Some of them, blessed with the right complexion, had even shaved their heads and sold the blond locks of their hair.

Not that there was anything special about either their hair or their merchandise. There wasn't. Other merchants haggled over such things every day in the thousand markets that lay between Kislev and Araby.

The thing about Pig Barter, though, was that it didn't lie between Kislev and Araby.

It lay between the Old World and Cathay.

And between Cathay and the Old World, the simple alchemies of distance and scarcity, and of supply and demand, grew into a great and wonderful magic. Goods that had been purchased for copper pennies were sold for silver shillings, or even gold crowns.

Or, even better, bales of silk. None knew from what strange eastern animal this stuff came, but it was as strong as steel, as smooth as liquid, and as beautiful as a setting desert sun. Only a poet could hope to truly explain the worth of the stuff.

The merchants didn't think about the worth; they just thought about the price, for the price was certainly worth thinking about. A single bale of silk was worth a house; a cartload; a palace.

By the time the caravan had left, every one of their score of carts was packed with the material. So it was that their owners, and even the squadron of their guards, were filled with a quiet joy.

Despite their ragged clothes and empty bellies, they knew themselves to be rich men.

Perhaps the richest was Franz Hansebourg. He certainly thought that he was. After all, the silks and ivories he'd acquired in Pig Barter were as nothing to his greatest treasure.

Now, as the caravan made its way home, his greatest treasure was sitting amongst his bales of silk as though they were no more than sacks of grain.

Katerina lolled on her father's wares, braiding her hair and listening to the squeaking of the wheels. They provided a constant rhythm, a wooden heartbeat that accelerated or slowed as the wagon train rattled towards the horizon. Sometimes, if she let herself, the girl could hear singing voices in that endless creaking, the words threaded through the noise like sunlight through a veil.

Not today, though.

Today she was too angry.

Her father saw just how angry when he came to check on her. He'd ridden around to the back of the wagon and climbed aboard, the column remaining at full march all the while. Like most of the merchants who took this road, he'd grown used to living his life on the move, stopping only when the weather, or the animals, demanded it.

'Hello princess,' he greeted his daughter as he re-tied the canvas flaps behind him and slipped into the shaded interior. 'I brought you some food.'

'Not hungry,' she scowled, and looked longingly at the slab of honeyed oatcake he'd brought her.

Even in the gloom of the wagon's interior, Franz could see the flush that burned on the white softness of his daughter's cheeks, and the fire that glittered in the green depths of her eyes. The expression matched the wild red flare of her hair perfectly, and the merchant felt a pang of affection.

By the gods, she was a beautiful child. And so sweet. Even when she flew into one of these rages he could barely stop himself from laughing out loud with his delight in her.

Especially when she flew into one of these rages.

'Are you sure you're not hungry?' he asked casually, pretending not to notice her clenched fists as he carefully settled himself down on one of the precious bales. 'We won't be stopping for supper tonight, you know. We have to use the full moon.'

Katerina scowled at the proffered food, then pointedly looked away.

'I don't want to eat. I want to ride with Jarmoosh.'

Franz smiled approvingly. Most children, even those a lot older than his eight year-old daughter, avoided his battle-scarred bodyguard like the monster he was. Not Katerina, though. If anything, the ogre's terrifying appearance just seemed to make him more appealing to her.

But, proud of her or not, Franz shook his head.

'You know that you can't ride with him today. You have to be punished.'

'It's not fair,' she snapped, punching one of the bales. 'Why do I have to be punished? Hermann Boes started it.'

'I know, but…'

'He pulled my hair!'

'Yes, but…'

'So I had to hit him.'

'You shouldn't have used a stone.'

'I was defending myself.'

'I know, sweetie. But you broke his nose.'

'Good. It serves him right.'

Franz sighed, knowing that it was pointless to argue. Apart from anything else, she was right. The Boes boy had pulled her hair. If only she hadn't hit back with a stone. By the gods, how he had wailed.

Despite himself the merchant chuckled at the memory.

'What's so funny?' his daughter asked, eyebrows furrowing with suspicion.

'I was thinking about Hermann. When you hit him he squealed like a piglet with an untwisted tail.'

Despite herself, Katerina smirked.

'In fact,' Franz continued, 'after he made the noise, Jarmoosh almost ate him. Said that he fancied a bit of bacon for breakfast.'

Katerina thought about this, then sniggered.

'Good thing he didn't,' she decided, and tried to reassemble her scowl. 'Herr Boes would have thrown us out of the caravan.'

'Yes,' her father nodded. 'He would.'

'If you hadn't punished me for hitting his son, would Herr Boes have thrown us off the caravan for that?'

'Probably not,' her father shrugged. 'But he might not have welcomed us back next year. It's not so much that you hurt his son, but that you made him…'

'Look silly,' Katerina finished for him. He nodded, surprised that she had grasped the situation so well. Boes hadn't minded his son's broken face. Not at all. But he had minded his humiliation. The boy's embarrassment, unlike his blood, upset his father, and the caravan master wasn't a man to let that sort of injury pass.

'You're exactly right, love. By the gods, I have a clever daughter.'

'Be quiet,' Katerina frowned furiously and pulled away from his hug.

'And a beautiful one.'

'Daddy!' she giggled in protest as he tickled her under the ribs.

'And brave.'

'Yes,' she nodded, flicking her hair back like a lion shaking its mane. Then she sighed and leant into his shoulder. The two of them lapsed into silence. They swayed with the rhythm of the wagon, listened to its wheels squeak and its canvas roof rippling in the wind.

'So, can I ride with Jarmoosh now?'

'Tomorrow,' Franz decided, and felt her pull away. 'Unless you'd care to apologise to the piglet now?'

'Ha!' his daughter replied, and recovered the treat he'd brought her. 'I don't think so.'

'No,' Franz smiled. 'Neither did I.'

Thank you, Shallya, for such a wonderful child, he thought as he climbed back out of the wagon a moment later. Although how you could have made her in the icy belly of a bitch like her mother is beyond me.

With the contented sigh of a man who knows not to examine a miracle too closely, he swung himself back onto his horse and returned to his post on the southern flank.

Above him, the sky slowly darkened as day ripened into dusk. Half an hour later, the first of the moons rose up to cast a frosty glow over the steppe. The oxen, nervous in the darkness, bellowed to each other for reassurance. Their cries were low and mournful, and so deep that the men felt them in their bones rather than heard them with their ears.

The wind picked up, and soon the snapping of canvas was added to the lowing of the animals and the creaking of the wood.

Beneath the cover of these sounds, the first of their pursuers closed in. Flitting amongst the shadows, their light bodies moved as quick and easy as dreams, they counted the wagons and the men, and watched the ripple of fresh meat beneath the oxen's hides.

Their stink sent many a rider's horse skittering nervously this way and that until the watchers, content with what they had seen, slipped silently away. One of the front pickets caught a glimpse of them as he drifted between sleep and wakefulness. In the moonlight the thing scarcely looked real, a hunched, black figure crouched on a bounding grey shape, so he said nothing about it.

It was the last mistake he ever made.

'LETS SEE,' NEFUD said, pulling the tip of a nose that looked sharp enough to cut his fingers. 'He won't dig. Hmmm. Interesting.'

'It's not that I won't dig, chief,' the goblin whined, struggling against his captors as he attempted to grovel even lower. 'It's that I can't. I lost my arm at…'

'Calm down.' Nefud grimaced, the gesture revealing a mouth full of jagged teeth. Moonlight glimmered on them, its white light stained brown. 'Nobody can expect you to dig with only one arm. Perhaps you'd give us a hand in some other way?'

'Yes, oh yes, boss. Anything you say. I'll give you a hand. I'd be happy to give you all a hand. Any of you. We're all brothers, after all. I'll give anyone a hand…'

Nefud's eyes twinkled merrily in the darkness beneath his hood as the captive babbled on. Then, with the perfect timing of a born comedian telling the punchline to a joke, he held up a single claw for silence.

'Excellent,' he said, happily. 'We're in agreement. You won't dig, so you'll give us your hand. Boys, bring a saw.'

For a moment the victim was struck dumb, silent beneath the approving howls of his fellows. A moment later he saw the first of the three saws Nefud's boys had so eagerly produced, and began to shriek.

The ragged mass closed in gleefully around their victim, and Nefud watched them with a wary contempt. He knew that they weren't really an army. They were hardly even a tribe. After all, most of their wars were fought without the need for an outside enemy, and almost all of their casualties were self-inflicted.

For a moment the sound of a saw grating against bone sent the mob into fresh heights of applause, and Nefud smiled. The sound was made all the sweeter by the knowledge that, had things gone a little differently tonight, the victim's increasingly hoarse screams could have been his own.

Tonight he had taken the biggest risk since he became chief. He had known it too. He was no fool, and he knew that if it wasn't for the twin gods of avarice and hatred, most of his kind wouldn't even steal, let alone stoop to the humiliation of toil. By asking them to dig, to strain and sweat like humans or animals, Nefud had effectively spat in their faces.

Of course, he had prepared by excusing the three most vicious mobs from any threat of work. In return they had promised to help him quell the inevitable mutiny that would follow his revolting orders.

Even so, the chief hadn't been sure they wouldn't use the occasion to get rid of him. Not until they'd attacked the first of the mutineers. It had been a short, vicious fight, his allies' assault on their grumbling brethren coming as a complete surprise.

Nefud knew that such enthusiasm had to be rewarded, and wracked his brains as he prowled away from the victorious mobs to supervise the night's labours.

The mightiest of these was the central pit, a huge ditch that was deep enough to swallow one of the humans' great wagons whole. Much to the disgust of the drafted diggers, it had to be hewn from the hard-packed earth of the merchants' road. Their snarled curses cut through the pale moonlight as sharply as their picks, punctuated by the occasional explosion of frustrated violence.

Above them, looking down with gloating eyes, one of Nefud's chosen mobs encouraged them to fresh efforts.

'Are they working hard enough?' Nefud asked, creeping up behind one of the overseers before barking out the question. Much to his satisfaction the goblin jumped.

'Yes, chief,' he stuttered, and took a step backwards.

Nefud watched him, nose wrinkling as he savoured the smell of his fear. It grew riper by the minute and the unhappy creature shrivelled beneath his chief's gaze like a punctured balloon.

'Why are you looking at me?' Nefud asked him at length, aware that the goblin's fellows were watching the unfolding scene expectantly.

'Sorry, chief,' he whimpered, and cast his eyes down.

'Why aren't you looking at them?' Nefud jabbed a thumb towards the ditch.

'Sorry, chie–'

'Get down there and start digging,' Nefud decided. It would have been more satisfying to take one of the fool's eyes, but he resisted the temptation. Dawn was fast approaching, and the pit was only half dug.

He waited until the guard had scrambled down into the pit and started digging before stalking away to inspect the other traps he'd ordered. He watched bundles of scrap being tied together and hidden beneath the brush that flanked the road; the positions of the rusty spikes were marked by the forms of their jealous owners. Amongst them other goblins worked, the poorest and the weakest. To each of these Nefud had assigned the task of digging a single rabbit hole, tiny pits narrow enough to lie invisible beneath a tuft of grass, but deep enough to snap a horse's leg.

The chief amused himself by imagining the sound that a horse's splintering bone would make should it run into one of these holes. Then he returned to where his allies had rounded up a fresh batch of mutineers.

The battered triangles of their heads were bowed low, and their green skins were black with blood in the moonlight. Lolling around them their captors sneered and squabbled, impatiently waiting for the chief to think of a suitably amusing punishment for these shirkers.

'Well, well, well,' Nefud said, stooping down to retrieve something from the shadows. 'It seems that even more of you don't want to work. Shame on you.'

He waved the severed hand towards them and tugged on one of the tendons, making the dead index finger rise and point. The darkness erupted with shrieks of laughter at this display of wit.

The captives, chastened by the gory glimpse of their futures, took the terrible risk of disagreeing with their master.

'We want to dig, chief, don't you worry about that…'

'It was all a misunderstanding…'

'I was just looking for a spade…'

Nefud shrugged, then used the severed hand to scratch his head. More laughter greeted the gesture.

'Are you sure you want to dig, then?'

The captives chorused their agreement enthusiastically.

'Excellent. In that case, you will pick a spot on the edge of the road, and bury each other. Not too deep that you can't jump out into the ambush, but not too shallow, either. I'm sure our brothers here will see to that.'

An approving roar went up from the captors and, giggling with the fun of it all, they rushed forward and dragged their victims off to bury them alive.

Nefud watched them, then went back to stare critically at the pit that cut across the road. He gazed into the blackness of its depths like a fortune teller into a teacup. The diggers were almost invisible now. Occasionally the moonlight would illuminate their grubby flesh as buckets of earth were passed up, but for the most part only the grunts, complaints, and the smell of freshly turned earth gave any indication of the efforts that were being made in the darkness below.

The chief was still gazing into the pit when the first of the wolf riders returned, the goblins scattering before the beast's bared teeth.

'Do they still come?' the chief asked as the scout dismounted and abased himself.

'Yes, boss,' the messenger whined. 'A great caravan, with the wealth of an entire city for our delight.'

'Our delight?'

'Yes… no. That is, for *your* delight, oh mightiest of leaders.'

For a moment Nefud enjoyed the sight of the scout wriggling.

'Shall we get him, chief?' one of his boys asked enthusiastically.

'You can if you can overcome his wolf,' Nefud said, then turned on his heel and left. Behind him a moment's uncertainty gave way to a chorus of jeers as the unlucky enthusiast was shoved towards the animal by his erstwhile comrades.

The wolf licked its lips and bared its teeth. In the shadows and moonlight the expression might almost have been a smile.

Nefud listened to the subsequent screaming with the bland satisfaction of a craftsman who has just finished some minor task. Then he noticed the first pink rind of dawn and frowned.

They were running out of time.

Grinding his splintered teeth with a savage determination, the chief stalked back into the horde, his crooked body shaking with barely contained malevolence. The yellows of his eyes gleamed as he prowled amongst his goblins, and he rubbed his bony hands together as he thought of fresh ways in which to encourage them.

THE NEXT MORNING found Franz riding alongside the walking ogre. The merchant had a threadbare grey blanket wrapped around his thin shoulders, a beggar's cape that snapped and billowed in the gusting wind. Despite the wool his teeth rattled as the frozen air battered him. He drew the blanket closer, twisting it as tightly about his shivering body as an old woman with a shawl.

Jarmoosh had a baggy pair of trousers, stiff with grime, and a huge leather belt.

Apart from that he was as naked as a new-born babe against the chill. Even his head had been shorn of hair, the better to display the crude tattoos that had been chiselled into his scalp.

It made Franz cold just to look at him. So instead, blinking away prisms of tears, he peered beyond his bodyguard and into grassy plains beyond.

It stretched away on all sides, an endless expanse of tufted grass and withered gorse. Occasional clumps of stunted trees, as black and twisted as covens of witches, made a stand against the desolation, their backs turned against the constant nagging of the wind. In other places the vegetation disappeared altogether, drowned by pools of sour, orange water.

And that was all there was in this bitter world. Only in the west, where the saw-toothed silhouettes of the World's Edge Mountains clawed their way towards the sky, was there any variation. Although those black spires were hardly any more cheerful than the rest of this wild kingdom.

Franz was glad to see them anyway. They were the last barrier, the gate beyond which lay the rewards for a year of hardship and danger. He grinned as he thought about what those rewards would entail, and cast his eyes upwards. A great herd of black clouds glowered back down at him, their bellies heavy with the weight of thunder yet unborn.

Another man might have found their brooding expanse oppressive, but not Franz Hansebourg. His attention had already been snatched by a hawk that hovered high overhead, its pale feathers ghostlike against the black thunderheads.

'It sees very well,' Jarmoosh rumbled, and Franz turned to him, a little surprised.

He was quietly amazed by the ogre. When Franz had hired Jarmoosh all those months back, the ogre could barely string a sentence together. Now he could hold a converstion with relative ease, when the mood took him, that was. The ogre's ability to adapt to its environment was astounding.

'The hawk, yes,' Franz replied eagerly, keen to encourage his bodyguard into the novelty of conversation. 'I suppose that it has to.'

Jarmoosh grunted, and the stubbled boulder of his shaved scalp furrowed in painful thought.

'Some in my tribe,' he eventually said, 'use hawks to see for them. In these places, you need to see from above.'

Franz nodded slowly and pursed his lips.

'I can see how that would help,' he allowed, diplomatically. 'But at least on these plains we can see whatever might be approaching us from miles away.'

'No.' Jarmoosh shook the great boulder of his head. 'You can't. Even now there are greenskins all around us. But they know how to hide. To wait.'

Franz stood up in his saddle and looked towards the horizon, half expecting to see the orcs that Jarmoosh had promised him. But there was nothing except wind-blasted scrub, none of it more than knee high.

'I don't see any greenskins,' he said, sounding apologetic.

'You don't see them,' the ogre agreed. 'They know how to hide. But they will attack soon. I can smell them.'

Once more Franz searched the surrounding ground and felt a bead of cold sweat tickling its way down his spine. All of a sudden he decided that he preferred the version of his bodyguard that contented itself with the occasional grunt.

'Oh well,' he chuckled uneasily. 'If they attack, just make sure Katerina doesn't get to 'em. I'd hate to see what she'd do if she thought they were trying to steal her sheet of Cathay cotton.'

The ogre turned to stare at his master, his eyes shadowy pits beneath the overhang of his heavy brow. Franz stared back, suddenly uneasy.

He had always thought, along with all the other merchants, that ogres were barely sentient, their unmoving features a sign of empty-headed stupidity. But now, as he gazed into eyes that were as deep and still as subterranean wells, he began to suspect that it was not stupidity that kept his bodyguard's face so blank.

He began to suspect that it was the watchful, impassive calm of complete and absolute confidence.

'I understand,' the ogre rumbled, his voice a dull baritone.

'Understand…?' Franz, who was turning over this new insight to see if it might be useful, vaguely repeated the word.

But then question and theory were both forgotten as the sound of a huge crash sent his horsing rearing up.

'Ulric's teeth, what was that?' he cried, and peered up ahead to where the sudden crash of splintering wood had given way to the screaming of horses and the bellows of stricken oxen.

'The ambush,' Jarmoosh rumbled, his expression unchanging, 'has been sprung.'

'Ambush?' replied Franz as he attempted to calm his horse.

'Don't worry,' the ogre said, dragging his massive, crudely forged weapon from behind his back. 'I will obey your command.'

And with that he turned to face the emptiness of the moorland to his side.

Except, Franz realised with a sudden jolt of fear, it was no longer empty. Far from it. A seething mass of bodies had sprung up as mysteriously as mushrooms from a freshly ploughed field. They even looked a little like mushrooms: their stunted, misshapen bodies small and squat beneath tall black caps.

Franz watched them from behind the granite bulk of Jarmoosh's shoulder, his mouth open in surprise as he tried to work out what they were.

For a moment he took them to be beggar children, but only for a moment. Whatever these things were, they were no youngsters. Their gnarled skins and crooked teeth spoke of years longer than his own, and the dirty yellow slashes of their eyes flickered with ancient malevolence. They twisted the blunt daggers of their noses into contemptuous sneers as they rushed forward, brave in their vast numbers.

Franz closed his mouth with a snap and drew his sword. Then he shouted a warning to the other merchants, just as they began shouting a warning to him.

Had they had time they would have pulled their carts around and lashed them together into the crude fort of a laager. But the ambush had been sprung so suddenly that there was no chance to do that. The first of their attackers had already scrambled into the road, spitting soil out of its mouth and shrieking a terrified war-cry as it waited for its fellows to catch up.

With a stab of fear Franz remembered his daughter. The thought of these inhuman raiders touching her squeezed his stomach into a tight fist of nausea, and a sudden slick of sweat sheened his skin.

Jarmoosh wasted no time on such anxieties. Instead he lowered his head and bellowed with unmistakable joy, the bone-trembling sound deeper than a bull's roar. The ragged tide of the attackers hesitated before him, brought short by the sound, but before they could run the ogre hurled himself towards them.

With careless ease he flicked the razored iron of his guillotine blade to one side, turning his hip as he thundered forwards like a farmer hefting a scythe.

Along the entire length of the caravan a hundred other men prepared to meet the ambush, their fear giving way to desperate courage. That, combined with their strength, might have been enough to save them from the swarming rabble of the goblins' assault.

Might have been.

Unfortunately, they were never to know. As the first of the greenskins, driven wild with terror and adrenaline, slashed at the defenders, the caravan boss's bugle rang out, calling the two tone note that gave the order to laager up the wagons.

'What's that idiot doing?' Franz roared, outraged at his leader's stupidity. There was no time to form a circle now. No time to…

Jarmoosh bellowed again as he reached the cowering enemy. With a great hiss of sliced air he swung his blade in a blurred arc. The hungry edge chopped through half a dozen of the enemy as easily as a cleaver through a rack of ribs, leaving a string of ruined bodies in its wake.

The creatures screamed or howled, or just bled. Incredibly, Jarmoosh laughed, the thunderous boom of his humour drowning the cries of the wounded. Then he lunged forward again.

But Franz had no more time to watch. The first of the enemy had already closed in behind the rippling muscles of the ogre's back and, seeing in the merchant softer meat, they rushed towards him.

Franz had never been much of a swordsman. Here, though, that didn't matter. The creatures that closed in around him had no particular skill either.

Nor did they have any armour.

Franz hit the first with a graceless lunge, his sword chopping down through cloth, flesh and bone. The merchant prised his blade free from the shrieking creature in time to wield it against the next. This one ducked, but too late. There was a thud of steel into bone, and it fell back with its head cleaved in two.

'Ha!' Franz cried, surprised at how effective he'd been. Then another trio of the creatures rushed him, and his satisfaction was forgotten as he lunged towards them.

At first it seemed that his luck would continue. The first two he killed with a single stroke, his blade slicing into their flesh easily. But even as their blood pulsed into the mud a flash of white-hot agony exploded in his thigh.

With a cry of agony he recoiled from the pain. The movement helped his attacker to pull its blade from his flesh, and it staggered backwards, the bloodied weapon held in its hands.

His cry of agony became one of rage and Franz hacked at the creature, cutting its spindly arm off at the shoulder. This time he felt no joy in the victory, though. Instead, grimacing with pain, he counted a dozen more raiders, the greenskins springing up to take the place of their fallen comrades. They slunk around him with the hungry caution of vultures, and he eyed them warily.

Franz, seized with a sudden fear for his daughter, snatched a glance back towards his wagon. He pursed his lips and thought about galloping back to take her on his horse. No matter how valuable his cargo, it might be better to leave it and run.

But even as he reached that decision it was too late.

Whilst he had been distracted, a pair of the enemy, as quick as arrows, had ducked beneath his sword arm to sever his horse's tendons. The mare let out a sudden, piercing scream as they did so, her body collapsing into a tangle of spasming limbs.

Franz barely managed to kick his feet free of the stirrups as she fell. As it was he just managed to throw himself clear of her thrashing hooves. Somersaulting over her head he hit the ground with a tooth-rattling impact. He felt something snap within his chest and the taste of copper filled his mouth, but by now he was beyond worrying about such details. Instead, numbed with the adrenaline rush of combat, the merchant spat out a tooth and looked back towards Katerina's wagon.

As he watched one of the raiders, as quick as a cockroach, slipped through the flap.

'Jarmoosh!' Franz screamed, the cry tearing itself from his throat with a sudden terror. Emboldened by the fear they heard in his voice, his enemies surged towards him, their rusty blades dull in the grey light.

Some of their blows glanced off the merchant's outfit.

Others struck home.

'Jarmoosh!' Franz repeated, ignoring the wash of warm blood that had suddenly slicked his sword hilt. It turned loosely within his grip as he stumbled to his feet, clumsily slashing about with wild, ill-timed blows that cut through nothing but air.

Behind him his tormentors closed in, gleefully stabbing at their victim before jumping back out of the way.

The merchant fell to his knees and watched more of the creatures swarming towards his daughter's sanctuary. His features twisted into a gargoyle's mask of pain, an agony that had nothing to do with the flurry of rusted steel that bit into his flesh.

Franz tried to lift his sword for another blow, but the hilt slipped from his nerveless fingers. A sudden sheet of blood blinded him in one eye, he reached forward, sobbing as more goblins swarmed towards his caravan.

'Shallya,' he whispered, the words lost amongst the shrill giggles of his killers and the wet, meaty impacts of their blows. 'Shallya save her.'

But Shallya didn't save her.

Jarmoosh did.

He appeared seconds before his master died. Sparing the man who'd hired him no more than a glance, the ogre charged towards the wagon, bellowing out a terrible war-cry as he ran.

The enemy fled before him like hens before a fox. Jarmoosh's massive blade lashed out at the stragglers, cutting them down or throwing them high up into the air in a bloody confetti.

When he reached the wagon he tore the canvas from its wooden ribs and reached inside. Franz watched as he threw the priceless bales of silk to the ground and plucked Katerina out of the wreckage.

Her scant figure dangled like a rabbit in a conjuror's grip, and she was screaming hysterically. She was wide-eyed, shaking, terrified. She was also sobbing, a heartbreaking keening that hurt her father more than the blades that bit into his flesh.

But she was alive.

And that, Franz decided, was all that really mattered.

Jarmoosh paused only long enough to swing the girl onto the muscled slab of his shoulder, and then he was off, cutting through another scrum of raiders like a lifeboat through the surf.

'Thank you,' Franz hissed, the words bubbling up in froth of bloody foam. Behind him an axe rose and fell, the blow bringing a squeal of delight from the scavengers that closed in on him.

KATERINA HAD BEEN half asleep when the attack had begun. Lolling comfortably amongst the baled cloth she had been snug beneath her furs, eyes half-closed as she dreamed of the puppy she was going to choose when they got home.

It was going to be a big one, she knew that much. Not one of those nasty little flea-bait things that her mother and her friends carried around, but a real dog. A wire-haired boar mastiff, maybe. Or an orc-hound. One with golden eyes and muscles as solid as bone.

Of course, daddy didn't know that he was going to buy her a puppy yet, but that was alright. She'd let him know in good time. Perhaps when they were over the mountains, and nearing the first market town.

She smiled with an expression of smug contentment, squirmed a little more snugly into her furs, and wiggled her toes.

Now, what would she call it?

Ah, of course. She'd call it Jarmoosh. That is, if he wouldn't take it amiss.

She didn't think that he would. One of the things she loved about him and his kind was how sensible they were. If she loved the dog, she knew that he would be happy if she gave it his name.

Almost asleep now, Katerina was turning over this thought when the first wagon in the caravan crashed into the pit. At first she scowled at the noise that followed, and silently cursed the wagoneer for disturbing her peace. Then the first cries of alarm rang out and her irritation became curiosity.

Slipping on her boots and wrapping her sleeping furs tight around her shoulders she snaked her way down to the peephole she had cut in the canvas of the canopy.

At first she couldn't see what all the fuss was about. From this angle she couldn't see much more than the hips of the riders that waited outside, or the occasional blasted tree trunk against the grey horizon.

Then she heard the unmistakable bellow of Jarmoosh. The sound reverberated through the timbers of the wagon and sent a deep thrill racing through her bones. Reaching forward, no longer cautious in her vandalism, she tore a great rent in the material, the damage letting in a draught of freezing air that brought tears to her eyes.

She blinked them away in time to see the first wave of the stunted raiders sweeping onto the road. She saw Jarmoosh bounding forward into the midst of them, his muscles rolling like barrels as he wielded the blade of his cleaver through the front rank. Then she saw daddy, his horse skittish and wide-eyed with fear, and even as she watched the first of the assailants reached him.

Katerina ground her teeth together as she watched the monsters that dared to attack her father. Forgetting the cold she let the fur slip off her shoulders. Two high red spots of rage blossomed on the pale ivory of her cheeks as she watched the bloodshed.

She knew what she should be doing now. Daddy had told her often enough. In the event of an attack she was to burrow beneath the bales until someone called her. It was a one-sided game of hide and seek that Franz had played with her often enough, knowing the value of making a game out of the drill.

Now that they were being attacked, though, Katerina found that she didn't want to hide. Her teeth were chattering with rage, not fear. Nor was there any reason for the racing of her heart but for anger. Anger and exhilaration.

Then she saw daddy's horse collapse beneath him, and the fear came.

With a startled scream she jerked away from the viewing slit, sick with sudden panic. After a brief struggle she regained her composure and forced herself to look back out into the turmoil beyond.

But before she could make sense of the confused scrum that now rolled across her father's dying horse there was a sudden hiss of indrawn breath behind her, and a rustle of cloth as the assassin struck.

Katerina turned in time to see the dagger plunging down towards her. She flipped out of its way with the instant, thoughtless grace of a dropped cat, and twisted back to seize her assailant's wrists.

The creature snarled with frustration as it tried to free its dagger from the bale that held it, snarled again when the child snatched at its arm. It tried to shrug her off as it struggled to recover its blade. Then her small white teeth closed on its wrist and it screamed.

Lurching back, the greenskin spun around in a complete circle. The manoeuvre whiplashed the girl's body through the air in a wide, clumsy circle that ended with a thump as she hit a bale.

But despite the taste of rancid flesh that filled her mouth, Katerina just bit down harder. The goblin squealed in pain and surprise, and tried to pull her off by her nose.

Katerina felt something crunch as he twisted it, the break followed by a sudden rush of blood. The shock of pain was enough to unclench her teeth and she fell backwards, her hand closing around the hilt of the buried dagger.

The hilt twisted in her hand as she scrabbled away. Then, with a hiss of ruined silk, the knife came free.

Katerina and the greenskin realised what had happened at exactly the same moment. Its bloodshot yellow eyes met the flaring green of the girl's, but it took the creature a split second too long to realise what Katerina had grasped immediately.

They were still predator and prey.

But she was no longer the prey.

The girl leapt forward with a piercing scream, and stabbed downwards with the dagger. Her attack was a single, fluid motion, the blade zipping though the air like a shard of lightning.

Before her prey could blink, the blade, razor-sharp despite the rust that marred the flats, sliced through the wiry tendons of its neck.

Again Katerina twisted the dagger, and this time she was rewarded with an explosive spray of blood, a victory banner of gore that painted itself across the canvas of the wagon.

'Ha!' she cried triumphantly, and blinked a misting of blood out of her eyes, the better to watch it die. 'That was fun!'

There was the tear of canvas and she turned to see two more of the misshapen things struggling into the wagon.

An angelic smile spread across Katerina's face. Still smiling, she darted forwards and thrust the knife with all her might into the face of the nearest creature.

There was a thunk as steel met bone and the creature fell backwards, eyes crossing over the blade that had been buried between them. Its fellow took one glance at it then rolled back out of the wagon.

Katerina threw her head back and laughed.

This *was* fun!

Then, the thought hitting her like a cosh: she remembered daddy.

The joy bled from her face and she scrambled back to the tear in the canvas, desperate to see what had become of him.

'He's alright,' she told herself with the savage determination of a girl who was used to the world bending itself to her will. 'He's alright.'

Clinging to the illusion, she scanned the bloodied world outside for any sign of him. At first there was none: just a mass of raiders that swarmed around his fallen horse, hacking slices of meat from its still living body or squabbling over bits of tackle. But then the mob parted, rushing clear as Franz Hansebourg lashed blindly forward.

Katerina saw her father for a split second before his killers closed back in. It was a split second that she would see for years.

Her wide eyes soaked up every terrible detail of her father's murder. The agony on his beloved face beneath sheeting blood.

The collapse of his strong body beneath a thousand vicious wounds.

His hand outstretched towards her as if to offer some final gift.

These and a hundred other details were scorched into her by the branding iron of memory. It was all the inheritance that he was able to leave.

The pain of it was too much. By the time Jarmoosh had reached her she was crippled by a grief that was close to madness. When he swung her up onto the meaty perch of his shoulders she hardly noticed, her skinny body shaking as she screamed up an agony that seemed close to tearing her apart.

Beneath her, his silence sundered by a sudden, bone-jarring roar, Jarmoosh ploughed through the raiders and out into the wilderness beyond. Few of the enemy dared to oppose his escape. Those that did he clove in two, or bludgeoned, or crushed beneath the iron heels of his boots, leaving them as carrion to be picked clean by their brothers.

DUSK FOUND THE two survivors miles away from the doomed caravan. The silhouettes of its wagons stood tiny and motionless against the dying light of the far horizon, as lifeless as the picked bones of a corpse.

The ogre set the child down as the night drew a merciful veil over the distant scene, and began to make a fire. Katerina sat slumped forward. She stared hollow-eyed into the flickering depths of its burning heart, unseeing as the first of the pursuing wolf riders closed in around her and her guardian.

CHAPTER TWO

IT WAS NOT every night that a completely new play opened in Bordeleaux. Of course there was a constant rush of theatres opening and closing, of actors hired and fired, of old plays reworked, or recast, or rewritten.

But a genuinely new play… well, that was a special occasion. Special enough to fill every tier of the great Theatre de Gisoreux with the glittering ranks of Bordeleaux's elite. Merchants and noblemen, governors and princes, pirates and assassins and landlords; the great and the good sat squeezed into their elegantly carved boxes as comfortably as perfumed hogs in gilded sties.

Beneath the scintillating lights of the amphitheatre's chandeliers they were a spectacular sight. Even the merchants had exchanged the solid black broadcloth of their counting houses to preen in a peacock array of bright velvets and shimmering silks.

But compared to their womenfolk, willing victims of the city's dressmakers, they looked positively drab. These martyrs to fashion suffered beneath costumes that made them look like the denizens of some fevered dream. Their hats alone were bigger than the small dogs which snapped and quarrelled amongst their stockinged legs, and their dresses looked as heavy as any squire's armour.

Struggling beneath this weight, the city's goodwives sweated like field hands, the moisture that sheened their plump faces as bright as their jewellery.

Not that all the women were dressed so expensively. Far from it. Some of the merchants, much to the jealousy of their rivals, had left their upholstered and upstanding wives at home. Instead they'd invited leaner girls in lighter clothing. They were as beautifully sculpted and as dia-mond hard as the chandeliers which blazed overhead, these girls, and they were young, these girls.

But despite their tender years, a wary cunning glimmered behind their carefree smiles and breezy ways. Nevertheless, if there had been an innocent amongst the mob that thronged the theatre, he might have taken them for the daughters of the men to whom they clung. Maybe even the granddaughters.

But not even the most unworldly could have made that mistake about the inhabitants of the great central box. A wide gondola of velvet cushions and carved cherubim, it loomed over the groundlings below, the mismatched pair who had hired it lolling about between girls whose affec-tions were anything but daughterly.

And why should they be? The men who'd hired them were Florin d'Artaud, the most celebrated adventurer of the month, and his manservant Lorenzo. It was on contracts like these that a courtesan's reputation was built, and the girls were as desperate to be seen in this rare opulence as the most socially ambitious merchant's wife.

'Sssssssh,' Florin told them, pushing one from his lap and leaning forward as darkness descended. 'Let's watch the play.'

The girls complied with the easy alacrity that was the hallmark of their trade. Florin's companion, however, proved less amenable.

'Theatres,' Lorenzo spat, in defiance of the relative hush that had fallen over the crowd. 'What a waste of money.'

'Sssssssssh,' his companion hissed again as the curtain lifted on the first scene. 'Look, there's me!'

And so it was. At least, it could have been. The figure that strutted across the stage below was certainly the right shape. He was lean and fit, and he sported a fashionable topknot. His clothes were right, too, as expensive and stylishly cut as the original's own.

He even swaggered in the right way.

'That pansy!' Lorenzo jeered, loud enough to draw several interested glances from neighbouring boxes. 'He's nothing like you.'

But Florin was no longer paying attention to either his companion or to the girls. Instead he was hunched forward, brows furrowed as he watched the stage as intently as an owl watching a wheat field.

'That's not right, for a start,' Lorenzo scoffed a moment later as the stage version of Florin fought a long and complicated duel over the honour of a damsel. 'It was gold we had to fight for. And look, they're using swords. We always used boot knives...'

This time Florin did turn to regard his companion. His face was hard despite the soft light. Lorenzo realised that it was time to stop talking.

He shrugged regretfully, then lay back into the unfashionably plump arms of his escort. Seizing her opportunity she fed him first one olive, then another. The third she let slip from between her fingers, timing the lapse so that the oily preserve fell between her fat, white breasts and slid slowly down between them.

Lorenzo, always the gentleman, turned to follow it down with his tongue. The evening might not be such a bore after all, he decided, a leer splitting the broken angles of his battered face.

Florin remained oblivious to his accomplice's efforts, his mind on higher things. Already his heroic alter ego had slain the wicked baron, and was preparing to go into Lustrian exile with a band of devoted followers. As he watched them pledge him their fealty, Florin could almost convince himself that this was the way it had happened.

Almost, but not quite.

Try as he might, he couldn't quite be such a fool.

The first act ended with a rousing chorus sung by stage sailors and soldiers. The score of greasepainted desperados sang the praises of their glorious new leader, who strutted amongst them as confidently as a lion amongst a pack of dogs.

Then the curtain fell, the chandeliers were lowered, and Florin found himself once more in the world of reality.

'Well, what do you think?' he asked delightedly, turning to Lorenzo. Then he looked hastily away. 'For Shallya's sake, do you have to do that here?'

'No, boss,' Lorenzo shrugged. 'But you know how it is...'

—Disentangling himself from his companion the older man glanced hopefully towards the stage. 'Has it finished already?'

'Only the first part,' Florin said. Then he turned to his own escort, who still remained mostly clothed. 'Did you like it?'

'I think,' she breathed, 'that it is wonderful. You are so brave. And so strong.'

Florin looked into her dark eyes, wide with admiration. His back straightened. His chest swelled.

'Oh, bravery doesn't come into it. You see, when a man is in tune with his destiny, he doesn't think of the terrible dangers, or the hardships involved.'

'But so few men are courageous enough to accept a destiny as great as yours,' her voice lisped into his ear, and she began to gently massage the nape of his neck with one hand whilst stroking his belly with the other. 'Or powerful enough.'

'Well, yes,' Florin allowed, swallowing. 'That's quite a good point.'

'That's why everybody respects you,' she continued, her breath warm against his neck. 'And why...'

Her voice faded to a whisper, and she was brushing her lips across her hero's when a sudden, insistent knocking began on their door.

Florin licked his lips and thought about ignoring it. Lorenzo, however, wasn't about to miss the opportunity of using his new 'master's' voice. He'd been practising it ever since their celebrated return from Lustria.

'Come!' he bellowed, with the cheerful rudeness of a true aristocrat.

Florin cursed inwardly. Then he drew away from his companion and turned to examine the squat figure that stomped in.

Its round body was clad in plain black clothes, its feet were shod in sensible black boots, and its pinched, florid face was creased into an expression of almost comical disapproval.

'Oh no,' Florin groaned upon seeing his guest. 'Not you again.'

A scowl creased the newcomer's mottled features into an even more bitter expression, and he squeezed his hat between his sweating fingers as though it were Florin's neck. Then, with an obvious effort, he dragged his features into the frightened snarl that served him as a smile.

'Master d'Artaud.' He bowed, jowls wobbling with the effort. 'I just came to congratulate you on your new celebrity.'

'Oh really?' Florin smiled. 'Well, thank you, Master Volavant. In fact, I'm glad you're here. I was just about to come and see you about selling the Lizard's Head.'

'Really?' The fat man said, his smile becoming almost genuine.

'No,' Florin said with a wink.

Lorenzo cackled appreciatively.

'As I've told you on every other occasion you've asked, the Lizard's Head is not for sale. It's my tavern, it's the best in town, and it's making far too much money.'

Volavant swivelled his eyes upwards, as if in silent appeal to the gods of unfair competition. Then he bullied his unwilling features back into a grimace, and attempted to sound reasonable.

'Perhaps you're right,' he allowed. 'But you should sell it to a man like me who can really make it profitable. For instance, you should use clay pots, not pewter ones. Of course they break, but just take that from the girls' wages. And you don't know how much to charge for wine. Or for ale. Or even for vodka.'

'On the contrary,' Florin replied. 'I know exactly what to charge. That's why I have so many customers.'

'Yes,' Volavant snarled, his forced good humour snapping. '*My* customers. My guild's customers. The honest businessmen who own every other tavern in the old quarter. You're driving all of our prices down. Do you want to ruin us? I ask you, one copper for a flagon of ale. It's criminal! If you won't sell, I insist that you at least charge a fair price.'

'Insist away,' shrugged Florin, whose attention was already wandering away to the small circular motions his escort's hand had started making on the small of his back. 'But I'll thank you to do it outside. I'm a little busy at the moment, as you can see.'

Florin nodded towards his companion, who smiled at his competitor.

'Don't worry, Poppi,' she told him, licking her lips as greedily as if they were coated in cream. 'I'll make you feel better this Wednesday.'

Impossibly, Volavant's face grew even redder. His cheeks darkened to an unhealthy purple. His eyes bulged. Rage and embarrassment warred upon his face, and for a moment he seemed on the verge of fainting.

It was only when the seams of his hat started to split that he pulled himself together. Suddenly remembering to breathe he straightened his back and his face.

'You'll sell, d'Artaud. You'll sell, or you'll suffer the consequences. And you, strumpet, this Wednesday's appointment is cancelled. So is every Wednesday's. I think that I prefer fresher meat.'

'How dare you insult my lady, sir!' Florin roared, spring-ing to his feet and snatching his sword belt from the back of his couch. 'I demand satisfaction!'

But the merchant had already fled. Popping through the door as neatly as a cork from a bottle he bolted down the passageway, thundering away from the famed swordsman, Florin d'Artaud.

'Come back!' the supposed duellist called after him, his eyes flashing. Then he kicked the door shut and turned back to his companions, a mischievous grin on his face.

'Nice one, boss,' Lorenzo told him. The girls just giggled.

'Ladies and gentleman, I thank you,' Florin boomed in a mock stage accent, and took a deep bow.

That was when the applause started.

It came from the boxes on either side of them, the occu-pants of whom had been eager voyeurs of Volavant's humiliation. Then it spread as others in the theatre joined in, not knowing quite why they were showing apprecia-tion, but guessing that they were supposed to.

Florin swaggered up to the edge of his box and took another mocking bow. The applause grew louder, and a wide, white grin split his face.

'You're a real hero, boss,' Lorenzo muttered sarcastically.

'Yes,' Florin said, without glancing back. 'I know!'

Lorenzo watched him as he took a swig of wine and felt suddenly uneasy. Perhaps it was because of all this fame, all this celebrity. Florin lapped it up like a pup laps up spilt milk, but it made Lorenzo feel uncomfortable. There was something not quite right about all of this exposure; some-times he felt that the carriage they now rode in was just one big archer's target, and their fine clothes markers in a drag hunt.

Well, to the hells with it, he thought, looking back at his companion. Let's just make the most of it while we can.

A moment later Florin, not wanting to outstay his applause, sat back down beside him.

'They'll be talking about this all week,' he decided, hap-pily.

And they were. But Volavant's humiliation was to be only the beginning of the story that would soon be spreading like a fire across the town.

Its consequences were to provide the real meat.

THREE HOURS LATER the play came to its spectacular climax. A horde of costumed monstrosities, their outfits a bizarre confusion of man, house lizard and snake, were routed by the stage Florin and his followers.

Their victory was lit by cannonades of fireworks, the smoke setting the first rows of the audience coughing like plague victims, and oiled with buckets of raspberry flavoured blood. The spectators cheered and stomped as the lizard king was pulled down, and hurled such thunderous applause at the final curtain that Florin himself was moved to go down and take a bow with the actors. As he waved his courtesan twined herself around him in the glow of the footlights with a delighted smile on her face, and the crowd went wild.

From the cooler environs of the box Lorenzo watched his master as he strutted about on the stage. When the curtain fell again he sighed and, his own re-dressed companion in tow, stomped down through the rat-run of connecting passages to the area backstage.

'Ah, there you are, Lorenzo,' Florin beamed when he saw the older man. 'I was just telling Joules here how superbly realistic his portrayal was.'

The director beamed so happily that a tear glinted in his eye. Lorenzo just grunted.

'If you say so, boss,' he griped. 'Funny, I seem to remember a lot more mosquitoes. And a lot more leeches. And even more running away. Still, I'm an old man. Perhaps my memory's going. I certainly can't recall any of those amazons, for instance. Or any of your speech...'

'Yes, thank you, Lorenzo.' Florin glared at him, then threw a brotherly arm around Joules and turned him away. 'Now, how about introducing me to my alter ego?'

'Of course,' the director gushed. 'Of course. He'd be honoured!'

'Yes,' Florin agreed. 'I suppose he would.'

Lorenzo watched his master disappear into the half costumed and half naked mob that thronged around him, and
grimaced.

'We'll be here all night,' he muttered. But although he had
been speaking to himself his companion answered anyway.

'If that's the case,' she told him, wrapping her arms
around him and crushing her voluptuous body against his
bony frame, 'let me help you pass the time. I happen to
know that there's a dressing room just around the corner.'

'You do?' Lorenzo asked, cheering up despite himself.

'Oh yes,' she giggled. 'An old friend of mine lets me keep
a key to it.'

'In that case,' Lorenzo decided, snagging a bottle of
cognac from a passing flunkey, 'lead on. I've always been
interested in the theatre.'

FLORIN AND LORENZO left the theatre long after midnight.
Exhausted and satiated by the night's entertainments they
paid off their companions and dragged themselves into
their waiting carriage.

'Home, Jaques,' Florin told their driver, then slumped
back into the plush upholstery.

'Not a bad night, hey boss?' Lorenzo asked, a worn-out
smile softening the hard edges of his face.

'No, not a bad night at all,' Florin nodded.

He peered through the carriage's windows, open against
the warm summer breeze, and watched the streets rolling
by outside. It seemed like a lifetime ago when he'd had to
walk them, nothing between him and the cobbles but
worn boots. Back then, these same streets had been a different world. A harder world, and a more dangerous one.

A night such as the one he'd just spent would have been
an undreamt of luxury back then. A pleasure so out of
reach that it would have been difficult even to imagine.

And yet…

Well, and yet that other world had held its own share of
pleasures too. Pleasures that he was starting to miss. There

had been the joy of small but vital victories, narrowly won. Or the exhilaration of hazardous plans, desperately conceived and recklessly carried out.

Even the hunger and the occasional bloodshed hadn't been all bad. In fact, the more the well-fed and richly clothed Florin thought about it, the more alluring these discomforts seemed to have been. They had been what had made his life so lively; the sour which had made everything else taste so sweet.

'Do you ever miss the old days?' he asked Lorenzo.

The older man looked at him in surprise.

'No,' he decided after a moment's thought. 'Not really. I'm happier rich than I was poor.'

'Yes, but do you ever miss, you know… the excitement?'

Lorenzo started to speak, then stopped himself. The truth was he did sometimes miss that rush, but it was a truth that seemed wrong. After all, he'd spent his whole life getting to this place, to this wealth and this comfort. It didn't seem right that sometimes the gain seemed more like a loss.

'I must admit, boss,' he conceded. 'I know what you mean.'

'And why,' Florin continued, suddenly philosophical, 'do you still call me boss? We're partners. You don't need that habit of deference any more.'

Lorenzo sniggered.

'It ain't deference. It's just a nickname. Do you know what "boss" means in Quenelles?'

'No.'

'Thought not.'

'Well, what does it mean?'

'I can't remember offhand.'

'As your boss I order you to tell me.'

Lorenzo cackled happily as the carriage rattled on.

'Look over there,' he said a moment later. 'Looks like some poor bugger's gone up in flames.'

Florin looked, saw the flickering orange of some house fire reflected on the white marble of the distant cathedral.

'Let's just hope it doesn't spread. I don't suppose it's that far from the Lizard's Head.'

Lorenzo cursed.

'Even if it is, I'm damned if I'm going fire-fighting tonight. That girl of mine certainly gave her money's worth. Just goes to show, the fat ones are always the best. She had one trick where she put her ankles all the way behind her neck and…'

The conversation descended into hideous detail as the carriage rattled across the cattle bridge. As soon as they'd reached the far side of the river the firelight grew brighter, reflections of its flames painting themselves across more roofs and walls.

Florin, trying to ignore the images Lorenzo insisted in conjuring up, caught the first whiff of smoke and frowned.

'So that's why she said she wanted extra,' Lorenzo grinned, but the punch line fell on deaf ears.

'I don't like this,' Florin muttered. His nose wrinkled as the smell of burning grew more acrid, and he shifted uneasily on his cushions. 'The direction of the fire, it's too near the Lizard's Head. I think we might have a problem. Driver, make haste!'

And the driver did. With a swish of his whip he sent the horses bolting forward. As they accelerated into a full gallop their speed bounced the delicately-crafted carriage along the broken cobbles as gracelessly as a dung cart. With a whoop of exhilaration he sent the whole contraption slewing around one corner, then another.

Inside his two passengers were tumbled around like wasps in a jar. Elbows cracked into the woodwork, shoulders cracked glass, and more than once their heads came together in a painful thump.

But despite the rattling misery of their journey, Florin had other things to worry about. By now he'd realised just how close to his inn this fire was. How ruinously close, perhaps.

Then, with a turn that sent sparks flying from beneath the carriage's steel-shod wheels, they were on the King's Road. It was the thoroughfare down which the Lizard's

Head leered, and they could see the bulk of it as soon as the carriage had stopped listing.

'Oh no,' Florin groaned as he saw his burning tavern. The flames whooshed up from chimney stacks to light the darkness of the night sky, or poured through the windows in a flood of fire. Here and there great slabs of blackened tiles had already fallen downwards, shed from the roof like a salamander's skin to reveal the inferno that raged within.

The carriage shrieked to a sliding halt as the horses stopped, the dancing flames of Florin's ruin shining in the whites of their eyes.

'Oh no,' he repeated, as he jumped into the street and stalked forward, the heat already warming his face. Lorenzo followed behind him, mouthing his own curses, as they pushed their way to the front of the crowd of bystanders.

For a moment Florin considered organising them into some sort of bucket chain, but only for a moment. His tavern was beyond saving. Even the ragtag band of unemployables that comprised this quarter's fire watch knew as much. Their backs were to the blazing tavern, their flickering shadows dancing across the neighbouring hovels they were flattening. Some of them held back the enraged occupants, whilst others were busy dousing the street with a bucket chain that stretched down to the river.

'Oh no.'

'Master d'Artaud, thank the Lady you've come!'

'Brigitte. Glad to see that you're alright,' he muttered, dragging his eyes away from the blaze for a moment to smile at his barmaid. She clung to his arm with a surprising strength, her fingers as strong as a vice.

'There, there,' he told her vaguely, and turned his attention back to the Lizard's Head. 'Don't worry.'

'But it's Nelly!' she shouted, tears glistening in her eyes. 'She's still in the ale cellar.'

'What's she doing down there?' Florin asked, horrified.

'She wanted somewhere to sleep. I said that it would be alright. Master d'Artaud, you have to save her!'

Florin and Lorenzo looked towards the leaping flames
that held the tavern in their jubilant grip, and the choking
black pillar of smoke that rose up from them. The front
door stood open, revealing the blazing timberwork of what
had once been the most popular tap room in the city.

The two owners looked at each other, and Lorenzo
shook his head sorrowfully. Florin took a deep breath and
watched one of the ceiling timbers fall down into the taproom with a sickening crunch. It would be pointless to
attempt to save the girl now, he knew that much. She was
probably already dead, roasted like a pig on a spit, or suf-
focated by the choking fumes.

No, she was beyond any help. Any attempt to rescue her
would be foolhardy. Vainglorious. Stupid.

Then he smiled. His teeth glittered like rubies, as bright
as any flame.

And suddenly he was racing forward, roaring with a wild
battle cry that served to blot out the doubts that hung
around him as thickly as the rolling smoke. A dozen paces
on he felt his skin tightening with the heat from the blaze.
It was a physical thing, a slap of burning air that slicked his
body with a sudden, greasy sweat even as it baked the air
in his lungs.

The door loomed up in front of him, the flames that
rushed out as hot as a daemon's breath. To the stink of burning wood and alcohol there was added the stench of burnt
feathers. Florin, hesitating on the brink, realised that the
plumage that graced his fine velvet hat was already burning.

This is insane, he told himself, peering through a stinging prism of tears into the inferno beyond. Nothing could
survive in that.

Although perhaps it could in the granite cool of the ale
cellar.

As he watched, another beam crashed down into the
ruins of the tap room, exploding into a storm of sparks and
splinters. A wave of liquid heat rolled over Florin and his
hair began to singe.

Forget this, he told himself. Run.

But somehow he found himself sprinting forward, stooping to avoid the smoke that roofed this hell. Despite the burning heat, he raced forward, knuckles dragging over the steaming floorboards as he charged. By the time he reached the trap door that led to the cellar he was as dry as a torch, his clothes a tinderbox just waiting for a spark to burst into destructive life.

Trying not to think about this, he grabbed the iron ring and pulled, his palm suddenly anaesthetised as nerve endings ceased to transmit the unbearable pain of melting skin.

Unaware of how badly he'd been hurt, Florin tumbled down the short flight of steps that led down into the ale cellar. It was cooler here. Still as hot as a roasting tin, but cooler than above. It was also blindingly dark, a void of smoking wood and steaming ale.

'Nelly!' Florin cried hoarsely, his voice lost beneath the gleeful roar of the fire above. He coughed, a painful hawking that ripped itself out of his tortured lungs. Then he tried again.

'Nelly!'

This time he thought he heard an answering cry. From one corner there came a muffled sob, a wordless gurgle that might have been nothing more than the bubble of boiling ale.

'Nelly?' he repeated, coughing again as he stumbled forward.

And there she was. Bundled in the corner, arms locked around her knees in a foetal position, the girl seemed tiny. As Florin stumbled nearer, squinting through the choking darkness, she looked up, her eyes wide and shining with tears. Florin met her terrified gaze and tried to smile reassuringly.

Unfortunately the girl saw the expression, saw the black silhouette of the demon who had come for her baring its teeth. As Florin reached out she pushed herself back against the wall, crying out in terror.

'Come on,' Florin told her, his voice a scorched hiss after all the scouring the fire had given his throat. 'We're going.'

The girl shook her head in denial, and pressed herself further back, as if trying to push herself through the sweating cobbles of the cellar wall. In the room above, another beam fell, crashing onto the floor above them with a bone-jarring thud.

Florin's patience snapped.

'Come here,' he hissed, and grabbed for the girl. His hands closed on her shoulders and he dragged her forward, only to drop her a second later as she bit down on his hand.

Beneath the pain, and the smoke, and the panic that was threatening to burst through the chains of his self-control, Florin's response was swift and decisive. Closing his bleeding hand into a fist he drove it forward. It was a short, efficient jab that connected with the girl's chin, rattling her teeth and knocking her senseless.

'Excuse me, madam,' Florin whispered with a jagged little cry that was somewhere between a sob and a giggle. Then he threw her over his shoulder as easily as a sack of onions and staggered back towards the quickening heat of the burning tavern.

In the seconds he had been below, the blaze above had blossomed into a forge of terrible, unbearable heat. As he threw himself back into the flames, Florin felt his skin stretch as tightly as the case of a frying sausage.

He screamed then, the pain of his burning body like nothing he had ever felt before. Stumbling towards the door his strength bled away, evaporating beneath the heat like water, and he fell to his knees. The doorframe, miraculously still standing, seemed to draw farther away as he crawled towards it, and he knew that unless he dropped the dead weight of the serving girl, he'd never make it.

But he wouldn't drop her. Even as his living flesh roasted he knew that his pride would no more allow him to abandon her than gravity would allow him to fly.

He almost took comfort from the thought as, with a final, painful hiss of breath he collapsed onto the scorched woodwork, the edges of his smouldering clothes beginning to blacken.

'HOW MUCH?' LORENZO cried, eyes widening in horror.

'Twelve hundred,' the crone repeated, 'and forty.'

'I'm sorry, grandmother.' Lorenzo calmed himself. 'I must have gotten mixed up. There is only one man who needs your skills, not a dozen. And perhaps a girl, if we can afford it.'

'Yes,' the old woman nodded, her eyes disappearing into the wrinkled folds of her podgy face. 'But that one man is the famously wealthy Florin d'Artaud. His life is obviously worth a lot more than that of another man.'

'Not really,' Lorenzo frowned. 'Every man's life is worth the same.'

The old woman snorted and spat into the brazier that lit her chamber. The phlegm sizzled on the glowing coals and then exploded into a gout of flame, as if her very spit was alcoholic.

And perhaps, Lorenzo thought with a glance at the bottles which filled the shelves of this room, it was. He didn't know what the contents of these grotesque containers had been pickled in, but he doubted it was water. He found himself studying a small, misshapen thing that floated in one. For a moment he took it to be some sort of shrivelled, hairless monkey, then he noticed the umbilical cord which trailed away from its belly button.

Grimacing with disgust he looked away from the foetus, letting his eyes rest on another shelf. The pale, drowned things which floated within the murky depths of the jars that ranked this one were mercifully unidentifiable. Except for the eyeballs, of course.

Lorenzo tried to persuade himself that they weren't human.

'No man's life is worth the same as another's,' the old woman said, watching the shades of revulsion that played across her guest's face with a certain satisfaction. Over the years a great many of her customers had been willing to settle on the most outrageous of fees just to be free of her little chamber of horrors.

'For instance, a month ago, I healed another patient, a man whose burns were twice as bad as your friend's. A longshoreman, he was. The naphtha barrel he'd been carrying split just as he brushed against a landing torch. Very nasty. Still, his life only cost him eight.'

The crone's eyes gleamed as she watched Lorenzo's face harden. Already, after only a couple of moments haggling, they both knew that she would get her way. There was nobody else in Bordeleaux with her reputation, or her abilities. And even if there had been, Lorenzo had no time in which to find them. The burns Florin had taken were scarcely any worse than they were rumoured to be, his hold on life scarcely less precarious.

If Lorenzo had reached him a moment later he would be hiring a priest, not a healer.

'Alright,' he said, bitter but resigned. 'How much for just Florin, then?'

'Twelve hundred,' the old woman said, 'and forty-one.'

'That doesn't make any sense.' Lorenzo protested 'How can it cost more to heal one than two?'

'I always charge the mean ones more,' the crone explained, and absently scratched her stubbled chin.

For the first time since he'd dragged his friend from the burning inn, Lorenzo felt himself smiling, the expression stinging the reddened skin of his face. The crone smiled back. A moment later they shook hands, and, dragging a battered leather satchel behind her, the healer followed him out to the waiting carriage.

THE PAIN CAME in waves that were as insistent as those of any ocean. Sometimes they lapped gently across the shining pinkness of his skin. Sometimes they surged between the tight claws of his hands, or pounded a heavy rhythm deep within the ruin of his lungs.

Occasionally the pain would reach such stormy heights that it would defeat itself, collapsing into a blessed numbness. When such a respite came, Florin would sink into an exhausted sleep, there to battle nightmares of blindness and drowning smoke.

When the crone saw him she pursed her lips and hissed as dubiously as a horse trader considering a purchase.

'You'll have to pay first,' she decided as she dropped her satchel onto the floor of the inn and bent further over the patient. He muttered through stiff lips, cursing from the depths of some terrible dream.

The old woman pressed a gnarled fingertip against one of the blisters which stubbled his singed scalp. It popped as easily as a rotten grape. She shook her head.

'Sure you want to pay?' she asked Lorenzo without looking back. 'I never lie, and I leave the false hope to the priests. I tell you now, this one is nearer to Morr than Shallya.'

'Never mind that,' Lorenzo muttered, and pressed his purse into her hands. 'This is all we have. Do all that you can.'

The witch dropped the purse into her bag, and peeled back another of Florin's bandages. It was stiff with a fluid that was as yellow and sticky as honey.

She grunted, and tapped her one tooth thoughtfully.

'What about the girl?'

'She's in the next room. But trust me, he needs your help first.'

'Alright,' she decided. 'Get out. I need space to work.'

'Is there nothing I can do?'

'Yes. You can eat and sleep. You've done your part. Just stay out of here unless I call you.'

'I'll be downstairs, then,' Lorenzo muttered, but the old woman ignored him. She was already stripping her patient's dirty bandages away, replacing them with a smear of evil-smelling lotion.

The sting of it woke Florin, and he sobbed with renewed pain. The witch looked up from her work, and gazed deeply into the young man's bloodshot eyes. There was hardly anything in them but animal pain, animal desperation.

But there was a flicker of something else, too. Something small, but as hard and bright as a diamond. She was glad to see it. The priests talked a lot of swill, but one thing they did know was this: that a man's soul was the strongest part of him.

It was almost with reluctance that she popped open the tiny vial of sleeping salts beneath his nose and sent him back down into oblivion.

'Rest,' she whispered to him. 'Rest and be well.'

Two hours later she was finished. Leaving him as neatly cocooned in her bandages as a fly in a spider's web, she stalked off, spider-like herself, to find the girl.

FLORIN OPENED HIS eyes and studied the beams that ran above his head. The plaster that sagged between them was marked by the shapes of islands and continents, a grubby cartography of mould.

He yawned and stretched. He had no idea where he was, nor did he care. Far from it. When these little moments of amnesia came to him Florin treasured them. They always gave him the sense that he'd been born again, given a fresh birth into a world whose possibilities remained to be discovered.

Even as he savoured the sensation, a door creaked open and one such possibility tiptoed over to his bed. She gazed down at him, the flushed face beneath her turban rapt with adoration.

'Good morning, Nelly,' Florin said, his voice sounding surprisingly hoarse.

With a little sob the girl put her hands to her mouth, and tears welled up in her eyes.

'Oh, thank Shallya!' she said. 'You made it through. I prayed that you would. Every night for three nights. And every day. The witch, that is the crone, told me that it might help. And it did! Oh, thank Shallya! But how do you feel? You look all right on the outside. I mean, a little red, you know, but she said that the burns on the inside were the worst…'

'Burns?' Florin interrupted her. Noticing how weak his voice sounded, he made an effort to deepen it. 'What burns?'

'From the fire,' she cried, seizing his hand and squeezing it hard. 'The inn. Don't you remember saving me? Oh, you were so brave. Everybody said so.'

But Florin was no longer listening. The peace of his waking had been shattered by a thousand shards of terrible memories, images of fire and smoke that could have come straight from one of the hells. One memory in particular surfaced, that of the moment when he'd seized the red-hot iron latch of the trapdoor.

He shook the girl away and lifted his hand to study it. The back of it was still red, although no more than if sunburned. That was scarce comfort, though. It was the palm that he'd left smeared across the metalwork, greased away like lard on a baking tray.

A sudden reluctance to look at the damage seized him. For a moment he could do no more than stare at the back of his hand, as hypnotised by indecision as a mouse beneath a cobra's gaze.

Then, with a deep breath, he turned his hand over and looked at the palm.

The lines of it, unbroken by even a trace of a scar, told the same story as ever. The flawlessly healed skin between them glistened with a cool sweat.

'It's not possible,' he said, looking at his other hand in case he'd been mistaken. But it was just as smooth as its brother. 'How long have I been asleep?'

'A week,' said the girl, reclaiming her grip on his hand. 'It's a miracle, isn't it? And all thanks to the witch. I came to see you only three days ago, and you still looked… ugh, I can't describe it. But she's strigany, you see. They know things.'

'What things?'

'All kinds of things.'

Florin looked at his hands again, not quite believing how lucky he'd been. Then he pulled back the sheets and studied the rest of himself. His skin was smooth and unblemished. Even his old scars seemed to have gone.

He lifted one leg up and wiggled his toes. Then, seeing how avidly the girl was sharing his appraisal, he pulled the sheets back over him.

'Well, Nelly,' he said, pleased to have remembered her name. 'I don't suppose you know where Lorenzo is?'

'In the taproom,' she replied. 'He's a hero too. Although not as much as you, obviously. Still, he saved us both. When you fell he came and got us. Do you know, even when you'd passed out you wouldn't let go of me. He was complaining about that before, but I think he was joking. Do you think that he was joking? I think that he was joking. He's funny. Anyway, some people are still buying him drinks.'

'Well then, let's not disturb him,' Florin decided. 'I'm just glad that I managed to save you. How could I have left such a beauty to Morr?'

For a moment Nelly seemed at a loss for words. The moment didn't last long.

'Oh, I'm not so beautiful,' she giggled. 'And now my poor hair's gone. The witch said I'll just have to wait for it to grow back, but I don't think she understands. It takes years to get the style right. It isn't just the hair, it's the way it flows. Tell me honestly, don't you think I look hideous with this turban on?'

'No, not at…'

'You still look wonderful though. Can I kiss you? I did before, when you were asleep. The witch said that it might help, and I think it did. Do you mind?'

'No, but…'

But Nelly had already pounced.

THE NEXT DAY Florin and Lorenzo, cloaked against the blizzarding rain that the east wind had chased into the city, returned to the Lizard's Head.

Its charred carcass lay sprawled over half an acre. Where once there had been stables and taprooms and boarding rooms, an entire hive of drunken activity and clinking gold, there now remained nothing but scorched timbers. Sodden with rain, they oozed soot-blackened water, polluting the gutters that ran past them.

Nor did the devastation end there. Around the inn lay the ruins of the hovels the fire-fighters had demolished. Some of the shacks had been shoddily tied back together by their inhabitants against the weather, whilst others remained abandoned. Despite the downpour some of their tenants were picking through the remains of the inn even now, pocketing everything from pewter mugs to door hinges.

'Maybe we should stop them.' Florin said, his voice as soft as the rain which pattered on his hood.

'No point.' Lorenzo shrugged. 'They'll have taken everything worth taking already'.

'I wish you hadn't sold the carriage.'

'I wish you hadn't cost us everything else we had by playing the hero.'

Florin grinned.

'And I wish you wouldn't look so pleased with yourself.'

'Lorenzo,' Florin smiled, the memory of a morning spent with Nelly keeping him warm despite the damp. 'You know me. I'm a man unafraid to seize his destiny.'

'Destiny!' Lorenzo spat. 'Poverty is what you mean to say. All that gold. All that wealth. Think of what we had to go through to get it. Or do you think it was as easy as in that damned play? May the gods curse that theatre, and the mollies that flounce about in it. I knew it was bad luck.'

Florin shook his head.

'I don't think that bad luck had anything to do with it. Or if it did, it came in the shape of that pig's arse Volavant. He told us he'd put us out of business. And so he did.'

The two men sunk into a thoughtful silence. It was Lorenzo who broke it.

'Do you want to kill him?'

Florin shrugged.

'That's easier said than done. He's got guards. He knows we're coming. Nelly said that it's all over town, how he threatened to do this, and how people are waiting to see what revenge I'll take. And even if we do manage to get him, his stinking guild will make sure we're for the chop.'

'Is that a yes?'

'It's an "I don't know". Ah, to the hells with this miserable place. Let's go back to the inn and think about it.'

'Ah, so that's what you were doing all morning,' Lorenzo jeered as they trudged off down the street. 'Thinking.'

It took them half an hour to squelch back through the rain to their inn. As soon as the owner saw them he rushed over, the filthy towel that served as his badge of office wrapped around one hand.

'There you are,' he began, relief showing in every line of his face. 'And about time, too. You have a visitor. A very important visitor. You should have told me he was coming, and I would have decanted some Estalian wine.'

'You serve Estalian wine every night,' Lorenzo reminded him, but the innkeeper waved his objection away.

'I mean the real stuff. But don't just stand here, keeping him waiting. I just wish you'd told me he was coming. Your rooms are filthy.'

'Before we go and meet this guest of ours,' Florin said. 'Why don't you tell me who he is?'

'Don't you know?'

Florin glared at him.

'It's Monsieur Mordicio, that's who. He said to show him up to your rooms. I thought you must be expecting him.'

'Mordicio,' Florin repeated, rolling his tongue around the name as though it were a bad tooth. 'What's that old vulture sniffing around for?'

'I don't know what you mean,' the innkeeper exclaimed, and looked nervously around the taproom. The half dozen patrons that sat nursing their flagons seemed to be paying no heed, which meant that they were probably listening to every word. 'I'm sure that Monsieur Mordicio is more than welcome here. He's a real gentleman, as I've always said.'

'Yes, yes, yes,' Florin said, impatiently. 'Well, let's go see what the philanthropist wants, then.'

'Philanthropist,' Lorenzo sniggered. 'I wouldn't put it past him either, the dirty old goat.'

The innkeeper hastened away from this dangerous conversation, and the two friends clumped upstairs to their chambers. A pair of guards were waiting outside, their shaven heads as smooth as their breast plates.

'Florin d'Artaud and Lorenzo,' Florin told the nearer of the two. 'Your boss wants to see us.'

'Wait there,' he commanded, and let himself into Florin's room. A moment later he returned.

'All right. Give us your weapons and go on in.'

'Such a courteous breed of monkey Mordicio's hiring these days,' Lorenzo said, brushing past the scowling guard and following Florin into their chamber.

Despite the fact that there were only three people waiting there was hardly room to move. Not that Mordicio took up much room. The old villain was as scrawny as ever, the patched black robes that covered his gaunt frame adding to the impression. His frail, gangling body was as insubstantial as a shadow beneath the grey tangle of his beard.

'Florin!' he beamed happily, 'My boy! It makes me a very happy man to see you so well. A very happy man. When I heard how badly you'd been hurt I wanted to come and see you. As the gods are my witness, so I did. But at my age I'm too frail.'

'Thanks for the thought,' Florin said distractedly, barely listening to the man who'd so effortlessly made himself a guest in his own chambers. Instead he was staring at one of Mordicio's companions, and wondering how loose his boot knife was.

Not that ogres were much more likely to attack than humans, of course. It was just that there was always something unnerving about being close to the things. Especially when they were as big as the one that squatted on Florin's creaking bed.

Above its blank slab of a face the ogre's tattooed scalp was pressed into the damp plaster of the ceiling, hard enough to leave a dent. Its legs jutted out across the room like a pair of small, hessian clad cows, and a huge cleaver lay across them.

Almost more distressing than the monster itself was its smell. Its breath alone was like an abattoir at high noon, and its unwashed clothes smelt even worse. In fact, the ammonia stench that clung to them was so strong that Florin felt his eyes beginning to water.

Nor was he alone in his suffering. The third occupant of the room seemed to be faring even worse. Middle-aged, well-dressed, and with a hairstyle to match, the woman sat beside Mordicio, a perfume-soaked handkerchief held up to her nose. Behind it, Florin saw a face drawn up into an expression of disgust that was strong enough to crack her mascara.

'Florin d'Artaud,' said Florin, turning to her with a click of his heels and a small bow. 'It's a pleasure to make your acquaintance, madam.'

'Ah, always so polite,' Mordicio beamed approvingly. 'He makes me very proud. Like a father.'

The woman shot Mordicio a stern glance for this interruption. Then, recovering from his breach of etiquette, she returned Florin's introduction.

'La Comtesse Hansebourg,' she said, offering her hand to be kissed.

'Enchanted. And may I ask what has brought a lady such as yourself to a place such as this?'

But before she could answer Mordicio cut smoothly in.

'Always with the questions, hey? Good, good. Always thinking. But before we get to that, I want to offer you my thanks.'

Florin frowned, then shrugged.

'No thanks are needed,' he told Mordicio. 'I was happy to pay back the money I owed you. In fact I should thank you for being patient enough to wait until I had returned from Lustria. And also, of course, for only charging three hundred per cent interest.'

Mordicio, as immune to sarcasm as he was to the ogrish stink that filled the room, accepted the thanks with a nod.

'Anything for an old friend. That isn't why I'm here though, not at all. I'm here because I want to thank you for saving my niece from that fire, even risking your life to do it! This boy,' he said, leaning close enough to the comtesse to make her lean away, 'is a hero.'

'Your niece?' Florin repeated. 'I'm sorry, Monsieur Mordicio, but you must have heard the wrong rumour. The girl I saved was only a serving wench.'

'Yes, yes,' Mordicio nodded happily. 'That's my niece. Little Nelly makes ends meet as a serving wench. It's a shame, really. Her father, that is, my brother, used to be quite well off. Then he borrowed some money from me to outfit a ship and... well, never mind. Suffice it to say that, what with the interest, and then the compound interest, he's been in the debtor's gaol these past five years.'

Mordicio shook his head sorrowfully as he contemplated his brother's financial miscalculations. Florin and Lorenzo exchanged a carefully blank look.

The ogre, its expression remaining as vacant as ever, broke wind with a sound like a tearing sheet.

'For Shallya's sake,' the comtesse snapped as the air thickened. 'Can we get this over with? I don't know why we had to come to this horrible place anyway.'

'To be polite,' Mordicio told her, eyebrows rising in surprise. 'Don't forget, we're here to offer Florin his reward for saving my niece. You don't think I could just summon him, do you? Whistle for him to come running, like a dog or a debtor?'

'Hmmmph,' the comtesse said, and pressed her handkerchief closer to her face.

'A reward, you say?' Lorenzo asked, speaking for the first time. 'That, Monsieur Mordicio, would be most appreciated.'

'Appreciated,' Mordicio said, 'and deserved.'

'I won't deny that we could certainly use some money to rebuild the inn,' Florin said, trying to keep the look of suspicion off his face. 'But unfortunately we aren't in a position to borrow anything.'

'Borrow!' Mordicio cried, appalled. 'Borrow! You don't think I'd make a man who's just saved my beloved niece borrow money, do you? What kind of uncle do you think I am?'

Florin, thinking of Nelly scrubbing benches whilst her uncle snoozed in the richest palace in town, said nothing.

'Borrow! No, you won't have to borrow anything. Instead, I have two gifts. The first is a small thing. An errand, you might say, that I've run for you. It was your competitor Monsieur Volavant. He admitted to me that he instigated the fire that's ruined you.'

'When did he admit that?' Florin asked.

'At about four o'clock this morning. I even went downstairs to hear it from his own lips.'

'I see. And did he sign a confession?'

Mordicio gave Florin a look that was almost pitying.

'No. No, my boy, he didn't sign a confession. Why waste the ink? Anyway, he had no need to. Between you and me, Monsieur Volavant has no need of anything any more.'

Mordicio winked, as if sharing some harmless joke, and Florin felt a chill run down his spine. Somehow he knew that, however Volavant had met his end, it hadn't been pleasant.

'And what was the second gift you mentioned?'

'Twelve hundred and forty-one crowns,' Mordicio smiled. 'And the chance to earn it.'

'To earn it?' Florin and Lorenzo repeated in perfect harmony.

'Of course. I knew you'd be too proud to accept a handout. Then, as luck would have it, the comtesse here came to me for help. She's a lady in peril, you might say. A damsel in distress. And who better to help her, I thought, than the conqueror of Lustria, Florin d'Artaud?'

'Who indeed?' Florin asked, straightening his back.

Lorenzo shot him a look of perfect disgust whilst Mordicio, a vulpine grin lifting his beard, popped his knuckles happily.

'Yes, it's a perfect quest for a man like yourself,' he said, and nodded to his companion. 'There you go, comtesse. Didn't I tell you that young d'Artaud is a man of honour?'

'Perhaps,' Lorenzo interrupted, 'you'd care to tell us what job requires such an honourable man?'

Mordicio, grinning as hard as a bearded death's-head, told them.

'IT'S A TERRIBLE tale,' he began, with the obvious relish of a born storyteller. 'Although not, alas, an uncommon one. This world is a hard place, after all, and unforgiving of human frailty. In fact, it reminds me of something which once happened to me. I was only a boy at the time...'

'Get to the point, would you?' Frau Hansebourg snapped, the handkerchief she kept pressed to her mouth doing little to soften her tone.

'For you, madame, anything,' Mordicio graciously agreed. 'Now, where was I? Ah yes, that's it. The beginning. Well it all began, as do many tales, with desire. Some may call it greed, but they would be foolish. What could be more natural than the instinct to acquire wealth? Look at me, for instance...'

'Oh, be quiet, you old fool,' Comtesse Hansebourg said, waving one bejewelled hand at the most dangerous man in Bordeleaux as though he were one of her serving maids. 'I'll tell them. It's like this,' she said, turning to fix Florin with a hard gaze. 'It's all the fault of my fool of a husband, Franz. Franz Hansebourg. You may have heard of him? He was one of the three brothers who built the Hansebourg trading house.'

'Ah yes,' Florin agreed. He vaguely remembered the Hansebourgs from one of his brother's soul-destroyingly dull banquets. 'They import cotton.'

'Cathay cotton,' the comtesse said reproachfully, 'and other fineries.'

'But mostly tar and salt pork,' Mordicio volunteered. Frau Hansebourg pretended not to hear him.

'Anyway,' she continued, 'ten years ago Franz was on a trading expedition to the east. He'd taken three wagons through the World's Edge Mountains, heading for distant Cathay. And, like the fool he was, he took our daughter with him.'

'Ah,' Florin said, diplomatically.

'Needless to say, I told him not to take her. I told him that Katerina was my daughter, and I didn't want her dragged around on a caravan like some strigany brat. But he wouldn't listen. Franz was a pig-headed man, never willing to listen to the opinions of those more sensible than himself. Well, he paid for his stupidity. He insisted on taking Katerina and that was the last I ever saw of either of them.'

'I wonder why?' Lorenzo muttered sarcastically.

'What!'

'My man here was just wondering,' Florin oiled in, 'why they didn't return? Did some catastrophe overtake them?'

'Yes,' the comtesse said, and turned the chill of her gaze back to Florin. 'Yes, some sort of catastrophe. We're not sure exactly what, but six months after Franz had promised to return another caravan found the remains of his wagons. They'd been stripped of all merchandise, of course. As if murdering my family wasn't enough, the swine were also thieves.'

I wonder what she missed the most, thought Florin, the gold or the girl?

He thought he had a pretty good idea.

'It must have been a terrible shock for you,' Florin said, voice lowered sympathetically.

'But what, exactly, do you want us to do about it?' Lorenzo asked.

'Don't interrupt when I'm talking!' the comtesse scolded him. 'I'm getting to that. Or rather, I'm getting to our guest here.'

She gestured towards the ogre, eyes narrowing with contempt. Its own eyes remained half closed, still pools of blank indifference. For the first time Florin noticed that the swirling tattoos which covered the ogre's scalp also scarred his eyelids.

'It was almost ten years from the day of Franz and Katerina's funeral service,' the comtesse continued, 'that our friend here appeared. Or rather, was introduced by Mordicio.'

Again Mordicio bowed.

'It was the least I could do, madame.'

'Yes. Anyway, he brought interesting news. In fact, why don't you tell them?' the comtesse decided, raising her voice and slowing her words. 'Yes, you. Krom, isn't it? Tell these two what you told me.'

'Her child,' the ogre Krom rumbled, the baritone of its voice sounding as deep as an earthquake after the comtesse's shrilling. 'I know where it is.'

'Really?' Florin said, trying not to stare at the ogre's false teeth. It was difficult not to. Despite the gloom, the lumps of quartz it had hammered into its gums glittered, an incongruous constellation of trapped light and running saliva. 'You mean to say, she's alive?'

Krom paused to scratch between his legs before replying. 'Yes.'

Florin exchanged a glance with Lorenzo, who shrugged.

'How do you know that it is this woman's daughter?' he said. 'All children look alike.'

'It is the woman's daughter,' Krom told him, his certainty as deep as his bones. 'She came from the caravan of this female's master. She is the right age. And she has the same red hair.'

'Auburn,' the comtesse automatically corrected him.

'Auburn,' the ogre repeated, his lips moving as if he were tasting the new word as well as pronouncing it. 'Auburn like blood on snow.'

To Lorenzo's delight the comtesse flushed.

'And where,' Florin asked, 'would this child be?'

'In the tribe of Jarmoosh.'

Florin looked blankly at the comtesse, who shook her head impatiently.

'Apparently, she's with one of these thing's tribes,' she told him. 'Beyond the World's Edge Mountains. And that, Monsieur d'Artaud, is where you come in. Krom can find her, but I need a man of honour and courage to go with him and recover my daughter from the wilderness. Will you do it?'

Florin should have hesitated. He should have consulted with Lorenzo, or at least have haggled over the price.

But he didn't hesitate. After all, he was Florin d'Artaud, and although penniless, he was still a hero.

That was all that the fire had left to him.

'It would be my honour, madame,' Florin said heroically. Lorenzo scowled first at him, then at the comtesse.

'Wait a minute,' he said, outraged at the decision that had been taken for him. 'Why us? Why don't your husband's brothers mount their own expedition? This Katerina is their blood, after all.'

'No.' The comtesse shook her head. 'Gilles and Bouillon aren't fools. The herring fleets are almost due. They'd never miss a season's trading just because of a rumour carried by some subhuman.'

The three men in the room, suddenly remembering quite how big he was, looked nervously at Krom. Fortunately the ogre, who had lapsed back into the stupor that seemed to be his natural state, gave no sign of having heard. But before their relief became too comfortable he shifted slightly across the protesting springs of Florin's bed, lifted his leg, and broke wind once more.

A smell like an exploded corpse filled the room. The comtesse, with a little squeak, flung a purse of gold at Florin and bolted from the room.

'What a woman!' Mordicio sighed after she'd left. 'Hips like a peasant and a mouth like a whore.'

'It will certainly be an honour to be of service to the comtesse,' Florin said, then wished he hadn't as Mordicio's leer grew wider.

'Well, my boy, before you do that you'd better find her daughter. I've already booked you sea and river passage to the town of Grummand. No, no, don't thank me. What are friends for, after all? In fact, you don't even have to pay me now, if you don't want to. You know your credit's always good with me.'

'How much?' Florin and Lorenzo chorused.

The ensuing argument spilled over into another about the next stage of the plan. An hour later this became a discussion of the equipment they'd need, then of the climate beyond the World's Edge, then of the availability of maps.

Only Krom seemed to have no opinions on these subjects. As the humans plotted he remained silent, as still and watchful as a carved totem. To men who knew no better, he appeared to be the very picture of vacant indifference.

CHAPTER THREE

'REMEMBER TO LAND your punches this time,' Sergei's father told him as he bound up his son's fists. 'Last time even some of the herd saw you pulling your punches. That won't do at all.'

'Sorry, pa,' the lad said, clenching one of his hands thoughtfully. 'But you know how I hate to hurt Colli.'

Squinting in the gloom of their wagon the older man tightened the bandages around Sergei's knuckles. Finally, grunting with the satisfaction of a true craftsman, he checked the padding around the knuckles.

Then, without a flicker of warning, his own fist flashed forward to crack against his son's jaw.

Sergei, surprise vanishing beneath trained instinct, rolled away from the punch, his stool clattering across the floor as he sprang back to his feet.

'What did you do that for?'

'For disrespecting your Uncle Colli,' the older man said. 'And to show you how it's done.'

His face crinkled into a smile and he winked. The eye that remained open was watchful, though. Sergei was seventeen now, and a tough, wiry seventeen at that. When he decided to hit back his father wanted to be ready. He wanted to give the lad a fight to be proud of, just as his own father had when he had come of age.

But today, it seemed, was not to be that day. With an obvious effort Sergei kept hold of his rage, perhaps saving it for the fighting ahead.

Good lad, his father thought, and got to his feet.

'All right then. Let's start fleecing,' he said, and stepped out of the caravan into the sunlight beyond.

'Right you are, pa,' the youngster nodded as the door swung shut behind the older man. He stretched as he waited, scant muscles rolling beneath the bare skin of his torso. It was this apparent frailty, especially when contrasted with Colli's bulk, that made their fights so lucrative.

There were other fights, of course, which Sergei won or lost according to the will of the caravan's bookmakers. But the final bash with Colli was when the real money was made. It was just a shame that they could only stage their mismatched battle once per town.

Outside Sergei could hear his father's voice booming a challenge above the clamour of the crowd. He spoke of gold to the bold, and of the shame of cowardice, and they listened. Then he spoke of how much gold, and they listened harder.

Only when he had their full attention did he call for his son. Sergei, with a practiced gesture, leapt out of the caravan and onto the raised stage outside.

The crowd quietened as they watched him, squinting with careful appraisal. He was fit, they assumed, and as tough as all strigany. But as to his skill, well, that was what made things so interesting. Was the broken angle of his nose a good sign or not? Until he fought, they had no way of telling.

As the crowd studied Sergei, so he studied them. They were the usual mob, more or less, a great mass hemmed into the circle of wagons like sheep between fences. Although most of them had the pale skin of Empire folk, the masters of this land, there were plenty of other types too. After all this was Grummand. The folk who were drawn to live within its sturdy granite walls lived here for a reason, and that reason was the Black Fire Pass.

Encircled by the towering crags of the World's Edge Mountains, the pass wound through the heart of them in a single, unbroken thread. Many a catastrophe had found its way through this high causeway in ages past. Sorcerers, armies, plagues: all had slipped through the mountains and into the Empire like rats from an open sewer.

Yet, as well as danger, the pass brought riches. Silk was the greatest of them, but there were others. Carvings of green jade, spices tart enough to flavour the most rotten meat, aphrodisiacs of dragon's blood and minotaur's horn. These and countless other treasures kept Grummand's monthly caravans rolling away to the east like so many sacrificial lambs.

The riches also kept a constant stream of the bold and the reckless flowing to this place, a tide of human flotsam that was drawn by rumours of eastern fortune.

Sergei studied them as he stretched and flexed, preparing to take the toughest they could throw at him.

Dark-eyed Tileans jostled with round-faced Kislevites. Halflings conversed with merchants whose hooked noses and oiled beards marked them out as Arabyans.

In one corner a group of dwarfs was busily devouring haunches of roast goat, whilst in another a blank-faced ogre gazed impassively out towards the east.

And amongst this throng, as innocuous as paving stones, lurked the caravan's three bookmakers. So far as appearances went they were no more than merchants or mercenaries, idlers with too much gold in their purses and too much ale in their bellies. One of them was even complaining, in a loud, drunken whisper, about the strigany and their thieving ways.

Sergei managed to keep the smile off of his face as he listened to Uncle Bogdan expound his borrowed theories.

'Athletes and gentlemen,' his father bellowed, his voice rolling over the mob's chatter as smoothly as honey over bread. 'I introduce my son, Sergei Chervez. I won't lie to you, he's a good boxer. Not only that, but he's been training for over a year. That's why, gentlemen, you don't have to knock him out. You don't even have to make him submit. All you have to do is to stay standing in the ring for three rounds.'

This generosity brought an appreciative murmur. Some of the onlookers, who'd had the good sense to decide against the challenge, began to reconsider. Others, their minds already made up, pressed forward.

'So, gentlemen, for the price of a single golden crown who will try to win a dozen? Who has the courage to take on a strigany?'

Even before he'd stopped speaking the first challenger had pushed his way forward. Despite his rough clothes he seemed healthy and well fed, and as red cheeked as any farmer's son. He was certainly big enough to have spent his twenty-odd years forking hay and breaking earth; his well-fleshed frame held more muscle than fat.

Sergei watched him as he handed over his coin and had the rules explained. For this fight he had no need to look for the bookmakers' signals. He always won the first fight, and always by a whisker.

Which wouldn't be a problem this time, he thought, as his opponent lumbered into the ring. His face was flushed with excitement beneath the pale thatch of his hair, the locks the same colour as the straw which had filled Sergei's first punch bag. A good comparison, he thought, as he squared up to this amateur.

His father stepped back.

The bell rang.

The fight was on.

The challenger hurled himself into the combat with a flurry of blows, each as slow and predictable as the last. Sergei fell back beneath the onslaught, weaving past most of the punches but letting the occasional fist glance across his shoulder, or swish past the side of his head.

The crowd roared its approval as the big man pressed his advantage, shoving the strigany back towards the rope.

Sergei waited until the hemp scratched his back before hooking his left fist up beneath the farmer's jaw. It was barely more than a tap, but a neat enough clip to daze the man for the second Sergei needed to dodge out and away.

A chorus of disappointed curses came from the crowd, and the cries seemed to galvanise the challenger. With an angry growl, he sent a wide punch flailing over Sergei's ducking head. Before he'd even drawn back his fist the strigany darted forward, and jabbed him twice in the ribs.

The cracking of the bone was lost beneath the ringing of the first bell, and the challenger stumbled back to his corner, pain and determination warring on his face.

Sergei slumped down onto his own stool and pretended to be out of breath. Despite the fact that the afternoon sun was warm on his skin, he had yet to break into a sweat, and so, to hide the fact, he poured a bucket of water over his head.

Then the second bell came and he was back on his feet, dodging away from the challenger's more powerful punches, clipping him back here and there. The farmer was gasping for breath, drawing in great lungfuls despite his cracked ribs, when the second bell rang.

Again, Sergei slumped onto his stool and panted for air he didn't need. When the third bell rang he got slowly back to his feet, and marched gracelessly into the centre of the ring. He let the challenger hit him once more, a spent blow that crunched painfully into the gristle of his nose. Then, seeing the sight of his own blood, he moved in to finish the fight.

With only seconds left in which to hold on, the challenger felt a single, agonising impact as Sergei drove his fist into the his solar plexus. Then, as he curled in on himself, a neat left hook sent white light exploding through his vision, and his body crashing onto the woodwork.

Sergei heard his father count to ten, and the first fight was over. Ignoring the pain he wrinkled his nose, encouraging a trickle of blood for all to see.

'A brave contender,' Sergei's father said, watching the lad stagger back to his feet. 'Now my son will rest for a few moments whilst we wait for the next challenge.'

And, despite the sound of the first contender's vomiting, there were plenty more lined up already.

Today was going to be a cinch.

SIX VICTORIES, TWO defeats and sixty-three crowns later, it was Uncle Colli's turn to take the challenge. He had arrived in town separately from the main caravan, a scarred old battler with no more than a well-sharpened sword and a hauberk of battered leather to pack onto his old nag of a horse.

Amongst the constant ebb and flow of men that fortune sent through Grummand's gates Colli had been practically invisible, just one more sellsword. He had found lodgings in a cheap inn, and spent the last two days guzzling cheap ale and wolfing down cheap stew.

Now, swaggering towards the bloodied boxing ring, he reeked of both. Sergei, who was sitting in his corner with his head in his hands, seemed not to notice him. Nor did his father, who was loudly bullying his apparently reluctant son to carry on fighting.

This little pantomime was made all the more convincing by the fortunate intervention of one of the crowd. The old woman was a laundress, a well-known and well-liked citizen whose hands were as hard as her heart was soft. As Sergei's father heckled the lad so she heckled him, cursing him for his cruelty and lack of parental concern.

It was great entertainment. The caravan's bookkeepers saw their chance and made dozens of small bets against Sergei fighting again, bets they knew they'd lose.

Then Colli climbed into the ring, and Sergei ended the argument by standing up. The bookmakers swore loudly as they paid out, sprinkling coins across the crowd as shrewdly as fishermen throwing bait across a lake.

'Gentleman,' Sergei's father cried out as the challenger stepped into the ring. 'It seems that my son still wants to fight. He's a real chip off the old block, and no mistake.'

Colli unbuckled his leather armour as the strigany spoke, his muscles bulging beneath a tapestry of scars and tattoos.

He stretched, rolling his head on a neck that was as thick as a bull's, and punched a fist into his hand.

Sergei swallowed and tried to whisper something to his father. The older man hushed him off with an angry scowl.

The crowd placed their bets.

The fight was a thing of beauty, there was no denying that. Not from an athletic point of view, of course. After all, what aficionado of the sport could fail to be disappointed by the clumsy footwork, the wild haymakers, the slipping and pushing and cursing? There was little skill to be seen, and even less grace.

But all the same, in terms of pure entertainment, it was beautiful. First one man was winning, then the other. The air was filled with the sound of bloodcurdling howls of pain and the impact of skin on skin.

In the final round, when Sergei floored the challenger with a lucky hook, even some of those who'd lost money cheered.

'...and ten!' Sergei's father finished the count, before helping Colli back to his feet. From the corner of his eye he could see the caravan's bookkeeper's collecting their winnings from those who'd pay, or sending their own sons trotting after defaulters.

'Well, gentlemen,' Sergei's father said, 'it seems that the fighting is over for today, at least. You Grummanders are tougher than the opponents we're used to.'

'I'll fight him,' a voice called out through the drunken calls of agreement. The strigany looked up, and for a moment he thought that the offer had come from the ogre. But then he saw the man that stood in front of the great beast raise his hand.

'Over here,' the challenger said, stepping forward. 'I'll try my luck.'

The ringmaster's eyes narrowed as he studied the man. He was fresh-faced, smooth-skinned, well-dressed. His hair gleamed with oil and was twisted up into a topknot, a typically decadent southern fashion. As he moved forward the strigany saw the pistol and cutlass that hung from his belt. Both weapons looked new and unused.

Another man, this one with the bearing and clothes of a mercenary, followed him. His weapons looked anything but new, and his battered face was obviously no stranger to violence. He must be a bodyguard, the strigany decided. And who but the most foppish of aristocrats needed a bodyguard here?

Blue blood, he thought as Florin approached.

Ripe for the picking.

But what he said was;

'Sorry, your lordship. My boy here is all in.'

'I'm not surprised, after all that dancing about,' Florin said, and winked at the strigany knowingly. 'But I'll give him a chance to catch his breath.'

Sergei looked at Florin, who was now leaning against the ropes. Then he looked at his father and nodded.

But his father wasn't so sure any more. What did this youngster mean by 'dancing about'?

'Of course,' Florin, seeing his hesitation, pressed on. 'If your boy's only good enough for ringers and peasants…'

'I don't know what you're implying,' the strigany hissed, 'but the answer's no. Sergei's fought nine men already today. We're finished.'

'Hmmm,' Florin grunted, and raised one eyebrow. 'So your prize-fighter is afraid. Thought so.'

'I'll fight him.'

'No, you're tired,' Sergei's father said, this time meaning it. Every instinct was now urging caution. Beneath this challenger's soft exterior there was something dangerous, he could almost smell it. Something as sharp and well hidden as a razor blade in an apple.

'Boss,' said the man's bodyguard, laying a hand on his arm. 'We haven't got time for all this arsing about.'

'It won't take a minute.'

'You're right about that,' Sergei said, and his carefully composed frown slipped. In its place, as bright and easy as the rising sun, came an arrogant smile.

Florin smiled back, his expression a mirror image. In that moment the two men might almost have been brothers.

'What a waste of time,' Lorenzo said, disgustedly. The ringmaster just spat.

'If you want to fight, it's evens. Put up a dozen crowns, and if you last three rounds, you'll win a dozen.'

'Wait a minute...' Lorenzo began, but Florin had already unbuckled his belt and handed it over.

'Just hold this, would you?' he smiled, and vaulted into the ring. Sergei, forgetting to look beaten, stood back to give him room.

'Rest for a minute,' his father told him, but the fighter shook his head.

'I'm all right, pa.'

The older man was aware of the sudden interest the crowd was paying them, and said something to his son in a strange, guttural tongue. Reluctantly, Sergei stopped bouncing up and down and drooped his head. Florin, who'd watched the exchange, laughed at him.

'Good to see how completely exhausted you are,' he said, sarcastically, and threw his shirt to Lorenzo.

Let's just get this over with, the ringmaster thought, and glanced over to the bookmakers. Even this late in the day they were doing a brisk trade, their eyes gleaming as the punters they'd already fleeced were replaced by fresh faces. In between the handshakes and arguments each of them found the time to sneeze, burying the gesture in bright red handkerchiefs.

So, thought Sergei's father, they want a win. Good. He turned back to his son, who was gazing through Florin as if he were a pane of glass, and checked the bindings that covered his knuckles.

'Take him down,' the old man whispered, and the lad nodded.

'I will.'

A moment later the strigany rang the bell and the fight was on.

For the first couple of minutes the two men did little more than edge around each other, feinting to one side or another as they sought for the best position. The sun had sunk low over the western horizon now, low enough to blind any man fool enough to face it. Neither Sergei or Florin were fool enough, and it was that fact that kept them dancing around.

The crowd soon grew tired of this footwork, however. They began to jeer and curse. Incitements to violence were matched by accusations of cowardice. Aspersions were cast on the two fighters' parentage. One man even threw an apple.

Had Florin been as level-headed as he thought he was, none of these jibes would have mattered. After all, he didn't have to beat his opponent, he just had to avoid being beaten himself.

But Florin wasn't. He managed to keep his cool for another few seconds of footwork before leaping forward into the attack.

Resisting the urge to swing his fists around, Florin launched a flurry of short, sharp jabs. They connected, but only with the strigany's shoulders, chest and fists. The boxer stepped backwards easily, letting the Bretonnian's punches bounce off him as harmlessly as hail off a tin roof. Then, as the first bell approached, Sergei ducked forward and struck upwards, the lightning strike of a well-practiced uppercut.

Incredibly, it missed. Somehow his opponent had seen it coming. Or perhaps he had just slipped at a lucky moment. Either way, Sergei's fist cut through empty air, pulling him off balance for the first time that day.

Seeing his chance Florin pounced, his left cracking into the strigany's ribs whilst his right clipped across the man's temple.

Sergei blinked with pain and sprang backwards, landing as lightly as a cat as he turned to watch his opponent. Even through the adrenaline of the sport he could feel the pain in his side, the sensation hurting his pride enough to turn it into anger.

But before he could take his revenge the bell rang.

'He's good, pa,' Sergei admitted as the old man checked his ribs and examined the bruise on his forehead.

'Yes,' the older strigany agreed. 'Take him down as quick as you like. Then we'll finish for the day.'

'I will.'

A moment later the bell rang again. For the benefit of the crowd, Sergei let Florin bounce a few more blows off him before launching his own attack. It was sudden and vicious, the punches flowing from his advance as hard and as unexpectedly as lightning from a clear sky.

He jabbed and hooked. He sent uppercuts slipping under wide haymakers in combinations too fast for the eyes of the spectators to follow.

But Florin, flitting this way and that, somehow seemed to avoid the worst of it. Blows that would have felled him if they'd connected glanced off his dodging form, or slid off his shoulders. From time to time he struck back, short jabs that Sergei hardly bothered to avoid as he closed in, grunting with the concentration of a demolition man at work.

Gradually this onslaught began to take its toll. It was a close thing but, battered and bruised, Florin made it through to the second bell.

'You've broken your nose again, I see,' Lorenzo said, in a told-you-so tone of voice. 'Keep hitting his fists with your face like that and you'll soon be as handsome as me.'

Despite the trickle of blood, Florin chuckled.

'Well then, there's something to look forward to.'

'Seriously, boss, why not quit while you're ahead? What's a couple of dozen crowns anyway?'

'That strigany certainly knows his business. Seems he's hit me hard enough to give you concussion.'

'I try to talk sense to him,' Lorenzo said, rolling his eyes upwards in appeal to the heavens, 'but he doesn't listen.'

Then the bell rang for the final time, and Florin was back on his feet.

This time there was no pause. Before the last clang of the bell Sergei, as quick as a terrier on a rat, was upon him. Three jabs found their way to the side of Florin's head, and when he stumbled away from them a hook was waiting.

Stars exploded in the blue sky as he desperately barged past the strigany, taking a blow to his kidneys as he did so. A second later he stumbled onto the ropes and turned.

Beyond the bright sparks which now swam through his field of vision Florin could see his shadow stretching across the ring. It looked as solid as a fallen man on the blood-stained canvas. Ignoring the feeling that this was a premonition Florin tore his attention away from it and watched Sergei instead.

That arrogant smile was back on the strigany's face as he crouched and closed in for the kill.

Florin prepared to meet him, thinking about how warm the sun felt on the back of his neck. Sergei stepped into his shadow, eager to finish the exhausted Bretonnian.

It was the mistake Florin had been waiting for.

Dropping to one knee he fell, and rolled away to the right. For a split second Sergei found himself gazing through the air where his foe had stood. Gazing directly into the sun.

The flare of it burned painfully in his eyes, which flicked shut. Blinking hard against a sudden rush of tears he leapt clumsily back, his raised fists invisible behind the sunspots which blossomed in his eyes.

Florin saw his chance and took it. Springing back to his feet he cracked a fist into the strigany's temple, the blow hard enough to crack his knuckles. Sergei stumbled away from the impact and Florin struck again.

This time, though, the boxer's instincts saved him. He caught the punch in the palm of his hand, then returned it.

Florin, his advantage gone, sidled back away from his opponent and wondered what to do next.

Not that he had much time to wonder. Even before the sunspots had left his opponent's eyes, the strigany was upon him, battering through his defences with a volley of punches. Sergei ducked forward and threw his left up in a vicious uppercut. It rattled Florin's teeth like dice in a cup and collapsed his legs beneath him.

The Bretonnian felt his knees hit the floor of the ring. Then his palms. Then he heard a count, somewhere far distant. But then, as sweetly as the voice of the Lady herself, he heard the final bell.

It was probably the most beautiful sound he had ever heard.

'Right then, boss,' Lorenzo said, handing Florin his shirt as he shakily got back to his feet. 'If you've finished enjoying yourself, perhaps we can get back to the task in hand.'

'Of course,' Florin lisped as, wiping blood from his lips, he turned to accept the approval of the crowd. He bowed and smiled, chest swelling with pride despite the bruises that covered him. Then he turned to shake the strigany's hand.

'You were lucky,' Sergei muttered as they clasped hands. 'Another minute and I'd have had you.'

'Any idiot can hand out a beating,' Florin agreed, 'if he practises enough. But it takes a real man to take one and carry on anyway. Don't you agree?'

'Another minute,' the strigany repeated, a scowl darkening his face. 'Perhaps you'd like to try your luck again?'

'Ignore him, your honour,' Sergei's father cut in, and handed Florin the winner's purse. 'We're finished for the day. Here's your prize and well done.'

'Thanks,' Florin said, relief smoothing his bruised features as he counted the money. 'By the way, this is the caravan of Domnu Chervez, isn't it?'

'Amongst others, yes. Why do you ask, your grace?'

'We need to see him. A friend sent us.'

'Who?'

Florin frowned at the man's abrupt enquiry. His eagerness wasn't just rude, it was suspicious. There was no reason why he shouldn't mention Mordicio's name here, of course. But then, there was no reason why he should.

Lorenzo, a shrewd suspicion furrowing his brows, had no such qualms.

'We were sent by a Monsieur Mordicio,' he said, watching for the strigany's reaction.

'Monsieur,' he repeated with a bark of mocking laughter. 'Last time I saw the old villain it was Menheer. And why, might I ask, did he send you here?'

'I hardly think that that's any of your...' Florin began, but the strigany cut him off with a single word.

'D'Artaud,' he said, with as much confidence as a magician casting a spell. 'I've been expecting you'.

'Ah,' Florin said. 'I see. Well, we're pleased to meet you, Domnu Chervez?' he asked, and cautiously held out one hand.

'Likewise,' the older man said, and gripped the Bretonnian's bruised knuckles with an obvious relish. 'And I must say, Menheer d'Artaud, you certainly know how to introduce yourself.'

'Thank you.' Florin winced. 'I'm just glad to have caught you in time. Mordicio said you wouldn't wait for long, even if the pigeon made it to you. And the river boat took forever. Typical bloody Marienburgers. We haven't even had time to buy horses yet.'

'Then you might have a problem,' the Domnu said with a shake of his head. 'We leave at dawn.'

'Don't worry, pa,' Sergei volunteered with a helpful smile. 'Me and Colli should be able to find them something.'

'Well done,' the Domnu said, then frowned as he caught sight of something over Florin's shoulder.

'Not for you, friend,' he said warily, releasing Florin's hand to stroll over to the edge of the ring. 'Only humans, see? Not you. Sorry.'

The ogre watched him impassively. If anything was going on behind the battered contours of its face it certainly didn't show. Then, a muscle the size of a triceps rippling in its forehead, the ogre lifted one eyebrow and turned to Florin.

'It's all right, Domnu,' Florin said hastily. 'He's with us. In fact, Domnu Chervez, let me introduce Krom.'

Krom grunted and inclined its head in a slight nod. The strigany muttered his own greeting, then turned back to Florin.

'Why don't you go and eat whilst Sergei finds you some horses?' he said. 'Then meet me back here. Mordicio didn't tell me quite why he'd sent your little expedition along, but I'm dying to find out.'

'Good idea, pa,' Sergei said. Pulling on his shirt he vaulted over the ropes into the dispersing crowd, as lively as ever despite the day's exertions.

'I'll come with you,' Lorenzo told him, and handed Florin the bundle of his weapons.

'No need.'

Lorenzo smiled ingratiatingly, all three of his teeth gleaming in the rays of the setting sun.

'Really, I'll come with you. We'll see these horses together. I've a feeling things will work out cheaper that way.'

Despite seeing his middleman's fee slipping away, Sergei shrugged good-naturedly. After all, these two seemed rich enough for more than one fleecing. From Florin's pistol to the thick golden chain that glittered amongst the curls of Lorenzo's chest, everything about them said wealth.

There'd be plenty of time to impoverish them in the days to come.

A WEEK LATER and the pain from the fight had been replaced by the pain in Florin's backside. It had been a long time since he'd ridden a horse, but even then it had been with the aid of a decent, well-tanned saddle. Compared to the supple leatherwork he was used to, this one felt as though it had been carved from a block of wood.

But even if he'd been a trained cavalryman, riding along with the best saddle in the world, the pace that Domnu Chervez set would have been gruelling.

It started every day in the first grey light of dawn. Before the sun had even risen, the strigany women and the merchant's servants would crawl reluctantly from their wagons, coughing and grumbling loud enough to drown out the birdsong. Huddled in ragged blankets they'd stumble about the camp, drawing water or shivering as they blew life back into their cooking fires.

Meanwhile, whilst the acrid smell of wood smoke mingled with that of honeyed porridge in the cold dawn air, the men would harness their oxen back to their wagons, whispering to them with a tenderness that their families could only dream of.

Then, with the sun still little more than a rumour beyond the black silhouettes of the mountains beyond, the day's journey would begin. The beat of the march was slow, but it was constant. The remorseless tread of the oxen stopped for nothing but a black thread that Domnu Chervez kept wound around his wrist. When the sky was so dark that this thread could no longer be seen against it, the caravan would stop.

Then, and only then.

And yet the trail oxen that pulled the wagons seemed perfectly content to grind along for hour after hour, day after day. Not only that, but so did the caravan's outriders. There were perhaps a dozen of them, two-man patrols that flitted around the caravan like bees around a hive.

It was only a matter of time before Florin and Lorenzo, both well-armed and mounted, were asked to join them.

'How about it?' the Domnu had asked them one night as they sat around his camp fire. 'We're coming up to the foothills now, which is where things start to get interesting.'

'Of course,' Florin had replied. 'We'd be glad to.'

And in fact, he had been glad to. Although picking his way through the wilderness was harder than just plodding along behind the caravan, it was also a lot more enjoyable. Even Lorenzo stopped grumbling, the better to study this land.

Although empty of human life, the rolling countryside was rich and bountiful. Fields of wild corn gave way to lush green meadows. Glades of autumn-ripened pear trees, their leaves alive with the buzz of insects, lay unguarded. Their fruit was left to rot where it fell, or was picked through by flocks of stringy-looking hens.

Occasionally, they would come across the remains of abandoned villages. The stubborn angles of their walls remained standing and, despite the wisteria that softened their edges, defiant. There was no telling how long the derelict buildings had stood thus. Perhaps decades. Perhaps centuries.

Either way, the two friends hurried through them. Accidental shrines to a population long since washed away by bloody tides of war or plague, they seemed best left undisturbed.

And all the while, the mountains loomed larger in the east. Despite the clear skies and bright sunlight they remained black, as though permanently overcast by a shadow of their own making. Only their highest crests shone, white tips of ice scattered amongst the hazy clouds.

As the weeks passed the mountains drew nearer. The ravines that splintered their craggy hides could be seen with the naked eye, as deep as the wrinkles of a crone's frown. Florin, frowning himself from saddle soreness and sunburn, was staring at them when they came across the ambush.

It was their horses that saved them. They'd been trotting along a shaded deer-path, the passing tree trunks rippling the sunlight into zebra patterns on their coats, when they'd reared up in a sudden stop. There seemed neither warning nor reason for the halt, and it came so unexpectedly that Florin was flung over his mare's neck.

He landed on his shoulder and rolled, cursing to himself as he tumbled through the undergrowth. The thorns scratched, but at least they broke his fall, and a moment later he was scrambling back to his feet. He turned to see that Lorenzo had seized his horse's bridle, catching her before she bolted.

'She's smelt something,' the older man said, keeping his voice calm as the horse shifted beneath him. Florin saw that he was right. Nelly's ears were laid back, her eyes white and rolling, her nostrils quivering as she sniffed at the breeze; he could almost see the fear rising off her.

'Wolves?' Florin suggested, matching Lorenzo's gentle tones as he went back to stroke her. Nelly whinnied and turned her muzzle into his hand, her ears lifting a little.

'Maybe.'

'The wind is coming from over that ridge,' Florin said, gesturing towards a rocky outcrop that cut across the path

ahead. 'Tell you what, you hold on to Nelly here and I'll go
and have a look.'

Lorenzo sucked his front tooth and looked doubtful.

'Maybe we should both go. It could be wolves. Then
again, it could be anything. It could a dragon.'

'A dragon!' Florin scoffed uneasily, his voice lowering to
a whisper.

'Who knows?' Lorenzo shrugged. 'Might as well say
dragon as wolf. Why do you think all the villages here-
abouts are empty? Do you think a few mangy old wolves
would scare farmers away from land this good?'

Florin frowned, and looked again at the ridge. It looked
a little like a dragon itself: a long, low shape that stretched
through the forest. Then he sighed and turned back to
Lorenzo.

'Probably not. But what can we do? We're supposed to be
on patrol. We can't just go back because one of the horses
jumped. No, I'll look. Just hold the horses ready. I want to
sneak up on whatever they've smelled.'

'And if it sneaks up on you first?'

'Then we'll see if this still works,' Florin winked, and
drew his pistol.

He'd bought it in Bordeleaux before setting out. It was
expensive, ornately decorated, and heavy. It was also fright-
eningly inaccurate. Despite hours of practice Florin still
couldn't hit anything farther away than twenty feet, unless
the target happened to be a barn door. But even though
he'd known of all these disadvantages when he'd bought it,
the lure of blackpowder weapons had been too much.

Besides, he thought, as he checked the firing pan and
pulled back the wheel lock, it's powerful. The bullets could
punch through steel plate as easily as if it were rusted tin.

At least, they could if they hit it.

Returning the gun to its holster he padded quietly off
through the leafy ground, his eyes already searching for
handholds on the stone outcrop ahead. It wouldn't be a
difficult climb, he could see that much. The surfaces
were sloping and uneven, almost stepped, and creepers

as thick as his wrist trailed across it like a tangle of ropes.

Slowing his pace, Florin began to slide his feet through the detritus of the forest floor, pushing it gently out of the way before stepping down so as to avoid crunching fallen twigs. Not that he believed in Lorenzo's dragon, he told himself, as he slowed his breathing.

Not at all.

He was just being cautious.

By the time he reached the outcrop his passage through the forest had become almost perfectly silent.

The stone was hot beneath his fingers, sun-baked despite the sweet scented breeze that blew across it. Florin crawled up it, pulling himself from ledge to ledge, his palms sticky as a chameleon's as he worked his way towards the top, damp with warmth and the effort of moving quietly.

The breeze whispered in the trees behind him, the sound as soothing as the stone was warm. As Florin climbed up to the last ledge he wondered if they should rest here. They could eat the frugal bread and water meal the Domnu had provided them with whilst arguing about imaginary dragons.

Then he crested the top of the outcrop, and suddenly he was no longer thinking of bread and water.

He was thinking of pork.

The sleeping herd below were surely wild boar, he decided. They certainly smelled wild enough. It was no wonder the horses had stopped; this close even Florin's nose wrinkled at the musk that rose up from their snoring bodies.

Cautiously flattening himself against the rock, he licked his lips and gazed down upon the animals. Their fur, the colour of rusty bristles on a wire brush, was coarse and ungroomed, and their tusks were jagged.

Still, there was no reason to suppose that the flesh within it was inedible.

Florin, visions of pork chops sizzling in his imagination, counted twenty-three of the slumbering animals. As he did so he thought back to the last time he'd seen their like. That had been on the other side of the world, and in much less happy circumstances. Then, he had been the hunted, not the hunter.

Shuddering at the memory, he drew his pistol and, biting his lip with the effort of maintaining silence, he slowly readied it. The single mechanical click of the wheel lock was lost beneath the grunting and snoring of the herd. Florin inched the hexagonal barrel forward, resting it along one arm as he wondered which one to take.

A young one, he thought, but not too young. We want meat that's tender, but we want quite a lot of it.

It really was a shame that he only had one shot. If he shot the grizzled old tusker which was lying nearest to him, sprawled out as if already dead, the younger ones would run. But if he shot one of them, would they provide enough meat?

Torn between one target and the next, he hesitated. And in this moment of hesitation, the boars' owners appeared.

They loped into the clearing with a clumsy grace, rolling along like sailors on a pitching deck. The gait set their shoulders rising and falling, and their trailing knuckles swung back and forth like drummers' fists. Although man-tall they were heavier than humans; their blunt heads were misshapen with mastiff jaws and their mottled green hides bulged with a deformed strength.

Some of the rags the creatures had stretched between their scraps of armour may well have been made for humans. Indeed, one of them was even wearing what could once have been the jacket from an Imperial soldier's uniform, the fine gold braid now as grubby as the strings of a mop.

But there was no mistaking these vile creatures for anything other than what they were. Not even for a moment. Even Florin, who'd never seen a live one before, knew orcs when he saw them.

He pressed his racing heart closer to the rock as more of them bundled into the clearing, and unhooked his finger from the trigger. Firing suddenly seemed like a very, very bad idea. In fact, perched above a clearing full of such beasts, even his breath seemed too loud.

The orcs were too intent on their business to hear him, though, or even to look up. As they dispersed amongst the herd, each seeking its own animal, the boars began to wake. And their mood, upon being woken up, wasn't sweet.

They squealed and snarled. They slashed their tusks at the legs of the orcs and at each other. One, a cunning old boar with a face that reminded Florin of Lorenzo, kept its eyes closed in feigned sleep, snoring away as the orcs approached. It waited for one of the smaller orcs to wander within reach and then, when he was no more than a foot away, it struck.

The blunt daggers of its teeth tore a piece of flesh out of the rider's leg, a fist-sized chunk of green meat followed by a gout of dark blood. The orc howled with pain and staggered backwards, dancing about to the raucous laughter of his companions. The boar chewed contentedly as its victim stumbled away, its blood darkening the ground.

But a moment later, the wounded orc had recovered. Florin winced as he watched it grind a handful of dirt into its wound, carelessly staunching the bleeding before resuming the search for its boar.

By now, most of the orcs had found their mounts. Whatever savage bargain the beasts had struck amongst themselves, it was obviously an individualistic one. It also seemed to be strangely democratic: the boars allowed their chosen riders to roll up onto their massive shoulders because it was their will, not because they were in any way cowed or broken in.

Florin, his sweat dampening the stone, watched the chaos below gradually resolve itself. Once they were mounted, the orcs, each armed with a thick stabbing spear, milled restlessly about. Florin was seized with a terrible suspicion that they were going to round the outcrop upon which he was hiding and head towards Lorenzo and the horses.

But even as he wondered whether or not to make a run for it, the leader, its skin as dark as ivy beneath its rusted plate mail, bellowed an order. Before it had time to finish the call, its mount decided to leave. With an impatient grunt the boar turned and trotted off towards the north.

The mob followed, a ragged stampede that crashed through the undergrowth in a graceless avalanche of snarling boars and cursing orcs.

Florin remained frozen as the noise of their progress faded. When it was no louder than the frightened chatter of the swallows that wheeled overhead, he turned and slithered back down to the forest floor.

'What was it?' Lorenzo asked as he hastened back to the horses.

'Trouble,' Florin said, wiping his palms before swinging back up into his saddle. 'Orcs. Dozens of 'em.'

'Ah,' Lorenzo nodded wisely. 'Orcs. I thought so.'

Ignoring Florin's raised eyebrow he turned and started to canter his horse back towards the caravan.

KROM HAD NO illusions about the men he was with. After only a couple of months in their lands, the ogre had no illusions about men at all. They were all weak, and most of them were cowards. He'd been shocked to see that even the most powerful amongst them, Mordicio, allowed a mere female to disrespect him.

And the fragility of their bodies... well, it would shame a gnoblar. The bruises that had covered Florin after his pathetically bloodless fight with the strigany had lasted for more than a week.

Still, despite this healthy contempt, Krom wasn't fool enough to underestimate his travelling companions to the extent that they underestimated him. Humans, he knew, were intelligent. It was a strange, overly complicated sort of intelligence, and was just as likely to tangle up their planning as to facilitate it. But it was to be respected, just the same.

Take Domnu Chervez, Krom thought, turning back on the ox he was riding to study the Strigany. He was weaker than most with age, but he had more power in his head than many ogres did in their fists. He seemed oddly immune to the human disease of fear, too. When he'd heard of the orcs that were gathering in the hills ahead, he'd just smiled.

Krom's face became blank with thoughtfulness as he remembered the scene. It had been evening when Florin and Lorenzo, their faces flushed and their horses winded, had brought news of the orcs. Within minutes, the entire caravan had gathered around them, the merchants fluttering about like a gaggle of frightened geese.

Chervez had waited for the fluttering to die down. Then, as confidently as if they were discussing something that had already happened, he'd told them exactly how they were going to deal with the orcs.

It was a good plan too, Krom reflected. So good that he'd seen no reason to open his mouth. Especially when every other traveller on the caravan had been doing just that.

Now, as morning drifted into afternoon, the ogre could see the place the Domnu had mentioned in his plan. It lay no more than half a mile ahead: a gap where the hills closed in on the trail like the posts of a cemetery gate. Oak trees, their foliage as thick as the hairs on his ox's back, covered the slopes of these hills, hiding the ambushers who waited there.

The leaves couldn't disguise their smell, though. To Krom's flattened nose, it was as sharp as an outhouse in high summer. He knew it for what it was too.

It was orcs. Full-grown orcs, and lots of them.

Some sort of animals seemed to be waiting with them, but he couldn't quite decide what they were. Goats, perhaps.

The sun sailed over the caravan towards the safety of the west, lengthening the shadows of the fifteen wagons and two horsemen who were following the ogre. The hills closed in towards them, as slow and eager as a pack of wolves surrounding a flock of sheep.

The smell of orcs became stronger.

Krom could already see where Chervez had guessed the attack would come. Up ahead, the trail wound through a meadow that was barely an acre across. On either side, the forested hills loomed as close as they could, the shadows they cast darkening the clearing.

As the caravan rolled into the clearing, Krom turned again to see that the wagons were keeping up and keeping close.

He knew that it was their fear, not their bravery, which kept the men following him into this trap. They knew they'd be safer facing the orcs this way than trying to outrun them. Even so, Krom half expected them to panic and flee.

Humans, he thought contemptuously, and lifted one leg to break wind.

A moment later, as though in answer to the obscene gesture, a harsh, discordant horn sounded out of the woods to their right. Krom stopped and squinted towards the treeline. Although the horn still sang out, the sound of it was lost in a sudden commotion. The noise of splintering branches, rumbling hooves, angry porcine squeals and fleeing deer.

But what it was mostly composed of was a terrifying chorus of inhuman warcries.

The noise of the boar riders' charge grew even louder as they crashed into the meadow. A terrible joy entered the orcs' voices as they caught sight of the caravan. It twisted their mouths up into snarls of glee, and the yellow slashes of their eyes narrowed with an unholy excitement.

Krom noted how the front-runners of this ragged charge leaned forward, lantern jaws hanging between the flapping sails of their mounts' ears as they closed in. The same bloodthirsty eagerness set them to swinging their short spears about in wild arcs, as if the weapons themselves were eager for battle.

Some of the spear tips were already bloodied, wet from accidental blows the riders had struck against their comrades. Two of the orcs were locked in combat after one such incident, the caravan forgotten as they tried to strangle each other beneath their boars' disgusted gaze.

But for the most part, the charge continued despite such distractions, the weapons continuing to whirl.

Krom swung to the ground, hefted his axe, and spared a single look down the line of wagons. The snapshot glance was filled with the blur of crossbow bolts and the sudden gleam of unsheathed steal. Contented, Krom turned all of his attention back to the task in hand.

And the task in hand was now. Despite their ungainly appearance, and despite the weight they were carrying, the boars had crossed the meadow with a frightening speed. Barely a minute had passed since their horn had sounded, yet already Krom found the anticipation of combat becoming reality.

With a bone-shaking roar he threw himself forward to embrace it.

If the nearest orc was surprised at this response it gave no sign. Instead it lowered its spear towards Krom's belly, the tip of the weapon weaving back and forth as it hurled itself towards the ogre.

Krom waited, holding himself in perfect stillness until the steel was a second away from spitting him. Only then did he move, spinning his bulk to one side and seizing the spear in one fist.

The boar continued in its charge, snarling as it barrelled through the space where the ogre had been. Its rider, however, instinctively refusing to let go of his weapon, was hoisted from its back and thrown up into the air.

Its warcry became a howl of surprise as it rocketed upwards, legs windmilling. Krom waited for it to begin to fall before he struck, swinging his axe in a one-handed blow that sent the falling orc's arm and head tumbling into the grass.

The ogre grunted with the satisfaction of a job well done. Then he slapped his free hand onto the haft of his axe and turned towards the enraged squeal of his victim's boar.

There was no subtlety in the animal's attack. No strategy at all. It just barrelled forward, tusks jutting up from the battering ram of its lowered head as it thundered towards the ogre.

Again, Krom made himself wait. Time stretched around him, a single second trickling past as slowly as a minute. At the end of it the boar was close enough to taste the cloth of the ogre's breeches. It bit down hungrily, but even as the muscles in its jaws were bunching Krom was moving, swinging away and cutting down in a single, liquid movement.

The axe blade rose and fell as easily as if it had been wielded by a servant splitting wood. As easily and as successfully. With a deep crunch the razored edge bit down through fur and skin, muscle and bone. Then it cleaved through the boar's skull, splitting its brain as neatly as a ripe apple.

The animal's squeal faded into a death rattle. Krom, with a wary glance around him, struggled to free his blade from the animal's carcass. But no matter which way he pulled it it remained stuck, trapped within the solid bone of the boar's skull. Even in death, it seemed, the foul-tempered beast was too stubborn to relent.

Krom felt a flicker of admiration for it as he abandoned his axe and picked up the orc's spear instead.

With a lick of his lips he searched for his next opponent, sniffing as eagerly as a hunting dog on the scent of its quarry. And there was plenty of quarry here, Krom thought contentedly, turning to select one. Most of them had made straight for the wagon train and were circling around the wagons, whooping with the joy of battle as the blood flowed.

Initially the high wooden sides of their carts had provided the travellers with some protection from the orcs' charge. Even now, most of the men remained perched on top of them, slashing down at the cavorting green figures.

Not all of the wagons remained, though. A couple of them, their oxen maddened with fear, had broken from the line and were now being dragged towards the opposite patch of forest, orcs in pursuit.

Another had been overturned. One of the barrels of wine it had carried had smashed open to bleed into the dust of the track. A boar was wallowing in the liquor, drinking greedily as its rider kicked at it and cursed.

Krom was about to go and put that particular orc out of its misery when, with a flash of movement, Domnu Chervez leapt into his line of sight. The Strigany hurled an empty crossbow at one of the attackers, then rushed forward to slash a cutlass across the nose of its mount.

It would have been a good tactic against a horse. The slash of pain across its muzzle would have been enough to send it rearing up in panic, probably throwing its rider down into a heap of broken bones. But against a boar the manoeuvre almost proved to be fatal. Far from frightening it, the pain just inflamed its temper.

With an almost human roar of anger, the animal lunged forward, its rider thrown off its back by the unexpected movement. Chervez leapt away from its first bite and scrambled back onto his wagon, losing the heel of his boot to the boar's snapping teeth.

The fallen orc, meanwhile, had scrambled back to its feet. Leaving its mount to distract the strigany, it ducked under the wagon and popped up to attack the strigany from the rear.

Krom saw its cleaver raise to strike, and threw his spear in a perfect, thoughtless reaction. The weapon hissed gleefully through the air. There was a meaty thump and the barbed tip punched through the orc's back and into the planking of the wagon. It scrabbled around as helplessly as a cockroach on a pin, howling in sudden terror as the ogre rushed forwards, drawing his belt knife.

Chervez felt the wagon shaking beneath him and looked up to see Krom's looming shape. The boar did the same. But it was a second too late; its teeth snapped on empty air as the ogre seized the wiry scruff of its neck and stabbed down between the first two vertebrae of its spine.

'Thanks,' the pale-faced strigany shouted above the noise of the battle.

Krom, his own misshapen features now freckled with sprayed blood, dazzled him with a grin full of quartz.

Chervez was glad to see it. As gruesome as it was, he couldn't think of another face he'd rather see.

Then their smiles faded as, just as another wagon fell crashing onto its side, the forest burst asunder with a fresh tide of attackers.

* * *

THE RIDERS HAD followed the Domnu's instructions to the letter. Drifting away into the morning mist they had slunk to the copse of trees he'd selected. Beneath their dripping boughs the horsemen had waited, shivering, until the breaking dawn showed them the path northwards.

It had been a rough path, hardly more than a goat track through the woods and meadows that blanketed these hills. In the chill of the morning, the dew had shone like the ice on the spider webs that crisscrossed it, and the temptation to gallop through them had been all but irresistible. They had soon left the caravan far behind.

The day grew warmer as they charged along, racing north until the morning was full and the dew drops had long since vanished. Then they had wheeled and turned to the east, squinting as their mounts had splashed through a river valley which seemed to lead straight to the sun.

An hour later and they wheeled again, turning behind their leader as neatly as a flock of sparrows as he trotted back up into the hills, heading south now to finish their manoeuvre.

There was no more galloping now. No more wild careering through bracken and gorse, or shallow, foaming water. On this leg of their journey there was just caution, stealth, and wide-eyed alertness.

Florin, already itching with frustration at being under somebody else's command, began to hate it even more. He knew why things had to be done this way. The Domnu had explained it all very carefully, and it had all made perfect sense.

Even so, having once seen their enemy, this long, tortuous route became a sort of torment. The waiting was the problem. The anticipation. It twisted his stomach up into tight knots, and strummed on his nerves even as it greased his palms with sweat.

If only they'd been able to charge, either towards the enemy or away from them. Florin knew that once the attack began he'd have no more time for fear. There'd be just the drunken rush of adrenaline and concentration, the gods' own drug that would see him through to either death or victory.

When the harsh cry of the enemy's trumpet rang out from beyond the next ridge, it was almost a relief.

'Right then, lads,' the strigany who was leading them said. 'Looks like we got here just in time.'

'Any rewards for the first kill, Colli?' Sergei asked, and Florin's ears pricked up.

'Not really.' Colli winked at him. 'Just the boasting rights.'

Although they'd barely spoken a word since leaving Grummand, Sergei and Florin exchanged a brief, hard look. Neither of them spoke of any challenge. Neither of them needed to.

The nervousness that had been twisting Florin's stomach into painful knots vanished, disappearing as completely as the morning dew. In its place was the decision that, whatever the costs, he'd take more heads than any arrogant little strigany.

Sergei, who was pointedly looking away, had already come to much the same decision himself.

'Time to move,' Colli said as the first, distant sounds of battle floated up from the valley below. 'Slow trot at first. Nobody to pass me until I give the word.'

He waited for the men to chorus their agreement before leading off into the slanting afternoon sunlight. Florin and Sergei soon found themselves jostling for position behind him.

'Let me go first,' Florin told his rival. 'I need room to fire.'

So saying he drew his pistol, flourishing it like a card player with an ace.

The strigany was unimpressed.

'No, I'll go first,' he said. 'There'll be no bell to save you this time, remember. Better let the real fighters do their jobs.'

Despite the angry flush that coloured his cheeks, Florin kept his tone light.

'Yes, you're a good fighter on a stage. But this is war, not entertainment. You should stay out of my way and let me show you how it's done.'

'I've seen your way,' Sergei said, adjusting his seat as the column speeded up. 'Falling down and bleeding. Not much good against orcs.'

As the Bretonnian struggled to think of a suitable reply, oak gave way to beech, and the forest thinned. A loud, piercing scream cut through the dappled light and Colli, taking it as a signal, broke into a canter.

'Watch and learn, my boy,' was the best Florin could come up with as the column became a line, and the line accelerated into a full gallop.

Eighty hooves beat a rumour of their coming on the rich loam of the forest floor, sending leaves flying up like confetti and filling the air with the smell of soil. Florin felt his heart swell, felt the blood singing through his veins and the breath of the quickening wind fresh on his skin.

For a moment his smile grew wide and white in the shade of the forest, and then the horsemen were clear, the thunder of their charge hurling them out into the brightness of the meadow beyond. The grass swished across their horses' fetlocks, whispering the same sibilant promise as the wind that hissed through their manes.

'Chaaaaaaaaarge!' Colli yelled with a wild abandon and, with barely a pause, the riders fell upon the rear of the unsuspecting orcs.

THE EVENING AIR hung still and heavy. Smoke from the cooking fires drifted upwards in tall, unbroken columns, only feathering away when it passed across the first of the stars. The men that sat around these camp fires were also still, also heavy.

At least, some of them were.

Others were too alive to rest for even for a moment. They laughed, and drank, and bounded from one fire to the next. They boasted and sang, stopping only to refill their pipes or their bellies. Despite their years, their excitement made them seem like new-born lambs, still drunk with the miracle of their own births.

Even the agonised cries that occasionally rang out from the circled wagons seemed to have little effect on their high spirits. If anything they merely served to fuel them.

Sergei, his back to the safety of the laagered caravan, seemed to share a little of every man's mood. Whilst his face was grim, his brows lowered in an expression as black as the approaching night, his movements were quick, restless. Somehow he didn't seem able to stop pacing around a corpse that lay tumbled in the grass.

A few hours ago it had been an orc.

No, not an orc, Sergei thought, bitterly. My orc.

It had been after the shock of their charge had sent the greenskins fleeing in confusion that Sergei had met this particular specimen. He'd already killed two others, cutting them down like cattle as they'd milled about between the hammer of the cavalry and the anvil of the caravan.

Unfortunately, so had that smug milksop of a Bretonnian.

That was why he'd been thankful to find his orc. It had been a lively specimen, full of fight despite the arrow through its leg. It had been big, too. So big that its death would have brought Sergei the victory over Florin that time had so unfairly denied him in the boxing ring.

But just as he'd drawn his cutlass back in preparation for a single, killing blow, the orc's head had exploded. A great gout of black blood and splintered bone had splattered back as it had collapsed, undoubtedly dead before it had even hit the ground.

When Sergei looked around there had been Florin, grinning like an overpaid whore over the smoking muzzle of his cursed pistol.

Florin, Sergei thought, and kicked the orc hard enough to make its corpse jump. What sort of stupid name was that?

'Weren't thinking of your old man, were you?' a voice said from behind him. It was sudden and close enough to make Sergei jump.

'No, pa. Not you.'

The two strigany lapsed into silence and looked down at the carcass. They were so intent that it might have just sat up and started telling them their fortunes.

'You fought well today, lad,' Domnu Chervez told his son after a moment. 'To kill a pair of orcs is something to remember. To savour.'

Sergei's forehead creased, and looked at the Domnu as he tried to find the right words.

'Just ask our friend d'Artaud,' the Domnu continued before he could do so. 'He knows it. He only killed one more than you, and now he's sitting around the fire, telling us all about it.'

'But he shot the third,' Sergei said, his voice deceptively calm. 'And it was mine. He shot it right out from under my cutlass.'

'Yes.' His father nodded. 'It was a good shot, wasn't it? Looks like he got it right between the eyes. And from horseback, too. Quite impressive.'

'Quite lucky,' Sergei grumbled, and the Domnu's eyes hardened.

'He killed three, you killed two. Can you change that?'

'No.'

'So what are you going to do?'

Sergei scowled down at the orc, as though it might know the answer. For a second the vicious yellow slash of its remaining eye twinkled in the light of the rising moon. It might almost have been winking.

'Accept it,' Sergei said, with a sigh of resignation. 'Get him next time.'

Domnu Chervez slapped his son on the shoulder.

'Good lad. Now, like I said, the Bretonnian is sitting at the fireside now, telling everyone about how he bested you. What are you going to do about that?'

'I'm going to go,' Sergei decided, 'and shake him by the hand. Offer my congratulations.'

The Domnu nodded approvingly.

'Good idea. I'll come along with you. I want to hear him tell the story again. Why are you looking at me like that? I do. He's only told the damn thing a dozen times. I want to hear it again.'

Sergei was still reluctantly smiling as he strode back into the camp. Once there he surprised everyone, most of all Florin himself, by shaking the Bretonnian by the hand.

'Well done,' he said. 'Good shooting.'

'Just lucky,' Florin said, bemused.

'I know,' Sergei replied, 'but never mind. I'll get you next time.'

'We'll see,' Florin allowed. 'We'll see.'

The next day the caravan left the last of the hills behind it and wound its way up into the mountains proper.

CHAPTER FOUR

ULLI KIRLSON STOOD on the high stone parapet, one gauntleted hand resting on the freezing metal of his axe, the other on his mailed hip. At these heights the wind was bold enough to tug at his beard, and sharp enough to frost his helm with the snow's breath. But despite the wind's best efforts Ulli remained unshivering at his post, as solid as the stonework of the ancient watchtower itself.

Below him, slicing through the jostling summits of the World's Edge Mountains, was the pass. Like most dwarfish masterworks its location had been chosen with the utmost care. There wasn't a place better suited for the construction of a road such as this for a thousand miles in any direction. Even so, the building of it had been hard, a work of centuries rather than years.

But that had been a long time ago. Since then, time had erased the runes and carvings with which the dwarfs had marked their masonry, scouring them away so thoroughly that the pass might almost have been an accident of nature.

Most of the human travellers that passed this way took it for just that and thought that the smooth bored tunnels through which the road passed were no more than caves. They thought that the bridges which carried them so safely across the mountain chasms were no more than freaks of geology.

They were mistaken, of course, although understandably so. After all, none of their own civilisations could have even dreamed of shaping the mountains in such a way.

Only the stones which cobbled the road were unmistakably hand crafted. They fitted together so neatly that, even after all these centuries, it was impossible to fit a dagger point between them. The quality of the workmanship was signature enough for the folk who had made it, and dwarfs that passed this way would spend many hours discussing and admiring it.

Unfortunately, the pass's main traffic came from human merchants, and their attention was usually too sapped by the thin air and icy winds for them to admire the stones which bruised their feet.

Ulli was watching one such party pass this way now. From the eyrie of his watchpost he counted the horses and wagons that filed towards the toll gate, and the men who drove them. They were so bundled up that they might have been almost anything, had it not been for their obvious frailty.

Only one of their number seemed immune to the cold, although Ulli soon realised that this was, in fact, an ogre. A bodyguard to one of the wealthier merchants, he guessed. Or maybe a guide.

A generation ago the dwarf would have sent a runner down to tell his thain of the caravan's approach. These days, there weren't enough of his kin to be spared for such tasks. Instead there was a lever, an iron-hard piece of oak that set an alarm bell ringing far below.

When he'd pulled it, Ulli unslung a crossbow from his back, and winched back the string. Then he slid a bolt into the groove and rested it on the parapet. His eyes gleamed as brightly as his armour as he sighted down the weapon, and his armour gleamed as brightly as the black ice which sheathed the battlements.

Just for once, Ulli wished that this party would refuse to pay the toll. Maybe even try to fight its way through the gates. Anything to break the endless monotony of this cursed posting. Sometimes it got so bad that he even considered becoming a trollslayer, spiking his hair into an orange mane and going forth to seek his doom. Anything for a bit of action.

The caravan stopped and its leaders, swaddled in shapeless bundles of cloth, hurried forward to make their obeisances and pay their dues.

Ah well, Ulli thought disappointedly. There's always beer.

Warmed by that happy thought the dwarf listened to the gates grind open and watched the caravan crawl through, bound for the barren lands beyond. The Ogre Kingdoms, some called them. Vast tracts of moorland and steppe, home to the gods alone knew what dangers; but also, great opportunities.

'Lucky bastards,' Ulli muttered, and spat neatly onto one of the wagons that was passing beneath his tower.

THE MASSIVE SLABS of the dwarfs' gates boomed as they swung closed behind the caravan. They cut across the pass as neatly as the level of a mason's balance, resting on the exact point where up became down.

Not that the knowledge did much to alleviate the bone chilling cold. It seeped up from the icy cobbles beneath them, and radiated out from the sheer walls on either side.

'Nippy, isn't it?' Florin asked.

'Not really,' Sergei shrugged, his words misting the air with a plume of frozen white breath.

Lorenzo, who was riding behind them, sniggered. Both men pretended not to hear him.

'That dwarfish gate is a pretty piece of work,' Florin continued. 'Have you seen it before?'

'Many times,' Sergei replied.

'I wonder how they keep the metal free of ice? Some sort of magic, perhaps.'

Sergei touched the hilt of his dagger, an unconscious gesture against sorcery. Then he shook his head.

'No. I've heard tell that there are pipes in the stonework around it. Pipes full of hot water pumped up from the depths of the earth.'

'Really?' Florin asked. 'I wouldn't be surprised. Dwarfs are certainly clever enough for that.'

'Have you ever known a dwarf?' Sergei asked, breaking a brief, awkward silence. For some reason Florin had chosen to ride beside him today, suddenly eager to make friends. The strigany wished that he hadn't. He was a lot more comfortable breaking jaws than making polite conversation. He was better at it, too.

Not that Florin seemed to mind this awkwardness. In fact, he quite enjoyed the opportunity it gave him to fill the silences with his stories.

'Yes,' he said, starting a new one now. 'I've known many dwarfs. There's one in particular I'll never forget. It was in Lustria, and his name was Thorgrimm. He was a great comrade. Loyal, strong. Very dry sense of humour.'

'Ha!' Lorenzo interjected, the sound snapping against the chiselled walls that loomed up on either side. 'Dry sense of humour. No sense of humour, is what you mean to say.'

'Lorenzo didn't like him,' Florin explained. 'They were too much alike.'

The older man swore at him, and Florin winked at Sergei.

The strigany looked back at Lorenzo with a bemused expression on his face. It was beginning to dawn on him that, despite appearances, these two Bretonnians weren't really master and servant after all.

Then he turned back to Florin, a sudden suspicion hardening his voice.

'Wait a minute,' he demanded. 'Did you just say you knew this dwarf…'

'Thorgrimm,' Florin interjected.

'…this Thorgrimm in Lustria?'

'Yes.' Florin nodded casually. 'Ever been there?'

Sergei snorted dismissively.

'No more than you have,' he decided. 'Nobody goes to Lustria. At least, nobody returns.'

'We have,' Florin said. 'That's why Mordicio chose us for this mission. He wanted the best.'

Sergei, unconvinced, turned back to Lorenzo.

'Is he telling the truth?'

'About going to Lustria, yes,' Lorenzo affirmed. 'About how many times I saved his skin there, never.'

Sergei turned back to Florin, and the two men studied each other.

'Tell you what,' Florin decided. 'Before this conversation becomes tedious, I'll swear it to you. On Lorenzo's soul, I swear that I've been to Lustria and back.'

'And I'll swear the same on his,' Lorenzo chuckled.

The strigany believed him. A new feeling of respect served to tie his tongue into even tighter knots.

'So,' he managed, at last, 'why are you coming with my father's caravan?'

Florin, leaning back in his saddle and gazing heroically into the middle distance, replied with a single word.

'Adventure,' he said, waving his arm in a perfect imitation of the actor who'd played him in the theatre.

Sergei struggled to look unimpressed.

'Why don't you tell the lad the truth?' Lorenzo said, spoiling the mood. 'It doesn't matter if he knows.'

'The truth?'

'That is the truth,' Florin said. 'But as for the specifics, well, it's a rescue mission. There's a beautiful girl who's been kidnapped by a tribe of savage ogres. We have to rescue her.'

'Which is to say,' Lorenzo, nervous of calling ogres savage with Krom just an earshot away, hastily chipped in. 'There's a certain girl, who has been rescued by a tribe of ogres. We have to bring her home.'

'And your ogre will guide you to this tribe?'

'Menheer Krom has agreed to do that, yes.'

'Is it far from the road?' Sergei asked, after a moment's thought.

'We don't know,' Florin shrugged. 'Maybe.'

'Then it might turn into an adventure, I suppose,' the strigany allowed. 'There are always greenskins waiting for us. They follow the caravans when they leave the mountains, waiting for stragglers. There's always one or two. Wagons with broken axles usually, or horses with broken legs. Unless you know how to shake them off they'll be on you before nightfall.'

Florin and Lorenzo exchanged a glance.

'I'm sure that Krom knows what he's doing. This is his land, after all.'

All eyes turned to the front, where Krom was plodding away in his usual position of point man. Somehow, without a word being spoken, he had made that honoured station his own since the outset.

'No reason why he should,' Sergei said, when it became clear that the ogre hadn't heard. 'The raiders would never bother with a lone ogre. With those horses and that metalwork they'll bother with you, though.'

Sergei smiled smugly, and peered towards the first smudge of distant green that a turn in the road had revealed. In a day, perhaps two, the mountains would slouch back down into foothills, and the dwarf-built road would fade into the packed earth of the Silk road.

Florin followed the strigany's gaze, then turned back towards him, his face alight with amused suspicion.

'And I suppose,' he asked, his voice heavy with sarcasm, 'that you know how to stop these greenskins from following us when we leave the caravan?'

Sergei nodded contentedly.

'It'll take a clipping of lucky heather or something, I guess. Or some sort of carved charm.'

'Nope.' The strigany shook his head. 'What it will take is me.'

'What do you mean?'

'I want to go with you.'

The statement, as unexpected as one of the strigany's uppercuts, was enough to silence the three men. Each sat wrapped in a world of his own thoughts as their horses clopped onwards.

It was Florin who broke the silence.

'Why do you want to come with us? I thought you were supposed to be guarding the caravan.'

Sergei shook his head.

'Pa can make do without me. What's one man? Anyway, I want to… oh I don't know. It sounds daft.'

'You want to become an adventurer?' Florin suggested.

'I want to make my fortune,' Sergei contradicted him, much to Lorenzo's amusement.

'The lad's not such a fool after all,' he snorted.

'I don't know,' Florin mused. 'We'd have to ask the Domnu. And we wouldn't be able to pay you much. Look, wouldn't it be better just to tell us how you think we can avoid any greenskins that might be following us?'

'No.' Sergei shook his head.

'We could just ask somebody else.'

'They wouldn't tell you. The merchants don't know, and we strigany never undercut each other.'

'I don't know. What do you think, Lorenzo?'

'Up to you, boss,' the older man said. 'It wouldn't hurt, I suppose. On the other hand…'

But suddenly Krom was speaking, the deep rumble of his baritone cutting through the conversation like an axe through kindling.

'This human,' he decided, twisting around on his saddle to give his judgement, 'has a valuable skill. We will take him with us.'

Then, without waiting for a reply, he turned back to the front, eyes once more scanning the hard road ahead.

Florin drew himself up to his full height.

'I think,' he began, his voice steady with a confidence that he didn't quite feel. 'That as commander of this party, that's a decision for me to make.'

Despite the tension that greased the air he let the challenge stand, watching the ogre's back as the men watched him. He gave Krom a single, impossibly long moment to respond before carrying on.

'However, in this case, I think that hiring Sergei is a good idea. That is to say, if his father agrees and if he will agree to a suitable remuneration.'

Krom's back remained turned as Florin spoke, his huge frame as silent and relaxed as ever. His only response came after Florin had stopped speaking, and that was only to belch. The gurgle was as wet as a blocked sewer sound, and loud enough to echo around the pass like some sort of obscene fanfare.

'Well, that's settled then,' Florin said, light-headed with relief as the echoes died away. 'So, young Sergei. How much do you think a lad such as yourself is worth? Twenty crowns is the usual, isn't it?'

'A day?'

'Ha!'

Krom listened to the negotiations unfolding behind him and smiled. They were annoying, these humans, but they were entertaining, too. He was already looking forward to getting them back to the tribe, and seeing how much they might be worth.

THE MOUNTAINS ENDED abruptly. Unlike their western approaches, which rose up out of the gentle swells of the foothills, the change between mountain and steppe in the east was immediate, the huge bulwarks of the World's Edge range collapsing into grassland as quickly as waves hitting the beach.

To the travellers, the descent from the heights into the world below felt like the change from winter to summer, although these false seasons took only two days to change.

As they followed the dwarf road, ice flowed into water, and the dead, black stone began to blossom. First with lichens, then with mosses, then with the grasses and shrubs which carpeted the plains beyond.

Buzzards began to circle overhead as they rattled along the last few miles of the mountain road, the birds' sharp eyes and sharper talons ready for the hares that lived amongst the undergrowth here.

By the time the road beneath the wagons degenerated back into hard, packed earth their owners had stripped off the furs they'd worn against the blistering cold of the mountain heights. They still remained wrapped in thick ponchos, or padded doublets, though. Despite the warmth of the autumnal sunlight the winds here were chill, harbingers of the season yet to come.

. Only Krom remained unaffected by the changing climate. As always he wore nothing but his boots and breeches, these held up by the wide belt that curved over the boulder of his stomach.

Leading the caravan, his eyes scanned both the distant horizon and the road ahead, his ears hearing every rumour the wind whispered, the flattened lump of his nose wrinkling as he sipped the scent it brought.

He wondered if anyone else realised what was following them as they blundered out into this seemingly empty plain. He doubted it.

Either way, the fleeting grey shapes which had begun to haunt both the dusk and dawn since they had left the mountains had not yet dared to strike. So far they had contented themselves with sniffing around, as quick and nebulous in the gloom as the clouds which scudded overhead.

They would eventually strike, Krom knew. They'd have to. If their chieftain let a prize as big as this slip through his tribe's fingers his reign would end, quickly and bloodily. At the very least he'd have to secure the frame of a broken wagon, or the horseflesh and metal of one of the caravan's outriders.

Or even better, Krom considered, his own little group. If the chieftain whose tribe was so silently stalking them could catch that tasty little morsel his future would be assured.

Krom turned over the possibilities in his mind, unconcerned. There was nothing he could do about such an attack until it happened, so why worry? Anyway, when the time came to strike out on their own, the Domnu's son might make good on his promise to throw the pursuers off their trail.

And if he couldn't, Krom thought with an easy insouciance, he couldn't.

He tipped back his head and smiled contentedly, his quartz teeth sparkling in the sunlight.

It felt good to be home.

'WHAT TIME IS it?' Florin asked, the question sounding like a curse.

'Middle of the bleeding night,' replied Lorenzo, who didn't seem much happier.

'Why are you waking me then?' Florin snapped. 'We're not on guard tonight.'

'According to friend Krom, it's time to get ready.'

Florin sat up, blinking in the light of Lorenzo's lantern. Beyond the little circle of light it cast the world was completely dark, as black as the inside of a cavern. Shivering, Florin pulled on his doublet and unbuttoned the hole in his blanket which let him wear it as a poncho.

'Has he lost his mind? Five minutes off the road in that and all of our horses will have broken legs.'

'We're to prepare and wait for dawn,' Lorenzo told him 'You get our stuff from the Domnu's caravan, and I'll get the riding tack ready.'

Florin cursed as Lorenzo lit a second lantern for him, and wandered off towards the horses. He was still cursing as he made his way over to collect the baggage they'd left with the Domnu.

But when he got to the strigany's caravan he found the saddlebags already waiting on the ground for him. Sergei was standing guard over them.

'Thanks,' Florin grumbled, putting the lamp down and slinging one over each shoulder. They were heavy and he staggered as he struggled to take their weight. 'Have you got your own stuff ready?'

'Yes,' the strigany said. Despite the strain the saddlebags were putting on his shoulders, Florin noticed something strange about the other man's voice.

'Pass me my lamp, would you?' he asked him, freeing one hand from his burden and holding it out.

Sergei did so silently, and as he bent down Florin could see that his cheeks were puffy, his eyes red. With a touch of amazement he realised that the young thug had been crying.

For a moment the Bretonnian considered mocking his tears. Then he considered consoling him. Then one of the saddlebags slipped, and he found himself staggering away into the night beneath their weight.

'Young Sergei looks even more miserable than I feel,' he told Lorenzo as they hoisted the first of their bags onto his horse.

'Not surprised,' Lorenzo muttered. 'It's never easy to leave your family for the first time. At least, so I've heard.'

Florin grunted as they walked to the second horse.

'Let's just hope he doesn't get cold feet. The wilder the lands gets, the happier I am that he's coming with us. I'm not sure, but I think that I saw something last night.'

'A sort of a hunchbacked wolf thing? '

'Yes, exactly. You too?'

Lorenzo nodded his head, then realising the gesture was invisible in the near-darkness, spoke.

'I thought that I was dreaming, to tell you the truth.'

'I hoped that I was. Now I just hope Sergei keeps to his word,' Florin muttered again, then fell silent as he went back to check his horses tack.

He needn't have worried. As the first grey rumours of dawn lightened up the eastern sky the strigany trotted up beside them. He sat tall on his father's best horse, his meagre bundle of possessions strapped to the saddle behind him. A new sword sat comfortably on his hip and his features were a mask of eager determination.

'Said your goodbyes, lad?' Lorenzo asked him as the three horsemen gathered around Krom's motionless form.

'Yes,' said Sergei. The tears which had so surprised him had passed, vanishing as suddenly as an April shower. In their place there remained only the tingling feeling that he

always got before a fight, the strange combination of fear
and excitement that made the world seem a brighter place.

Exactly the same way Florin was feeling, in fact.

Their horses shifted nervously as, on the eastern horizon,
the smouldering gloom of the sky burst into the fiery hues
of a rising sun. It seemed to push a chill wind before it, the
cold air rustling unfelt through the humans' hair and lifting Krom's topknot like some barbaric banner.

The ogre waited until the sun had cleared the horizon
before raising his hand as if in greeting, and signalling their
start into the untracked wilderness beyond.

Of the four companions, Sergei was the only one not to
look back.

WHEN NEFUD HEARD that four of the humans had left the safety
of their cursed caravan, he could scarcely believe his luck.

In fact, he didn't believe it.

Why should he? His luck had become dangerously con-
sistent of late. Consistently terrible. The last few months
had been a catalogue of bloody skirmishes, every one of
which his tribe had lost; of laboriously planned ambushes,
which had all somehow failed, and of almost constantly
scheming underlings.

This last was the worst, for the treachery of his tribe
seemed to mirror the treachery of Nefud's own body. The
years that had passed since his last victory over a human caravan had been long and harsh, and they had taken a heavy
toll. The old goblin's muscles had become so weak that he
had to rely on others to wield his whip, and his reflexes had
become so slow that the only goblins that he could cut were
the ones too terrified to dodge out of his way. Even his teeth
had rotted away like age blackened mushrooms.

Oh, he still had allies from amongst the warring factions.
They had gleefully littered the plains with the remains of
those he'd suspected of treachery. But somehow the more
traitors he killed the more there seemed to be.

But now, just as his whole world was beginning to disin-
tegrate around him, the gods were dangling the chance of

a victory in front of him. A big enough victory, perhaps, to keep his scrawny old carcass safe from younger claws for one more season.

That is, if this truly was a chance, and not part of another plot.

'And you say,' he mused, sucking thoughtfully on a filthy fingertip as he questioned the scout, 'that four of them just decided to wander off, away from the caravan, all alone?'

'Yes, boss,' the owner of the fingertip whined. He was clutching his mutilated hand to his chest as he swung gently beneath the tree, his wolf waiting below him. Its yellow eyes were intelligent enough to see that its rider's problems were his alone, and cold enough to enjoy the fact.

'And why,' Nefud continued, 'do you think that they'd do that?'

'Don't know, boss. Please let me down. I can't feel my feet any more.'

Nefud watched the hanging goblin as if considering the request. As he did so he absentmindedly tossed the scout's dismembered finger to his wolf, which eagerly snapped it out of the air.

'It doesn't seem to make much sense,' Nefud mused as the wolf gulped the titbit down. 'And yet, on the other hand, not everything does make sense. Look at me, for instance. Why did I cut that finger off instead of another one?'

The old goblin's face creased like a rotten apple as he posed the question. Then, baring the mouldering ruins of his gums in a toothless snarl, he drew his knife and hobbled forward. The crescent of steel gleamed in the afternoon sunlight. The edge was more than sharp enough to make up for his lack of teeth.

'Honest, boss, I'm not lying. That's just how it was!'

Nefud paused. By now there was no mistaking the ring of terrified truth in the scout's voice. The old goblin's smile faded as he pursed his lips thoughtfully, the horrible sphincter-like expression squeezing his whole face.

He didn't think for long. After all, what did he have to lose?

'Very well. I think that you're telling the truth. But I'm getting old, so I might be wrong.' Nefud paused, keen to see if any of his gathered brethren would be fool enough to agree out loud.

They weren't.

'So I'm going to give you a chance. When dusk comes, we'll go to the place where the humans separated. If we find their track, we'll follow it. If not, I'll feed the rest of you to your wolf. From the feet up.'

'Thank you, boss, thank you, thank you. You won't regret it, I promise you.'

The scout was still babbling thanks as Nefud turned and hobbled away. Behind him he left the scout swinging in the breeze like a hung pheasant. He didn't let him down until the coming of the night and the beginning of the hunt.

'TELL ME YOU'RE joking.' Florin said as he watched Sergei working on their tracks. 'Tell me that you're not really relying on lucky heather.'

The strigany looked up from his task with a flash of irritation. He had been waiting to find a watercourse before deploying this particular weapon, and he was afraid that he might have had to wait too long. Already his shadow was lengthening across the moorland, as tall as the stream that they'd found was shallow.

'All right then. I won't tell you that.'

So saying, Sergei pulled another sprig of dried herb from his satchel and began to prepare it. It was tempting to point out to that arrogant coxcomb of a Bretonnian that this wasn't heather, it was wolfbane.

But to hell with it, he decided with a grin. Let him fret.

'Don't worry,' he said, as he pulled the stalk through his clenched fist, then opened it to reveal a palm full of tiny soap-green leaves. 'It's an old custom. Bound to work.'

Florin lowered his head and pinched his nose between thumb and forefinger, and Sergei took the opportunity to wink to Lorenzo. Without waiting to see if the older man returned the gesture he squatted down over the hoof print he'd selected. It was good and deep, the depth and angle of it full of information to those with the skill to read it.

And their pursuers, Sergei knew, would certainly have that skill.

Shielding the dried fragments of the herb in the cup of his hand he took a pinch of them and, as carefully as a farmer sowing seed, sprinkled them into the shelter of the imprint.

Satisfied with the quantity he walked forward, hunched forward as though sniffing the trail himself, and selected another. Again he poured a few more leaves into it before prowling farther back down their trail to repeat the procedure.

Five minutes later he was done. He trotted back to his horse, swinging himself up into the saddle before turning to the ogre.

'Krom,' he said. 'Now we need to walk along the stream for a mile or so. It should wash away any sign of our trail.'

The ogre considered the proposal, his face as blank as always. Then he nodded.

'Yes,' he rumbled, goading his ox into the gurgling water even as he spoke. The others followed him in single file, their horses whinnying unhappily as the cold water chilled their fetlocks.

'This at least makes some sort of sense,' Florin admitted, twisting in his saddle to speak to Sergei. 'But I can't see why you wasted time back there. These old superstitions never work.'

'It'll work,' Sergei told him, his confidence almost ogrish in its intensity.

Florin sighed.

'We'll see,' he muttered, and looked wistfully back in the direction of the Silk Road. Right now that single dusty and overgrown cart track seemed like civilisation. In the distance, among the quilted expanse of gorse, heather and stunted trees, he thought that he saw movement. A moment later it was gone.

Could have been anything, Florin told himself uneasily. Somehow, he didn't find that a comforting thought.

* * *

EVEN BEFORE DUSK the tribe had begun to move, scurrying after the caravan as eagerly as rats after a bread wagon. Although their stunted forms were weighed down beneath countless misshapen bundles they moved swiftly, driven on by the anticipation of loot.

Ahead of them a score of wolf riders moved more swiftly still. Their mounts loped through the lengthening shadows with an easy grace, their mangy hides loose over frames made gaunt by long hunger. Even as they ran they began to slaver, the breeze tormenting them with agonising scents of cooked food and horseflesh from the caravan ahead.

The lead rider, his feet still numb and his hand still bleeding from the day's miseries, had other things on his mind than food. His mount, for one. Ever since it had swallowed his finger it had been acting strangely towards him. Its usual attitude of snapping belligerence had gone. In its place was the same sort of watchful patience with which a cat studies a wounded bird.

The goblin knew that, whatever happened tonight, his wolf would eat. The only question was what.

Between the contemplation of that fact and the certainty that that vicious old wart Nefud would certainly make good on his threat, he was shivering towards nervous collapse when he found the spoor of his quarry.

His face creased up into an expression of sheer joy and he began to giggle as he waved his filthy cap above his head, shrilling with impatience for the other members of the patrol to catch up.

'Lucky,' the first one hissed, his voice hushed against the last unpleasant light of the day.

Behind him, squatting on his litter like a poisonous toad on a lily pad, came Nefud.

'Look boss, here it is, I told you. Didn't I say, four of them, all four, they went this way, see, now the...'

The chieftain raised one withered claw, silencing his hysterical underling.

'Find these humans,' he snarled with barely repressed excitement. 'Kill 'em if you can, stop 'em if you can't. Me and the rest of the boys will be right behind you.'

'Yes boss!' the goblin riders chorused, the first of them already edging away from the chieftain and towards the relative safety of their prey.

By the time the pale sliver of the moon had appeared in the star-vaulted sky above, the wolves had halved the distance between them and their quarry. Their eyes gleamed through a darkness that they couldn't see, and occasionally they'd lift their heads to study their monochrome world. Despite the dimness of the moonlight they saw the landscape as easily as a man would on a cloudless day.

But mostly they left the seeing to their riders. What the wolves did was to smell. They followed their snouts up the heavy river of scent that flowed back through space and time, a blazing trail of scent that led inevitably to their prey.

For every mile, every yard, every foot that their quickening pace devoured, that scent grew stronger. Soon they could almost taste the meat that waited ahead; the man-flesh especially. It was as succulent in their noses as it would be upon their tongues.

Their leader whined with anticipation and, head still bowed down, broke into a gallop. His rider held on to clawfuls of lice-ridden mane as the rest of the pack followed him, their snouts wrinkling to suck every trace of smell from the trail.

They were still hurtling along when the leader brushed his nose across a hoof print full of wolfbane.

The effect of the herb was immediate and terrible. It exploded in the wolf's muzzle like a thousand hornet stings of agony, the pain beyond anything it had ever felt before. With an ear-splitting squeal the wolf sprang into the air, hurtling straight upwards in a desperate leap that sent its rider tumbling off into the grass.

But the wolf's agony had only just begun. The tiny spores of wolfbane remained lodged in the delicate flesh of its sinuses, burning through them like shards of molten steel through a slab of butter.

It was unbearable. Even as the wolf landed back on the ground it was snapping around in a blind panic, teeth flashing in the moonlight as agony blossomed into madness.

The wolf's rider, lethally distracted by its fall, saw the insanity that gleamed in its mount's eyes a moment too late.

Even as the goblin turned to run the beast was upon it, the sharp daggers of the wolf's teeth tearing through the back of its rider's neck to fasten onto its spine. It shook the life out of the goblin as easily as if it had been a rat, then threw it high into the night air.

That done the wolf raced away into the night, yelping and howling and lunging at the invisible enemy that was still scouring its way through the nerves of his nose.

Behind him, other wolves had also discovered the wolfbane. Screaming with pain they joined their leader in his madness, chasing after their brethren as ferociously as if they'd been chickens in a coop, or tearing at their noses with bloodied claws.

But if the wolves were panicked, it was even worse for their riders. The terrified goblins clung on to their mounts with a desperate strength, their eyes wide with horror. The luckiest amongst them were carried off in wild, breakneck chases. The rest were dashed onto the ground, there to be savaged with their hands still clutching tufts of fur.

In the distance Nefud heard the screams and the howling. Taking it for the sounds of battle he urged his bearers into a run. Behind him snapping whips drove the rest of the tribe through the gorse, the sound twisting the chieftain's sunken mouth into an evil smile.

Moments later his bearers stumbled over the first of the riders the crazed wolves had left behind them.

'Charge!' Nefud cried, and the goblins beneath him obediently slowed down. They were well aware of what the punishment for carrying Nefud into the first wave of battle would be.

They dragged their heels past another corpse as the rest of the tribe caught up with them, gasping and staggering beneath their loads.

Already the commotion the poisoned wolves had created had vanished, swallowed up by distance. Occasionally, the lingering scream of a crippled goblin floated through the darkness, but the battle itself seemed to have finished.

'Where did they go?' Nefud hissed, glaring down from the perch of his litter. The assembled mob shifted nervously beneath his malevolent gaze, eyes downcast as they tried to become invisible.

But then, incredibly, a voice answered him.

'Looks like you've brought us bad luck again,' it jeered. For a moment Nefud froze with pure amazement.

'Who said that?' he snapped, scanning the resentful mass of goblins below him.

'What's it to you?' another voice asked, this one coming from the opposite direction.

Nefud whirled around, the violence of the movement almost unbalancing him.

'Stand forward!' he shrieked, his rage all the greater for the twinge of panic that lay beneath it. 'Stand forward, or I'll have you boiled!'

But the only movement came from beneath his feet as, without a word of warning, his litter was unceremoniously dropped to the ground.

'You'll pay for that!' Nefud screamed, staggering to his feet as the bearers disappeared into the crowd.

But suddenly, he knew that they wouldn't pay for anything.

Suddenly he realised that tonight's misfortune had been one misfortune too many.

'Stand back,' he whimpered as his tribe closed in around him. They seemed to have grown impossibly big as they loomed over his crooked form, and their faces were sharpened with a terrible new confidence.

Nefud glared back up at them, but for the first time in a decade it was he who cowered when their eyes met.

A high-pitched whine squeezed its way out of his tightening throat. Then his bladder emptied in a spray of fear, the reflex as unthinking as that which made him draw his knife.

The blade twinkled once in the starlight. A semaphore message of pure panic, it was enough to snap the last of his underlings' reserve.

With a single, throbbing howl of vengeful glee the tribe fell upon their former chieftain. He screamed once, a piercing shriek that rose above their jeering voices. A second later the sound was cut off by a thousand frenzied blows.

Even when his last breath had left him Nefud's kin stayed at their task. Hacking, biting and tearing, they were driven by a vengeful rage that left nothing of their leader but for a few scraps of flesh.

To FLORIN'S SURPRISE, he awoke on the morning of the second day in one piece. A cold, damp, shivering piece, it was true, but at least unharmed by the monsters that had haunted last night's dreams.

And last night's dreams had been haunted indeed. More than once he had awoken with phantom cries ringing in his ears. Luckily the blood-curdling symphony had always faded, leaving Florin to persuade himself that the dreadful noises had been no more than the dregs of his nightmares.

Even so, despite the chattering of his teeth, he decided against making a fire. Apart from anything else, he wasn't even sure if that would have been possible. The stream they had been following had ended in a soggy expanse of tiny, reed-choked islands. Muddy flats separated these patches of dry land, seeming to stretch away until the very ends of the earth.

'Sleep well?'

Florin blinked the sleep out of his eyes and looked up. Sergei was standing over him. The strigany looked as well rested as if he'd just rolled out of a feather bed. He also looked as clean as if he'd bathed in a tub of hot suds, rather than out of a tin cup of brackish water.

The observation filled Florin with a flash of irritation, which he covered by dragging a comb through the rat tails of his own hair.

'Yes,' he lied, clenching his jaw against the chatter of his teeth and trying not to look as bad as he felt. 'I slept like a baby.'

'You didn't hear the wolves, then?'

'Um… no,' he lied again.

'Shame,' Sergei said, with an evil grin. 'Seems that the "heather" I used was lucky after all. Although not for the wolves, of course. They put on quite a chorus for us, while you were sleeping like a baby.'

'Didn't they just,' Lorenzo grumbled, and sat up from his nest of blankets. 'For a minute there I thought that they were even going to drown out Krom's snoring. At least, I suppose it was snoring. The big clod sounded as though he was strangling a herd of pigs.'

Krom chose that moment to open one eye. He rested it on Lorenzo.

As always the smeared expanse of the ogre's flattened features remained as blank as a watermelon. This inscrutability made his appraisal more threatening, letting Lorenzo's imagination decide what brutal thoughts churned behind those brutal features.

Despite the chill of the dawn Lorenzo found himself starting to sweat.

'Ah…' he began, but before he got any further Krom began to growl. It was a low, rumbling sound, like the slide of rocks beneath the skin of the earth. The timbre of it remained unchanged as he rose to his feet, the sound as constant as the threat which the humans saw in his eyes.

As Florin surreptitiously drew his pistol, Krom squelched across to Lorenzo. He leered down at him, jaws opening to display the crystalline blades of his teeth.

'Good!' the ogre boomed as the terrifying growl of his laughter faded away. 'Strangling a herd of pigs. Very funny. I like you!'

'Great,' Lorenzo muttered as the ogre, still rumbling with laughter, padded away to saddle his ox. 'Now my breeches are wet inside as well as out.'

Much to Florin's relief the wetland they had spent the night in soon dried out, the ground becoming firm enough to thump beneath their horses' hooves. In the distance, a wood rose up out of the rolling moorland, the trees stunted and bowed beneath the scourge of the east wind, but offering shelter all the same.

The Bretonnian was glad to see it. In the past days there had been no mistaking winter's rapid approach. The blooms that he'd seen after his descent from the mountains had vanished, leaving the wilderness they'd once graced as dour as a merchant in a winter cloak. The clouds had begun to move faster, too, shreds of them scudding across the sky as if eager to escape from a sun that grew ever colder.

All in all, Florin was looking forward to even a single hour spent in shelter.

'Krom,' he said, galloping up to keep pace beside the ogre. 'Those trees. I want to stop there and eat. Cook some food, perhaps.'

The ogre considered the idea in silence.

'Better to ride on,' he said after a moment's thought. 'We're still far from the tribe of Jarmoosh, and your female.'

'Nevertheless, I have decided to stop,' Florin told him. Without giving Krom the chance to disagree, he turned his horse's head towards the woods and cantered away. Lorenzo followed him and so, after a glance at the ogre, did Sergei.

By the time Krom had caught up with them the three men had already lit a fire at the edge of the wood. Its yellow tongues crackled and hissed as they fed it more wood. The smoke that rose from it was thickened with steam from the dirty grey socks that had been placed around it.

'Told you it would be worth a stop,' Florin told the ogre as Lorenzo put a pot of porridge on the fire to heat.

Krom said nothing. Instead he dismounted from his ox and, leaving it to wander towards the horses, he marched past the camp fire and into the gloom of the woods beyond.

'Where's he going, do you think?' Sergei asked as he dumped another pile of twigs by the fire.

'I suppose he doesn't want to frighten the horses,' Florin said.

Sergei's look of puzzlement gave way to laughter, and the two Bretonnians joined in. Whether it was the warmth of the fire, the smell of cooking porridge, or just the prospect of dry socks, the three men felt their spirits lifting.

For one brief moment the cold and the damp didn't seem to matter. Nor did the fact that they had no idea of where they were, or even where they were going.

For one brief moment all that mattered was that it was good to be alive.

'How are the oats doing?' Florin asked Lorenzo, who was stirring the pot with a stripped twig.

But, before he could answer, there was a splintering crash and their brief moment of tranquillity was shattered. The three men leapt to their feet, fumbling for weapons as the forest exploded into a confusion of teeth and fur.

KROM HAD KNOWN that stopping in the forest would probably be a mistake. Still, he had refrained from denying the humans their shelter. They were frail creatures, he'd reasoned. Perhaps even frail enough to sicken from a little cold and wet.

What he hadn't known was that they'd be fool enough to light a fire. The sharp smell of smoke had filled him with a contemptuous amazement as he'd plodded along in their wake. How the race of men could combine such heights of intelligence with such depths of stupidity was a constant puzzle.

As it was, the tang of smouldering wood had choked out virtually every other smell. It was only the sounds of the struggle beyond, the violence almost inaudible amongst the creaking of the branches and the whine of the wind, that had alerted him to the fact that they weren't alone.

Ignoring the mobile faces and pointless chatter of his companions, Krom had strode through them, ready to face whatever beasts were locked in the combat beyond.

He quickened his pace, relying on the sound of approaching violence to hide the crash of his boots through the undergrowth. Ignoring the whiplash of the branches he barrelled onwards, gradually slowing his pace as he came to the final stand of trees. Once there, he waited, but before his breathing had had a chance to slow two struggling animals blundered into the clearing before him.

The first to emerge was the victim. It was a huge animal. Its four legs were thicker than the trunks of the trees through which it had stampeded, and its jagged horns were as long as the splintered branches.

Krom froze in his cover as the beast rumbled on towards him. The thick hair of its pelt rippled like a field of corn beneath a gale as it thrashed from side to side, shaking a rain of detritus from its heavy coat.

Yet despite its wild energy the beast was obviously close to exhaustion. Steam rose from its cavernous nostrils like smoke from a funeral pyre, and the stink of its fear hung heavy in the cold air.

Behind it, as small as a child compared to its prey's bulk, came its nemesis.

Krom wasn't surprised to see that it was an ogre.

He smiled, a crystal flash of spit-soaked lightning against the gloom of the wood. The other ogre saw it and smiled back.

'Ho!' Krom called, pleasure lightening the rumble of his voice.

From across the clearing the hunter opened his mouth to reply, but it was too late. Before he could speak his body was whiplashed through the air, a blur of movement that ended against a tree trunk.

The impact shook a rain of frost-scorched leaves from the boughs above, and there was a snap that could have been either wood or bone.

Despite the blow, the hunter kept a firm grip on the chain which wound around his wrist. On the other end of it were a pair of sprung steel jaws, the mechanical teeth clamped into the bloodied hide of the beast it was hunting.

The huge mammal, three times the ogre's size, spun around and, despite their smearing of blood, the rusted links jingled. Then it caught sight of Krom and its eyes rolled with terror.

Although it couldn't have weighed less than three tons the beast leapt back, then spun around as nimbly as a gazelle. The movement pulled its captor off of his feet and sent him hurtling through the air once again.

This time it was his head which broke his fall.

'Want help?' Krom asked.

But the hunter had his pride. The misshapen bullet of his head shook, the gesture dislodging a patter of blood drops, and he lurched towards his prey. Perhaps hearing its doom in the clinking of the chain, the animal lowered its head and charged away.

White flecks of exhaustion sprayed from its muzzle as it staggered into a gallop. Mindless of the saplings that blocked its path it smashed through them, painting their splintered stalks with gore as it crushed them under its hooves.

And yet, no matter how fast it fled, the beast fled in vain. The hunter still held tight to the chain, and he was pulled through the ruin of his prey's passage like a plough through a tilled field.

The ogre seemed not to mind the skin-smearing speed of this stampede. Nor did he mind the thorns that tore through his bare skin, or the exposed roots that coloured his burly form with one fresh bruise after another.

All the ogre cared about was crawling up the chain.

Inch by inch, hand by hand, he worked his way up it. The steel jaws that completed the weapon remained fastened in the beast's tortured flesh, just as surely as the hunter's eyes remained fixed on them.

Despite the battering he was taking the ogre was actually grinning when the beast burst in amongst the humans.

Blinded with panic, it thundered through their scattering forms. it thundered through the fire, dragging the grinning ogre through the burning embers behind it, and barrelled away towards the freedom of the open steppe beyond.

But that freedom was never to be. With a final lunge the ogre swapped his grip on the chain for two handfuls of fur.

It was as slippery as blood-slicked heather, and he had to use all of his body to wriggle onto the thing's back.

There was a sudden bellow of panic as the beast realised what this new weight on its back meant, and it bucked wildly from side to side.

The hunter paid it no heed. Instead he improved his hold with a mouthful of flea bitten skin, and pulled a large spike from his belt.

For a moment he paused, heavy brows furrowed as he selected the right spot. Then, even as the panicking beast began to roll, he struck. The blow combined the force of a sledgehammer with the precision of a chirurgeon's scalpel, and the spike punched neatly through the back of the beast's skull.

The animal died without a sound. For a few moments the stubborn mass of its body staggered on, its legs carrying the lifeless body towards a horizon it would never reach.

When it finally collapsed, the tons of bone, fat, muscle, and fur fell so heavily that the humans could feel the thud of it through their feet.

Beneath the massive corpse lay the victorious hunter. His bloodied hands remained locked around fistfuls of his prize's hide, as if he were afraid that it would wake up and run away.

'A good size rhinox,' Krom commented when he'd caught up with it. With a grunt of effort the hunter slithered out from beneath the carcass, his tribal tattoos completely hidden beneath a black and red smearing of filth.

'It is,' he agreed as he staggered to his feet. The two ogres studied the slaughtered animal and a low, gurgling round of applause sounded from both of their bellies.

'If you tell those thinlings to build a good fire, we'll eat.'

CHAPTER FIVE

'THIS,' FLORIN EXCLAIMED through a mouthful of food, 'is fantastic.'

Sergei swallowed before correcting him.

'Delicious,' he belched, and waved the great club of the chop he was eating towards Lorenzo. It glistened in the light of a roaring fire, the flesh pink and succulent beneath the scorched outer layer.

'It's fantastic and delicious,' Florin compromised. 'Lorenzo, when it comes to cooking you're a genius. Even for a Bretonnian.'

Lorenzo nodded his agreement, and licked his fingers clean before replying.

'It could have done with a little salt,' he mused, but his companions hastened to disagree.

'No, those herbs were enough. Who'd have thought you'd find rosemary growing in this blighted place?'

For once Sergei agreed.

'He's right. And the way the meat is so tender. It almost melts off the bone.'

Lorenzo wrapped a rag around his hand and, squinting against the heat of the roaring flames, pulled another chop from the grill stone. It had been charred as black as coal, and the tips of the sprigs of the herbs he'd pressed into it were glowing red sparks.

Not that that mattered. The lesson that he'd learned twenty hungry years before was that inside this scorched shell the meat would be perfect.

'So this is how you eat in Bretonnia,' Sergei sighed approvingly, and smeared the grease from his lips with the back of his hand. 'I thought it was all fancy stuff with slugs and snails and the gods know what.'

Lorenzo barked with laughter, and tested the heat of his freshly incinerated chop with a grimy thumb.

'This is how we eat in Bretonnia,' he said, 'if we're in the wilderness and we've got a single night to get through a cow.'

'Why would you want to do tha... oh, I see.'

'Before he entered my employ, Lorenzo tried several other careers,' Florin told the strigany, raising one eyebrow in an ironic gesture. 'Nowadays, of course, with my example to follow, he's completely respectable.'

'That's a shame,' Sergei said, and Florin laughed delightedly.

'By Ranald's nose, the lad's made a joke!' he crowed, and slapped Sergei on the back. 'Didn't think you had it in you.'

The strigany flushed, his embarrassment invisible in the darkness, and busied himself with his meat. As he so often did whilst talking to Florin, he wished that they could box instead of making conversation.

Sometimes he got the sneaking impression that that was sort of what Florin was doing anyway.

Bloody Bretonnians.

'If you want real entertainment,' Lorenzo said, dragging the conversation back to safer areas, 'you should take a look at our two friends over there.'

His comrades obediently looked through the dancing flames towards the ogres. They were eating with the single-minded determination of marathon runners, the muscles of their jaws clenching and unclenching with the same constant beat as the muscles in an athlete's legs.

Occasionally one of them would glance back towards the pile of dismembered joints that was his share. The two heaps glistened from black to red in the dancing flames, grisly monuments to ogrish appetites. Minute by minute they grew smaller, shrinking behind owners whose whole attention was focused on the task in hand.

And, the way these ogres ate, the task did require attention. Not for them the fussiness of weak-stomached humans. When they ate, they ate everything. Hide, hoof, bone; it seemed all the same to Krom and his new friend.

As the three men watched, Krom stripped the last piece of meat from the bone he was holding, then reversed his grip and bit down on the top of the bone. It splintered beneath his teeth as he chewed and swallowed, crunching the bone down as easily as if it were an apple.

His opponent, meanwhile, was munching his way through a sheet of burned hide, the fur still thick despite the clumps that had been singed out of it. When he'd finished it, he reached behind him and drew out a length of spine.

Without even bothering to warm it he snapped off the first pink knuckle and shoved it into his mouth.

'Hardly a suitable diversion for civilised diners, are they?' Florin muttered, and put his half-eaten chop down.

'It's better than your damned theatre, anyway,' Lorenzo said, and took a tentative bite out of his own cooling joint.

There was a sharp crack from between them, and both men turned to see Sergei digging the marrow out of the splintered halves of his bone with a twig.

'What?' he asked, looking up as he sensed their scrutiny.

'Nothing,' Florin told him. 'We just didn't realise that you were as keen on etiquette as Lorenzo.'

'What's etiquette?' Sergei asked suspiciously.

'It's something these aristos do,' Lorenzo told him, with a disapproving shake of his head. 'One of their unnatural practices.'

Florin's smile glittered in the darkness, and he sighed contentedly. Unbuckling his belt he leant back against his saddle, yawning as he looked up into the night sky. Above him the moon, which was growing fatter by the night, flickered between a flock of silver grey clouds.

He was just beginning to wonder if he could smell snow in the air when, lulled by the crackle of the flames and the constant crunching slurp of the two ogres, he drifted off to sleep.

Sergei soon followed him, and then Lorenzo.

The moon sank gradually towards the far horizon and the fire died down to a mound of flickering embers. Occasionally a gust of wind would brush them back into flaming life, the sudden bursts of light flickering across the squat forms of Krom and the hunter.

Although sitting as still as piles of rubble, these two had no intention of resting. Instead, as one hour slipped into the next, the two of them ate. They chewed with a relentless, mechanical efficiency that had nothing to do with hunger, or even greed.

By now all it had to do with was honour.

That was why, even as they began to sweat with the pain of their gluttony, they forced down more meat, more bone, more hide.

Krom had already felt something tear deep within him, but he gave no more sign of the discomfort than had his opponent when a splinter of bone had lodged in his gullet.

They paused only once, and that was to unstrap the vast, broad belts that covered their stomachs. For a moment they looked at each other, their sweltering faces framing eyes that were deep with the mutual respect of two prize athletes.

Then, without further ado, they recommenced their duel.

Although the humans slept on, the two competitors were not without spectators. The vast distances of the moonlit heath behind them were alive with a thousand creatures to whom the smell of smoke, and of warm-blooded animals, and especially of roasting flesh, was irresistible. As the night wore on they thronged around the feasting ogres like moths around a flame, their eyes shining like torches in the darkness.

Occasionally, overcome by the sight of so much meat, one of them would slink forward, its jaws or its muzzle slavering.

None were successful. Each time one of the scavengers emerged into the clearing, the ogres, still chewing, would warn it off with a growl deep enough to tremble in its bones.

Hungry as they were the animals' fear always proved greater than their desire, and so they slunk away, preferring to wait for the remains rather than become remains themselves.

But they waited in vain. As dawn approached, the last of the kill disappeared between the trembling jaws of the exhausted ogres.

Honour satisfied by this draw, they managed to exchange a respectful nod before collapsing backwards into a blind stupor. It stilled their breathing, and clouded their half lidded eyes with a corpse-like sheen.

It also softened the acidic agony of their hugely distended abdomens, which, as their stomachs now contained their own body weight in raw meat, was a blessing indeed.

IT TOOK THE ogres two days to sleep off their excess. Two days which saw the first flakes of snow fall through the forest's shivering boughs. Two days of skies swarming with migrating birds, and of streams crackling with ice.

Two days in which autumn finally died.

But when the ogres did wake up, they were no longer strangers. After the agonising competition of the feast they had become firm friends.

Whilst the humans scraped around for wood, grumbling with impatience whilst they prepared to spend one more night in the teeth of fast-approaching winter, the ogres sat and talked. Buoyed up with the energy of so much digested meat they chattered as shamelessly as females.

And that was just as well, for it was after Krom had told him of their goal that the hunter broke the news.

'The tribe of Jarmoosh,' he'd said, not looking up from the scrape of the file with which he was sharpening the blood-rusted teeth of his trap. 'They are no longer north of here.'

'I'm surprised,' Krom replied, although his tone and face looked no more surprised than a block of wood. 'Last year that was their range.'

'It was, before the over tyrant came,' the hunter agreed, testing the spring of his weapon before moving on to start on the second jaw.

Krom watched his friend work as he digested this piece of news.

'I know nothing of an over tyrant.'

The hunter looked up, and something that might almost have been disbelief clouded the battered moon of his face.

'You have no need to trick me,' he said, turning back to his task. 'By the Great Maw, I am no more than a hunter. I have no tribe or loyalty, least of all to Bashar.'

'Bashar?'

Again the hunter looked up, fixing the other ogre with a long, unblinking stare. Krom stared back, his own face remaining impassive, and eventually his friend looked back down.

'Bashar Zog calls himself the over tyrant. The Scourge from the East. He says he has crawled out of the Great Maw itself, born into the world to unite the tribes to himself. Some believe him.'

'A strange thing to believe,' Krom suggested, and the hunter's stomach rumbled agreement.

'It is a strange thing to believe. More so as this Bashar makes alliance with the greenskins against his own kind. I will never follow him. It's said that when he swallows a tribe he slays the half grown, and the unwhole, and any females that are past breeding.'

'A traditionalist,' Krom observed.

The hunter shook the great boulder of his head, his top-knot swishing away the flies that had settled on the dried blood that covered it.

'More than that. He kills even a tribe's gnoblars. And their animals.'

Krom thought about the object of their journey here. If this over tyrant was prepared to waste good rhinoxen and valuable gnoblars, he would certainly never have spared some worthless human female.

He looked to the north, eyes narrowing as he studied a vision of the possible past, and the futures it might bring.

'But tell me of the tribe of Jarmoosh,' he demanded, uncomfortably aware of what the answer might be. 'Have they joined this Bashar?'

'Not Jarmoosh,' the hunter replied and was surprised by Krom's sudden, face-splitting grin. He bared his own teeth politely back as he continued.

'No. Not Jarmoosh. I know him of old. He has the heart of a true ogre, and a good fear of the Maw. But neither is he lacking in guile. I think that that is why he has gone to Skabrand, to the great snow feast. Who knows? Perhaps there he will find allies to help him stand against this over tyrant.'

'Perhaps,' Krom agreed.

'Although it is possible that Bashar will reach Skabrand first.'

With this warning the hunter slipped his file back into his belt and wound the chain of the terrible hunting weapon around his wrist. Its jaws he held open by squeezing the mechanism in his fist, ready to punch its mechanical teeth into his next victim.

Satisfied with his work he got to his feet, stretched as luxuriously as a half ton cat, and yawned. The great barrel of his chest swelled as he did so, and his voice boomed out against the wind.

'Now I will go,' he decided with a final roll of his shoulders. 'The herd I have decided to follow through the winter will be far to the east by now, and getting further all the time.'

Krom stood, and slapped the stretched skin of his gut appreciatively. Even now it bulged out over his belt, heavy with a stew of half digested rhinox.

'Thanks for the food and the news.'

'Not needed,' the hunter replied dismissively, then turned and jogged away into the trees.

When he had gone Krom sat back down, jaw dropping open with the drooling slackness of deep thought. He was sitting thus when the humans returned, bringing with them firewood and half a dozen skinned rabbits to cook over it.

'Tomorrow,' Krom said, his mouth snapping closed, 'we go west.'

And he said no more until the afternoon of the following day.

'IT CAN'T BE seen, or touched, or smelt, but it can wrap around you as tight as a belt,' Florin said, twisting back in his saddle and raising his voice so that the wind couldn't snatch the words away.

Sergei, his face screwed up against the sleeting snow, screwed it up a little more. He glanced upwards, blinking against the ice that fell from the low grey roof of the world.

'Easy,' he shouted back, as though he'd seen the answer there. 'Darkness.'

Florin mumbled something that could have been an admission that darkness was indeed the correct answer.

'Am I right?' Sergei pressed him, leaning forward after his comrade's departing back.

'Yes, yes, yes,' Florin said, waving the question away as though he didn't mind. A wolfish grin split the tired grey of Sergei's face, and he shouted his own riddle into the wind.

'I can climb, and swim, and sleep and bite, but I have no legs to fold at night.'

Florin's brows furrowed in thought, but only for a moment. He came from the warmth of the south, and from a town full of juicy rats.

'A snake,' he said, and, without even waiting to hear if he was correct, asked his next.

'In the summer, it's clothed that I go, but in the winter, I stay naked in the snow.'

Sergei fidgeted in his saddle and glanced about him. There was nothing to see but a desert of frozen moorland, punctuated here and there by drifts of dirty grey slush.

Clothed in summer... naked in winter...

For a moment the word 'Krom' balanced on the tip of his tongue, but that wasn't quite right. The ogre was at least wearing trousers in the snow. And a belt.

'In the summer,' Florin repeated, turning back again, 'it's clothed that I go, but in the winter, I stay naked in the snow.'

'I heard you,' Sergei snapped. In the past three days they'd slept for a total of twelve hours, and the strain was starting to show. This game had been started to take their minds off aching joints and exhausted nerves, and if it had been played with the right spirit it might have done.

As it was, the riddles had soon become a battle between Florin and Sergei. Lorenzo had long since given up, leaving them locked in competition as he dozed in his saddle.

'Just say if you don't know the answer,' Florin chipped in, trying to break the strigany's concentration.

'I do know the answer,' Sergei chipped back.

'What is it then?'

'Could be any one of a dozen things.'

'No it couldn't,' Florin said smugly. 'There's only one answer.'

'It could be oak,' Sergei began, counting off one finger. 'Or ash. Or elm. Or...'

Florin scowled.

'The answer is tree,' he said before his opponent could go any further.

A sudden gust ripped along the line of riders. It sent the damp blankets of their cloaks fluttering upwards and breathed ice chips into their shirts and down their collars. Only the ogre, the muscles of his back glistening with melted sleet, seemed unaffected by the cold.

'Shallya's mercy,' Florin cursed miserably, but Sergei didn't notice. He was too busy trying to think of another riddle. He'd already used the ones he'd memorised, and it was getting tough to think of anything fresh.

'Come on,' Florin told him, angrily trying to brush the snow back out of his collar. 'Do you have another one, or do you want to quit?'

'I can't be hurt by axe or bow, but a friendly hand will... will make me go.'

Florin was actually looking at the snowflakes melting off the back of Krom's neck as he listened to the riddle.

'Snow,' he said. 'Too easy.'

'No,' Sergei told him.

'What do you mean "no"?'

'I mean, no. You're wrong. I win.'

'How can I be wrong? It's snow. Axes can't hurt it but it melts in the palm of your hand.'

'The answer,' Sergei told him, 'is ice.'

Florin swore long and loud.

'Ice, snow, what's the damned difference? It's the same cursed thing.'

'No it isn't,' Sergei shook his head stubbornly.

'But you can't tell from the riddle which one it's supposed to be!'

'It's ice.'

'How do you know?'

'Because I made it up.'

Florin leant forward, closed his bruised eyelids and pinched the bridge of his nose. He took several deep breaths. Then he turned back to Sergei.

'A riddle can only have one answer. That's how it's played. Your riddle could have two different answers, so it doesn't count.'

An expression of doubt flickered across Sergei's face. He supposed that the Bretonnian was right. But then, he was damned if he was going to try and think of another riddle.

'It does count,' he insisted, averting his eyes guiltily.

'It doesn't!'

'It…'

'Silence.' The command rumbled back down the column. Krom hadn't spoken loudly, but the depth of his voice rolled over the whine of the wind and the tired bickering of the human's voices.

They fell silent, and their horses drifted to a stop behind the ogre's ox. Florin, resisting the temptation to rest, rode up to take a position on the ogre's right. He cupped his hands into a funnel and leant towards the chewed-up lump of gristle that was the ogre's ear.

'What is it?' he whispered.

Krom swivelled expressionless eyes towards him and frowned.

'Blood,' he said. 'Spilt blood.'

Florin sniffed. Apart from the sharp sting of the wind he couldn't detect a thing.

'Another hunter?' he asked.

'We will see.'

Once more Krom led the way forward.

Florin passed the news back to Sergei as he fell into step behind the ogre, and Sergei woke Lorenzo with it. The old man grumbled for a while, but soon fell silent.

Soon they all fell silent. The riddles and the quarrel were both forgotten now that they had something real to worry about.

The voices in the wind, for instance, whispering rumours that their straining ears couldn't quite catch. Or the blurred shapes that drifted through the falling snow, each of them almost visible.

Quietly, barely realising that he was doing it, Florin checked his weapons, loosening them in their holsters. Behind him the others did the same, following his example in an unconscious show of respect that would have pleased him had he been aware of it.

But he wasn't aware of it. None of them were. The only thing they were aware of was the suffocating sleet that wrapped itself around them, and the things which they imagined were within it.

It wasn't long before their horses began to fret. Florin's mare was the worst. Nelly dug her hooves in and refused to go on until he pushed his spurs into her side. As if in sympathy her sisters whinnied. It was a fearful, miserable sound that fit their riders' mood perfectly.

Ahead of them, as if conjured by the noise, a gaggle of shapes loomed out of the blizzard. They rose from the snow with the relentless inevitability of corpses rising up to the surface of a pool.

Along with the sight came the smell, the heavy, ripe stench of bad meat on a hot day. It washed over Florin in a nauseating rush. Despite the fact that flies couldn't possibly live in this season he half imagined their greedy buzz, half expected them to be swarming over whatever corruption lay ahead.

As suddenly as it had come the vile smell was blown away by a change in the wind. With a sigh so deep that even Lorenzo could hear it, Krom kicked his ox into a trot, heading towards the unmoving silhouettes.

By now Florin had decided that, despite the smell, they must be megaliths. Such standing stones littered this wilderness like teeth on the floor of a boxing ring, and it wouldn't be the first time they'd ridden through a cluster of them. The forms ahead were certainly tall enough. They also shared the same lumpen construction, as though they'd been built by gods who were only just learning to shape the clay of the world.

But the blizzard was too cruel to leave him with the comfort of his illusions. It faded away with a breathless whisper, revealing the silhouettes for what they really were.

'Sigmar,' Sergei exclaimed behind him, horror and wonder mingling in his hushed voice. 'Shallya and Ranald and Ulric.'

Silently adding the Lady's name to the pantheon, Florin followed Krom's example and dismounted. His mare jittered nervously as he did so, her eyes rolling fearfully as he handed her reigns to Lorenzo.

This close, the smell was constant.

Constant and revolting.

Florin clenched his fists, knuckles whitening against the lazy roll of nausea that threatened to overwhelm him. Nails dug ever deeper into his palms, he walked up to the first of the grisly monuments.

It was, he supposed, an ogre. At least, it had been an ogre. Now it was just a corpse, and a mutilated one at that. The great barrel of its stomach had been torn open as easily as a gutted rabbit's, leaving its stinking innards to hang down in a grisly tangle. Its eyes had been taken too, the bloodied sockets wide with surprise as it lolled upon its crucifix.

Florin saw something squirming within one of the cavities. He hurriedly looked away, catching sight of the next spread-eagled form. Despite the choking, liquid stink of the rotting flesh he took a long, deep breath. Then he straightened his back.

Then he strolled over towards the next victim with a carefully constructed nonchalance.

This one had been gutted too. With a wince Florin looked past the horrific injuries and studied the cross upon which the carcass had been tied. There was something out of place and yet naggingly familiar about the weird lumber the thing had been built of.

Ah yes, Florin thought. That's it. That dirty yellow polish, and the way the beams taper. It makes them look like tusks of ivory rather than beams of wood.

Chance would be a fine thing, he told himself. But unfortunately elephants live in Araby, not this freezing place. And even there, none are big enough to grow tusks as long as these.

All the same, he began to wonder how much the offal-smeared crosses would be worth if they were ivory. It wouldn't just be the weight of them, although that would be valuable enough. It would be the rarity. The absolute, incontestable rarity.

Florin arrived at a tentative figure. Then he dismissed it as too low and began again.

An auction, he thought, the rotting ton of crucified ogre forgotten. I could get the guilds to compete for the biggest tusk as a nameplate.

Scarcely daring to believe his luck, he brushed the frozen tips of his fingers across one of the beams. It was as smooth as a billiard ball. That could just be the blood, Florin told himself, and looked up at the huge carcass that was suspended on this treasure. The eyes on this one were intact, and as glassy as a taxidermist's model.

Florin pursed his lips, and looked into the orbs with the calculating expression of a strigany studying a crystal ball.

'Could this be ivory?' he asked the corpse as he tapped the crucifix it rode. 'If it is…'

The ogre turned its head towards him and blinked.

With a yell Florin stumbled backwards, and instinctively dragged his pistol out of its holster. The mutilated ogre turned its head to follow him, gazing down as he scrambled away and waved the muzzle towards it.

'What is it?' Sergei asked, trotting over. Florin looked down from the ogre's frozen eyes to the ruin of its stomach. Once more he saw how thoroughly it had been gutted. Whoever the butcher had been he'd cut his victim lethally open. The knuckles of its spine could even be seen through the void of its gut, white as the frost that encrusted its spilled entrails.

'Nothing,' Florin lied, realising that the ogre's wink must have been a trick of the failing light. It couldn't possibly have survived such a trauma, not even for a moment.

'It was nothing, I just slipped.'

Sergei looked at him with open suspicion. The he looked towards the ogre.

'Looks lively, don't he?'

'I don't know…'

But before he could finish, the crucified ogre opened its mouth and cried out, a hiss of wordless agony that set the spill of its guts shaking around its feet.

The two men leapt away from the beast, watching warily as it struggled against its bonds.

'Unbelievable,' Florin said, the initial rush of fear lost in a terrible wonder. Even now, with its entrails wrapped around its ankles, this ogre was not just alive, but fighting.

'Let's cut him down,' said Sergei. Florin tore his eyes away from the gory giant and studied the strigany, who studied him back.

A test, he thought.

Fine.

Knowing that this was madness, Florin nodded his agreement anyway. He slipped a knife from his boot, and together he and Sergei edged towards the struggling monster.

After the initial explosive burst of energy its strength was failing, the battered lump of its head already slumping forward to rest on its chest. Florin was glad. He guessed that even at the best of times it would be dangerous to approach a bound ogre with knives drawn. Now, maddened with pain as it must be, their reward for freeing him was liable to be a crushed skull.

A gallows smile tightened the Bretonnian's face as he began to saw through the first of the ropes. Careful to avoid cutting either flesh or ivory he glanced towards Sergei. The strigany scowled back at him.

'Stop,' a voice rumbled from behind them. Reluctantly the two men stopped, and turned to find Krom standing behind them.

'We're cutting this one down,' Florin explained. 'He's still alive.'

For a moment something flitted across Krom's face, a half glimpsed expression as fleeting as cloud shadow on a granite cliff.

Then it was gone.

'No. He lives because of the position the ropes hold him in. It is an old... custom.'

Florin frowned doubtfully. Then he shrugged and sheathed his knife. As he backed away he slipped on the spill of entrails. It brought a fresh cry to the ogre's lips.

Krom lurched forward and gripped the head of his crucified counterpart. The scarred paws of his hands pressed against the dying ogre's cheeks, and he tilted his face until their eyes met.

For a long moment they stood thus, silent and face to face. It was Krom who broke the silence, his single word cutting through the whine of the quickening blizzard.

'Who?'

The other ogre tried to speak, failed, cleared his throat with a great coughing gout of bloody phlegm.

'B… Bashar Zog,' he gargled at last. 'The… easterner.'

'I understand,' Krom nodded. 'The Maw will take you,' he promised and, biceps suddenly bulging, he twisted the ogre's head in a violent movement. There was a crack, the sound as sharp as an axe stroke despite the muffling of snow, and the last of the crucified ogres was dead.

The four companions stood in respectful silence, a makeshift funeral in the heart of this bitter wilderness. By nature none of them were particularly respectful. They weren't even particularly compassionate. Even so, it was impossible not to admire the strength of the ogre to whom Krom had just given the final comfort.

It was Lorenzo who broke the silence.

'We'd better get that ivory stowed away and find some shelter,' he murmured.

'Take the ivory,' Krom told them. 'But we won't find shelter. We won't rest. Now we will ride to Skabrand, and there I will leave you.'

'What?' Florin snapped 'That wasn't the deal. You're to take us to find the Hansebourg girl. You know that. You…'

'The deal,' Krom told him, the low rumble of his voice as certain as the turn of the seasons, 'is no more.'

Florin thought, and thought fast. In a heartbeat he decided against the threat of Mordicio's wrath, threatening though that could be. He also decided against bribery. After all, the ogre didn't even seem to want his share of the ivory.

Instead he played for time, aping the ogre's own terse argot with the single question.

'Why?'

'Because I must avenge my brother.'

'Which brother?'

Krom looked at him, the slabs of his features seeming almost contemptuous.

'This brother,' he rumbled at last, nodding towards the cooling corpse of the crucified ogre. 'Argut. I will make a trophy for him, from Bashar Zog's corpse.'

Florin studied Krom's face. It seemed emotionless. Unconcerned. Blank.

And he knew that there was nothing he could say to change the ogre's mind.

CHAPTER SIX

WHEN THE CUSTOMER stooped into its burrow, the gnoblar merchant's heart fluttered like a bat in a cage. It wasn't the silk of her young flesh that set its black blood racing, of course. It was the gold that was wrapped around it.

Bracelets of the stuff twined around her wrists in spirals of serpentine glory. Chains of it roped her neck in a noose of wealth. Combs of it glimmered amongst the braids of her hair, shining almost as brightly as the glorious fire of the hair itself.

The merchant felt itself falling in love.

'Come in,' it wheedled, and rubbed its hands together as enthusiastically as if it was strangling a kitten.

'Thank you,' Katerina said, bowing her head as she came further into the gnoblar's lair. There was no way of telling how big it was; in every direction valuable merchandise, unpleasant refuse and everything in between blocked her line of sight. The clutter could have reached back five feet or five miles.

'Sit, sit,' the merchant said, shoving a wobbly stool forward in a paroxysm of good manners.

'Thank you,' Katerina said once more, and settled herself down. She squatted easily on the stool, thighs parting in a way that would have disadvantaged any human trader. It didn't distract the gnoblar, though. He was too busy drooling over her jewellery.

'So,' it began, running the dagger of its tongue over the yellowed stubs of its teeth. 'What can I give to you?'

'Oh no,' Katerina said, eyes widening into deep pools of innocence. 'I can't accept any gifts. I want to buy something.'

'Ah,' the gnoblar said. 'If you say so. What is it that you want to buy?'

'I need some deathcaps. Toadstools, you know.'

The gnoblar almost asked why. Instead it shook its head, and hissed regretfully.

'Very rare.' It frowned. 'Very, very rare. In this place? At this time? Difficult.'

It shook its head, glimpsing up in time to see Katerina's horrified expression.

'But I must get some!' she pleaded. 'My tyrant told me to get some. I must!'

The tip of the merchant's tongue moistened the green flesh of its lips.

'Hmmm.' It scratched his head and pretended to consider. 'I could give you some. A dozen, say. But it will cost you, yes, cost you dear.'

Katerina frowned. Then, as if struck by a sudden inspiration, she looked down at the bracelet that gleamed around her wrist.

'Look at this,' she said, eagerly slipping it off. 'It's gold.'

The gnoblar tried to look unimpressed as it studied the heavy twist of metal. It was gold all right. Pure gold, by the weight.

'Perhaps I can find some deathcap,' it said, carefully placing the bracelet beside its own stool. 'Let me see what I have back here.'

'But do you need to take my whole bracelet for it?' Katerina whined unhappily.

'Yes,' the gnoblar nodded. 'Deathcap is very rare here. Very valuable.'

'Oh. Well, all right then.'

The gnoblar managed to keep the smile off its face until it had turned away from her. Then, teeth glinting in the light of the oil lamp, it made a great show of searching through first one pile, then the next. After the pantomime had gone on for long enough it produced one of the twists of deathcap it always carried with it.

'Here,' it said, finally turning back and showing the humaness a handful of the toadstools.

'Thanks,' she said, her hand whipping out in a blur of speed. The gnoblar glanced anxiously down towards where it had left the bracelet. It was still there.

But then a healthy paranoia made it pick it up.

'You switched!' it cried as it hefted the worthless thing in its hand. It didn't take a jeweller to tell that what had been gold was now bronze. Not even good bronze.

'Well,' Katerina said casually. 'You said you wanted my bracelet. That's it.'

'No,' the gnoblar snarled. 'The gold one.'

'Don't be a fool,' she snapped. 'Who'd give a gold bracelet for a handful of toadstools?'

But the gnoblar wasn't going to waste any more time trying to reason. Instead it whistled, a piercing shrill that should have brought his guards running.

It didn't.

'If you're waiting for those pathetic things I saw skulking outside,' Katerina told him, carefully stowing the deathcaps in a pouch, 'they're still there. Entertaining my cat.'

The merchant hissed angrily. If its guards were wasting time torturing some stray when they should have been guarding him, they'd suffer. Spite sharpened its hatchet face as it darted past Katerina and, as swift as a cockroach, scuttled vengefully out into the passageway beyond.

What it saw was enough to completely freeze the fire of its outrage.

True enough, there was a cat there. At least, the merchant supposed that it was a cat. It had the right sort of whiskers, and the right sort of ears. It even had a twitching tail. The tip of it swished playfully through the air as it watched the cowering bodyguards with feline concentration.

Unlike most cats, though, this one stood as high as a small pony. Slabs of muscle slid beneath the liquid smoothness of its pelt as it turned to study the merchant.

The sabretusk's emerald eyes narrowed hungrily at the sight of it.

'Here,' Katerina said, pushing past the frozen merchant and thrusting the worthless bracelet into its unresisting hand. It closed its fingers around the bracelet very slowly, never once taking its eyes from the daggers of the big cat's fangs.

'So, are we all square?' Katerina asked. The gnoblar opened its mouth to reply, and the cat growled. Or perhaps it was purring.

The gnoblar decided not to take the chance. Instead it snapped its mouth shut and nodded dumbly.

'Good,' Katerina, who was already strolling away, murmured. She passed the sabretusk, leaving the gnoblars pinned by its emerald gaze until she was about to turn onto the main thoroughfare. Then she whispered something, a murmured order that brought the beast padding silently after her.

Now that she had made good her escape, she allowed herself to smirk, a wicked grin that gleamed in the torchlight.

Weak fool, she thought gleefully as she pressed on.

The soot-covered stone of the ceilings grew higher above her. It was blackened granite, and it arched up high enough to allow even the tallest ogre to march through with his head held high. The girl stood to one side as a dozen of them did just that, the bulls as silent as the dead as they led their newly arrived tribe towards its quarters.

Their silence wouldn't last, Katerina thought. A contented smile played on her lips as she let the last of the

hulking figures stride past. As soon as he had done so she
barged out in front of their retinue, baring her teeth at the
lead gnoblar in an automatic gesture of pure aggresion.

No, she thought again as she followed in the ogres' wake,
the silence never lasted. Even the most taciturn of this taciturn race became talkative at Skabrand. Talkative, wild,
joyous. That was the point of the festival, and of the place,
and she loved it.

Even now she could hear the constant roar that reverberated from the central chambers, a fusion of violence and
voices that sounded like the devouring heart of some vast
furnace.

Katerina picked up her pace, eager to get this errand over
with and return to the fun.

The way was tangled, and lit only by the flickering light
of blubber-soaked torches, but she followed it easily
enough. Her tribe had been coming to this glorious place
every year for the past decade. And even when she hadn't
been here she had often dreamed about it. Skabrand was
always a wonderful adventure.

By the time she slipped into her tribe's chambers she was
almost running. The body of Duzrog was collapsed against
the door post, his belly rising in snores deep enough to
bring pride to any tribe. The sickly smell of beer hung
around him, as sweet as honey and as rotten as a sewer.

Katerina's sabretusk slunk past the drunken ogre with its
flanks pressed to the wall.

'Silly thing,' its mistress told it. The beast wrinkled its velveteen muzzle anyway.

The two of them marched hurriedly past the chained door
of the females' quarters, waded through the debris of the
deserted main hall, and entered Katerina's own little den.

It was dark in here, without even the sizzling fat of a
torch for light. Katerina didn't mind. She'd carved out this
place, and knew exactly where everything was. Even the
object of today's exertions.

The object, which had also been the object of yesterday's
exertions, whimpered when it heard her approach.

'Stop that noise,' she snapped at the gnoblar, who obeyed immediately. 'Here, I brought your medicine.'

So saying she squatted down in front of the creature and held out the offering. The bundled shape stretched out a shaking claw and cautiously retrieved the toadstools. From beneath its hood there came the sound of snuffling, then of chewing.

'What do you say?' Katerina demanded. The gnoblar, its puzzlement invisible in the darkness, wondered what could be going through its chieftain's head. It was almost always a mystery.

'Don't hit me again?' It finally volunteered.

'No! It's "thank you."'

'Thank you,' the gnoblar quickly said.

'And I will hit you again. If I catch you bleeding the rhinoxen one more time, I'll hit you twice as hard.'

'But they weren't the tribe's rhinoxen.'

'I don't care. Its cruel.'

The gnoblar thought about this. Cruelty wasn't a concept that fit easily into its world view. Despite the incomprehensible lessons Katerina had inflicted upon it and its brothers since she had taken over, 'cruel' still seemed like just one more way of saying 'fun'.

Even so, it agreed with an easy alacrity. Survival was something that did fit into its world view, and over the past years, Katerina's incomprehensible whims had become pretty much the beginning and the end of that.

That's why she was the chieftain.

'Good. Now that we understand each other, I'm leaving. Do you want to come with me?'

On another occasion the gnoblar might have said yes. Katerina often led her bemused followers to loot, which was another reason why she was their chieftain. But the toadstools were already beginning to work their healing magic, soothing the painful injuries that the gnoblar's cruelty-hating chieftain had inflicted upon it.

'No,' it muttered, the sheer unnaturalness of saying that to a chieftain sending a ripple of instinctive fear down its crooked spine. 'No. I want to rest.'

'Suit yourself,' Katerina said, flicking her hair back in perfect time with her sabretusk's tail. She prowled back out into Skabrand, looking for trouble.

And, barely an hour later, trouble arrived at Skabrand looking for her.

AFTER THE DISCOVERY of Krom's crucified brother, even Florin and Sergei had fallen silent. They had cut down the ogres from the other crosses with barely a word, severing the cords which bound them to the tusks and laying the ivory out. Then, each selecting a single piece, the men had tried to tie their share across the backs of their horses.

It had been a heartbreaking affair. Once the tusks had been cut down and laid out they looked a lot bigger, and when they were compared to the horses, they were bigger still.

Far too big, in fact, to carry.

But Florin was damned if he was going to leave all of this wealth out here to rot. Ignoring Krom's impatient rumblings he had taken a hand axe to the things, cutting as much length off as he thought their mounts could bear.

Their horses still weren't happy with the arrangement. It wasn't just the weight that sent them dancing rebelliously away, although the shortened tusks weighed enough. It was the smell of blood that really spooked them. Somehow they knew that the copper tang, still sharp despite the humans' half-hearted efforts to wipe it away, would draw every predator for a dozen miles.

Florin ignored their whinnies just as he'd ignored Krom's grunts. He knew that he'd never find this treasure again; even if there had been a landmark, the withering sheets of sleet that harried them would have hidden it as well as the blackest night.

As it was, he contented himself with loading a single five-foot piece on each horse. He would have tried to load two, but he guessed that Sergei would have protested.

The strigany would have been right to do so, too. Out here, their horses were more valuable than any amount of treasure.

So, with tears in his eyes, Florin left the find with no more than three medium-sized tusks. He tried not to think about all of the ivory they'd left behind, another fortune lost to the devouring elements of this merciless world.

The miserable procession plodded on through worsening weather. Soon after leaving the dead ogres, the blizzard began to darken, and the humans started to cast about anxiously for a place to pitch camp.

But Krom had no intention of stopping. Instead he let his reins go slack, content to let his ox find its own way forward. It was a good animal, he judged, sensible enough to avoid any potholes that might lie in its path.

Whether or not the burdened horses behind him would show the same good sense made no difference to the ogre. Nothing did, except the desire for revenge. It burned deeply within the cavern of his gut, this desire, keeping him warm despite the ice that froze in his topknot and armoured his breeches.

When the humans complained, he ignored them. When they threatened to stop anyway he paid them no heed. Skabrand lay ahead, and in Skabrand he would find allies. Or perhaps enemies.

Either way, he would be content.

Overnight the mood of the snow changed. No longer willing to melt away it became bold enough to lay claim to its new territory. It stacked up in towering drifts, burying heather and shaping gorse bushes into half formed snowmen. It crunched beneath the travellers' hooves and gathered thickly around their hooded shoulders. An occasional fit of shaking loosened it, but there was a constant fall of fresh snow to take its place.

By the time morning came, Florin no longer even shook. He didn't have the energy. The best he could do was to sit slumped in the freezing leather of his saddle, numb with both the cold and the red-eyed desperation of exhaustion.

He was almost comfortable. There was no more pain, just a weird feeling of being outside of himself. It was as though his frozen body was no more than a mannequin in a puppet show, and his soul no more than a spectator.

The snow had at least stopped falling, content with its work. On all sides a white desert rolled away. Here and there blinding patches of light shone like elven gold, but it was only the sun breaking through the clouds above.

Florin began to doze, slipping into a stupor that wasn't quite sleep. Fantasies of mattresses and hammocks danced through his imagination, the images conjured up by a desire as strong as lust. Unfortunately the dreams always ended almost as soon as they had begun, snatched away by the sudden jolts of wakefulness that kept him on his saddle.

After one such jolt he found himself looking back. His mouth falling open as he tried to understand what he was seeing. It was Sergei, walking beside his horse.

It took Florin a moment to realise why that seemed so strange.

'Why aren't you riding?' he asked at last, a stranger's voice emerging from his throat.

Sergei lifted his hanging head. The shadowed pits of his eyes were as dark as a skull's against the pallid expanse of his face, and the whites were as bloodshot as a drunkard's.

'To rest the horse,' he explained, his tones flat beneath the weight of his exhaustion. 'And to keep awake. It's too cold to sleep.'

'How can it be too cold to sleep?' Florin exclaimed, feeling like a drowning man who's been told that the lifeboat was too dry to use.

'Frostbite,' Sergei told him. 'Hypothermia.'

These were new words to Florin. Usually he would have asked the strigany to explain further, but he was too tired. Far too tired.

'You should walk too,' Sergei offered a moment later, speaking with an obvious effort.

'Why not Lorenzo?'

'I wrapped his legs in some cloth.'

At first Florin didn't understand. The words refused to sink into his consciousness just as stubbornly as the snow refused to melt off Krom's bare shoulders.

Then inspiration struck, and he leaned back to study Lorenzo's slumbering form. With a twinge of envy he saw that the old villain seemed to have mastered the trick of sleeping in the saddle. In fact, now that Florin thought about it, he could even hear him snoring.

Then his eyes were attracted by a flash of gold and blue, the kingfisher colours unique in this desert of snow.

'That's trade cloth,' Florin stated.

'No matter,' Sergei said. Florin looked at the strigany for signs of false modesty. He saw none.

'Where did you get it?'

'It's mine.'

'Why did you give it to Lorenzo?'

'To stop frostbite,' the strigany said. Florin found that he was grateful on his friend's behalf.

Not grateful enough to say thank you, though. He didn't have enough energy for that.

'You should walk.'

Florin nodded, knowing that the lad was probably right. The problem was that as soon as he had thought about getting off his horse and walking, the frozen lump of saddle leather had begun to feel wonderfully comfortable. At least as comfortable as the beds which had graced his imagination. He cursed himself for not having realised it sooner.

The ground, by contrast, looked as distant and as hostile as the surface of Mannslieb.

If Sergei hadn't been with them, Florin would have carried on riding, and to Morr with the sense of it all. But Sergei was with them, the cocky little buck, and the Bretonnian had long since decided that he'd be damned before he'd show him any weakness.

Quickly, before he could change his mind, he swung his stiffened frame out of the saddle, and landed heavily in the snow. Grimacing with pins and needles he pushed himself

into a march, trying not to stumble as he dragged his feet
through snares of snow and frozen heather.

'Very bracing.' He tried to sound light hearted. He
failed.

Sergei ignored him.

They walked on.

Soon the crunch of feet and hooves through the snow
merged into a single sound, the throb of it as constant as
a toothache. From time to time Florin raised his head and
looked around. He saw nothing. No structures jutted up
from the endless expanse of the snowfield. No megaliths.
There weren't even any trees to break the monotony of the
far horizon.

By midday Florin had begun to hear voices. Some of
them he recognised. Some of them belonged to men long
dead. One of them belonged to his mother, although why
she should choose now to start calling from her grave was
beyond her son's understanding.

And yet for all their variety they were curiously unimag-
inative, these phantoms. They were content to do no
more than chant his name, reciting the two syllables in
perfect time with his marching feet.

Florin supposed that he should have been frightened by
the invisible speakers. Terrified, even. If they weren't
ghosts then they were hallucinations, and who knew
what insanity they might herald?

But he was too tired to be afraid. Too tired to do anything apart from put one foot in front of the next, then
pick it up and put it down again.

And again.

And again.

And if his horse hadn't stopped, he would have walked
straight into Krom. As it was he just staggered to a halt,
the bite of his reins against his frozen flesh momentarily
silencing the voices.

'We have arrived,' Krom rumbled, gesturing ahead.

Florin followed the gesture. It led to absolutely
nowhere. There was nothing in any direction except for

the laundry grey sky, and the silvered expanse of the snow with which it had smothered the world.

The Bretonnian hoped that he had misheard his guide. Struggling through the mists of fatigue he tried to form a question. But before he could he did see something.

Several somethings, in fact. They had no form, nor even any colour, but they were certainly there. Beings of pure movement, they flickered up from the snow, tall enough for their heads to ripple against the sky.

Florin, too numb to feel anything stronger than mild alarm, remembered tales of the djinn which haunted Araby. Vengeful spirits that were said to prowl the caravan routes of the southern sands, wrenching their existence out of the sand and the air which surrounded them.

Could these be the northern version?

Struggling against the skin of ice which held it Florin drew his pistol, and checked the firing pan.

Then he barked with laughter at his own stupidity, and replaced the weapon.

The half-seen things ahead weren't any threat. Far from it. They were just rising columns of smoke. What had confused him was that they were belching up from holes that lay sunken in the ground rather than from chimneys.

Florin rubbed the gum from his eyes, and saw that these serpentine twists of smoke were everywhere. They rose from the snow-covered earth in a forest of venting air, the charcoal smears of rising smoke soon lost against the granite bleakness of the sky above.

The Bretonnian sniffed, and his eyes watered at the acrid stink of so many fires.

So many subterranean fires.

Skabrand, it seemed, was a city dug out rather than built up.

'Let's go and knock on a door,' he told Krom. His voice carried a note of pleading which he didn't quite like, so he tried again.

'Krom. Let's introduce ourselves.'

But suddenly there was no need. Without even a creak of warning one of the nearest snow banks erupted outwards. Snow plumed up into the polluted air, and before it had had the chance to fall back down a score of ogres had been vomited out into the world.

Despite the shock of their appearance, Florin felt the hot breath that rolled out of the trapdoor. He turned to bask in the blast of heat like a heliotrope turning to the sun.

The first of the ogres, his drooping moustaches waxed into walrus tusks that were long enough to brush the tattoos on his chest, cast an eye over Krom and his followers. He swaggered forward as he did so, his reckless confidence undiminished by the fact that he seemed to be unarmed.

'Why do you come to Skabrand?' the guard demanded, his flat, immobile features almost managing a scowl. Krom drew himself up to his full height.

'To feed the Great Maw,' he replied. 'And to drink until I can no longer move.'

The whole company began to howl and gurgle, a savage chorus that made Florin's blood run even colder.

As the guards led their guests to the city below, he knew that he'd never get used to ogre laughter.

CHAPTER SEVEN

JARMOOSH WAS GETTING old. Every winter, when he led his tribe back to this great gathering, that knowledge grew heavier. The season's pilgrimage drove home the fact that another year had passed. Another year which had brought him closer to the Great Maw.

But somehow the festival never made him feel older. Quite the opposite. There was something about the cheerful violence of Skabrand's celebrants, the stink of their blood and the roar of their voices, that made a youngster out of the tyrant.

Which, considering the size of today's opponent, was just as well.

The two of them had been locked in combat for the best part of the day. Gut pressing against gut and fists locked onto each other's belts, the whole of their existence had been rendered down to one, single objective.

The will to win had become the whole of their lives.

There was no particular skill to this contest. No cunning manoeuvres, or winning strategies. There was just strength, and weight, and the sheer, pigheaded determination to remain standing.

Jarmoosh watched fresh marbles of sweat rise like boils on his opponent's forehead. He smelled the stink of his breath and the ammonia tang of the urine that dampened his breeches. The other ogre, its face as expressionless as Jarmoosh's own, chose this moment to push harder. Jarmoosh pushed back.

Inside of them, sinews snapped as easily as bailing twine. Organs tore beneath agonising pressure. Bones bruised.

No matter.

The vault that surrounded their struggle was full of onlookers. Some bellowed encouragement to the two athletes, their voices blurred with ale or ragged with exhaustion from competitions of their own. Others were deep in conversation, or content to watch in silence.

One, however, her sabretusk pressing against her legs as if for protection, was wide-eyed with simple hero worship. The expression made Katerina look a lot younger than her eighteen years.

Jarmoosh didn't notice her until half an hour after she'd arrived. When he did, some sort of magic seemed to take place. It flowed from her rapt green eyes into his black ones. The spell filled the ogre's tired muscles with a bulge of new strength, and fanned the flames of his belligerence into a volcanic heat.

A savage cry tore itself from Jarmoosh's throat and he bore down on his opponent with fresh determination.

At first it felt like pushing down on an anvil, a mountain, a world. But then, somewhere within that immovable bulk, there was a deep tearing rumble.

An internal injuy, Jarmoosh thrilled.

Maybe even a ruptured kidney!

His face creased up into a horrible smile, and he shifted his weight another inch forward. Now he was sweating with agonies of his own; his muscles burned from hours of strain and his joints throbbed with the crunch of crushed cartilage.

Jarmoosh snatched another glance at Katerina. She'd been coloured as pink as picked bones by his rupturing capillaries, and he saw her for only a blink.

But it was all he needed.

To the deafening applause of his audience Jarmoosh crushed the last of his opponent's resistance. The combatant's ton of bone and muscle was no match for Jarmoosh's desperate energy and, with barely a flicker of warning, the ogre collapsed.

The victor stumbled over his foe's prone form, black suns swirling through the air around him. The onlookers, knowing that the best part of the competition was yet to come, surged forward as he gathered himself and turned back to his vanquished foe.

The ogre's defeat had been complete. He lay gasping on the packed earth floor like a landed fish. A big, edible fish.

Jarmoosh licked his lips as he lurched back towards the fallen form.

'Take his hand,' a voice boomed out behind him.

'No, his foot.'

'Take both.'

But as Jarmoosh stood over the fallen ogre another voice, ice sharp, cut through the tectonic rumble of ogrish advice.

'Don't be cruel!' it ordered him, as confidently as if he were one of her gnoblars and not the tyrant of her tribe. 'His ear is enough.'

Several misshapen heads turned to examine Jarmoosh's legendary female thinling. Standing only about a head taller than a goblin, she stared back at them fearlessly, her expression defiant.

'It was only a friendly match,' she scolded them, ignoring the fact that any one of the gathered ogres could have torn her in half as easily as a rabbit.

They grinned appreciatively.

Jarmoosh would have grinned too, but he didn't have the strength. Instead he bent down, closed the razored pebbles of his teeth around his opponent's ear, and tore it off.

A trickle of blood, a chew of crunching gristle, and it was all over.

'Oh, well done!' Katerina told him, rushing forward to wrap her arms as far around his gut as they would go. 'You are kind!'

'Yes,' Jarmoosh agreed, and swallowed.

FROM THE BACK of the crowd a bundled shape watched the tyrant and his humaness embrace. It was almost as stooped as a gnoblar, this figure. Some might even have said that it was almost as ugly.

Not that Lorenzo would have minded. In the burnished copper of Katerina Hansebourg's hair he saw his ticket home, and that was all that mattered.

As he watched, the ogre grabbed his ticket by her hips, hefted her as easily as a doll, and flung her high into the air. The girl twisted as neatly as a dropped cat and screamed as she fell back into his hands.

Then she laughed.

Lorenzo breathed again. Although reluctant to let her out of his sight, he knew that their first approach to the girl was vital. He could also guess who this girl, or any girl, for that matter, would prefer to have approach her.

With a final backwards glance Lorenzo hurried off to find Captain Florin d'Artaud, Hero of Lustria.

DEEP WITHIN THE fabulously warm stink of Skabrand, Florin lay sprawled amongst his baggage. Beside him, equally bedraggled, lay Sergei. Despite the heat of the place both men clung to their blankets, the rough cloth wrapped around their sleeping forms as tightly as the smoke from the primitive torch.

A single, guttering flame lit the burrow Krom had secured for them. It was small, as such burrows went; a twenty-foot cube that had been scraped out from between two of the stone arches that ribbed the complex. Even the ceiling seemed to be nothing more than soil and shale, its weight apparently supported by no more than good luck.

A crop of toadstools sprouted from this dark material in luminous clumps. The weird goblin fruits looked more flesh than vegetable, and more poisonous than either.

The only other feature was the untanned hide that served as a door. Matted remnants of fur alternated with withered leather, the material stiff with permanent rigor mortis.

And yet, to its shattered occupants, this squalid hole had all the qualities of an earthly paradise. It was warm. It was dry. And, best of all, here there was no need to do anything except lie and rest.

Florin was doing just that when the groping hand woke him up.

'Not now, Magellana,' he muttered from the depths of some dream. The hand paused for a moment before slipping spider-like beneath his jerkin. Florin growled, and batted the hand away without opening his eyes.

He was already sinking back down into the dream when the fingers began tugging at his belt.

Although he was tempted to ignore them, somewhere in the back of his mind the barking dog of suspicion forced him back into wakefulness. With a sudden start Florin sat bolt upright, eyes snapping wide open in the gloom.

The gnoblar that had been so industriously robbing him stared back, the stolen pistol held like a club in its claws.

'Hey!' Florin yelled.

The gnoblar squeaked with fright and turned to flee, bolting towards the hanging skin of the door.

'Come back!' Florin cried, jumping up and lunging for the thief. But as soon as he was on his feet he was down again, snared in the tangle of his laces. With a vicious curse he realised that his boots had been tied together. He cursed again when he realised how tightly.

The flap slid shut behind the thief. Florin, rage lending him inspiration, drew his sword and clumsily sliced through his laces. Ignoring Sergei's sleep-thickened voice he kicked his boots off and charged out after the gnoblar.

After the grotty confines of their quarters the passage beyond seemed huge. It was also surprisingly well built.

No bare earth floors or mouldy walls here, instead the ground underfoot was paved with great slabs of stone, and the walls covered in simple masonry.

Stretching away in both directions rows of torches burned, the light they cast shadowed by a great throng of figures. Some of them Florin recognised. The hulking shapes and tattooed hides of ogres were difficult to mistake for anything else. There were other, stranger denizens though: diminutive figures that nipped around their masters as neatly as rats in a pig sty.

As stunted and gnarled as the withered trees which blasted the plains above, they scurried about their business. Although as greenskinned as their orcish cousins, they were thankfully much smaller, much weaker. Perhaps that was why their beady eyes flitted around so cautiously. Yet, as well as with caution, the yellow slashes were also alive with the dangerous resentment of dogs which have been kicked too much.

Taken aback by the presence of so many of the things Florin hesitated. But even as he dithered the crowd parted and he caught sight of the thief rounding a corner ahead. Snarling with sudden anger he patted the empty holster at his hip and took off after it.

The Bretonnian dodged past the ogres then found himself amongst a group of gnoblars. Without a second's thought, he smashed through them, cursing them as they cursed him. They gave way easily enough, though, and he was soon through, legs pounding as he closed in on their thieving brother.

Oblivious to the yells from behind him, Florin skidded around the corner the thief had ducked around. It looked back, its face twisting in alarm as it saw him, and the chase almost ended as it tumbled in panic.

But even as it fell it reached its objective. Like Florin's own quarters, the mean tunnel had been scraped out of the side of the main thoroughfare. Chips of gravel stung his feet as he followed the gnoblar into its shadowed depths, and he had to duck his head as he ran, bowing down in obeisance to the low roof.

Ahead, little more than a blur in the poorly lit catacomb, the thief ran on. Its fleeing form led its pursuer past the mouths of other, even narrower passageways. Occasionally, sharp nosed and hooded heads would emerge from these to peer after the running figures.

Now Florin could make out the detail of the stolen pistol that hung from the thief's hand.

Now the swish of its fallen hood, and the stitching on its boots.

A hungry grin creased his face as he narrowed the gap between them to a few feet.

'Gotcha,' he whispered, and reached out to snatch at the fleeing creature's rags.

He was a moment too late. Even as his fingers brushed cloth his quarry turned and, as slippery as an eel, dived into the foetid blackness of another dugout.

With a snarl of frustration Florin pulled himself up, sliding to a painful halt on his bloodied soles. The steel of his sword hissed a warning as he drew it, and he paused to look into the darkness which had swallowed the gnoblar. Breath rasping in his lungs, he took a moment to regret the fact that he had no torch. Then he followed the thief into its lair.

A dozen steps later the first of the lights flared into life behind him.

Florin squinted against the sudden light. Then his eyes adjusted enough to see what it had revealed, and his laboured breathing froze in his lungs.

SERGEI HAD BEEN roused by the commotion of Florin's hasty departure, although not soon enough to see what had actually happened. Yawning into full wakefulness he'd rubbed a hand across the stubble of his no longer shaven head, and stretched luxuriously.

Next, remembering the blizzard they'd escaped, he checked his fingers and his toes, dreading the blackness that winter sometimes brought.

With a mutter of thanks he realised that his digits were all present and correct. Stretching again he cast his mind back to their arrival. He had some vague memories of stabling horses and dragging himself to this hole. Unfortunately, exhaustion had blinded him to any other detail. Apart from the fact that he was underground, Sergei had no idea of where he was.

No matter, he thought, rising and making for the door. That's easily rectified.

Like Florin before him he was shocked by the sight of the gnoblars in the ogres' stronghold. Unlike the Bretonnian, though, he wasn't particularly perturbed. A typical strigany, his world was neatly divided between those within the extended family of his caravan and those outside it. Whether those outside of it were men or animals made no difference to him.

Armed with this happy philosophy; Sergei stepped out behind a gaggle of passing gnoblars, eager to explore.

Used to being a stranger in a strange town (although never one quite as strange as this) he walked with apparent purpose, a gait guaranteed to put off all but the most desperate of beggars. He also tried to keep the curiosity off his face as he soaked up every fascinating detail. His eyes were never still and his thoughts never distracted as he left his quarters far behind him.

Already drawing a map of this new city in his memory, Sergei studied the masonry that rolled beneath his feet and arched above his head, always looking for memorable patterns by which to navigate. More interesting than the structure, though, were the denizens of this place.

There was no mistaking who were the masters here. As the ogres, the beasts growing ever uglier as Sergei's eyes adjusted to the light, swaggered through the gnoblars, the gnoblars scurried meekly out of the way.

And yet, the gnoblars didn't really act like slaves, or even servants. Some of them even dared to stare at Sergei, despite the fact that he was twice their size.

The strigany watched them in return with a hidden intensity. The way that they dodged amongst the ogres reminded Sergei of the caravan's dogs; they'd play the obedient pet readily enough, but for the most part they lived their own lives, invisible to those who supposedly owned them.

Sergei doubted if these evil-looking things led quite such innocent lives as the dogs. Still, he decided that the analogy was a good one, and soon found himself striding through them as easily as the ogres.

After a while Sergei noticed that this tunnel, which had at first appeared straight, was actually curving in on itself, spiralling inwards like a nautilus shell. A myriad of offshoots, either stone-built or scratched from the earth, branched off from it like capillaries from an artery, but Sergei ignored them. He wanted to see where this road led.

He also wanted to find out what was making the noise.

At first he hadn't noticed it. Beneath the chatter and bustle which filled the highway, it was easy to miss. But the further along the spiralling road he got the louder it became, a deep, constant groaning that sounded like the distant voice of a far-off ocean, or the thousand-throated cry of a battle.

The sound grew louder as the curve of the tunnel grew tighter. The crowd had begun to thin now, as though driven away by the dismal roar of whatever it was that lay ahead. As he passed the last little clump of gnoblars, their hoods drawn tightly around their heads as if to deafen themselves, Sergei felt a little like turning back himself.

No, he told himself sternly. You're strigany.

And a strigany fears nothing.

Thrusting his jaw forward as if inviting the world to take its best shot, Sergei marched on, the click of his boot heels audible above the alien voice which filled the emptying tunnel. By now the spiral of the passageway was obvious and unbroken by any offshoots. The few ogres that remained here were solitary and silent. Some of them pushed past Sergei, oblivious to him as they hurried towards the roar of whatever lay in the dark heart of their stronghold. Others, returning, he was careful to avoid.

It was these returnees that filled Sergei with the most unease. Each of them, without exception, was bleeding from lost fingers or ears. One was even weeping tears of blood from the freshly plucked socket of his eye.

Whatever lay ahead, the strigany considered, was obviously hungry. It even affected the air, sucking the atmosphere along the passageway like wine from a bottle. For the first time since he'd awoken, Sergei felt this warm breeze, and shivered as it caressed the nape of his neck. It tugged at the flames of the torches too, teasing them out into fluttering streamers of light.

The spirals grew tighter, and the hair on the back of Sergei's neck began to bristle like a hound's before a thunderstorm. It wasn't just the fact that the throbbing sound had mutated into a sort of inhuman sobbing. No, it was more than that. It was a feeling that gravity had become horizontal, that whatever lay just a few twists away was somehow dragging him towards it as surely as the bottom of a precipice.

Sergei's pulse quickened, and he came to a stop. The sense of vertigo passed, although not completely. Rather it seemed to be waiting, biding its time as patiently as a fisherman who is fearful that his catch will snap the line if he pulls too hard.

Despite his determination to fear nothing, Sergei knew that he should have stopped there, turned back while he still could. But as well as with bravado, his was a nature cursed with curiosity. The eerie keening of whatever lay ahead; he felt that he could almost understand it. Almost.

If he could only see what was making it...

Without making a conscious decision he found himself walking forward, rounding the last curve of the passageway.

And there he found the beating heart of Skabrand.

FLORIN HAD NO idea how many of the gnoblar's kin were gathered here. They were packed into an almost solid mass, the carpet of their filthy bodies stretching back into further darkness. Another torch flared into light and, wriggling like maggots on a corpse, the entire tribe began to wake up and look about them for the source of the disturbance.

Slowly, with the dreadful inevitability of blood trickling from an assassin's dagger, their eyes found Florin.

He suddenly realised how unimportant the stolen pistol was. How unimportant everything was except for getting out of this lair in one piece.

Face composed into a blank mask, Florin began to edge backwards. Moving slowly, he kept his gaze fixed on the mass of grotesque figures beyond. Poisonous yellow eyes glared back at him, the spite within them as sharp as the blades which appeared in their hands. Whispers hissed through the stooped figures and, without any command being given, they began to follow Florin.

Most of the tribe shuffled forward with the cautious patience of wolves that have cornered an animal they know might fight back. Others, bolder than their brothers, slunk around to take up position behind the retreating man.

It was one of these that threw the dagger.

Although accurate, it was a weak shot. The steel point sliced through cloth and skin, but bounced off a shoulder blade, leaving no more than a scratch behind.

The nip of steel was enough to snap Florin's nerve though. A wild battle-cry tore itself from his throat and he turned, following the lighting flash of his sword through the scattering gnoblars and towards the door.

Don't panic, Florin told himself as his scalp scraped painfully on the lintel.

Another stab of pain pinched his shoulder, but at least he was back in the tunnel. Hunched over into a knuckle-scraping gallop he bolted down the passageway, as stooped as an orc beneath the cramped ceiling. Although there was hardly any sound from behind him Florin could sense the mob that was following him. He could hear their pattering feet and the swish of their rags against the tunnel wall.

He could even smell them.

Dimly, beneath the exhilarating rush of fear and adrenaline, a part of him was calmly deciding to stop at the end of this return. Better to keep the pursuing mob bottled up, he decided, than to let them surround him and bury him with numbers.

And if he couldn't keep them bottled up... well then, he was finished.

The thought brought a hysterical grin to his face, the expression dripping a trickle of sweat into his eye. Blinking against the sting of it, Florin scraped against a wall, bounced around a twist in the passageway, and found himself almost upon the junction with the main thoroughfare.

Blinking again, this time against the prism of bright tears, he put on a final burst of speed, finishing this desperate race by leaping out into the light. As soon as he felt the cold flagstones beneath his feet he pirouetted back around to face...

To face nothing. There was nothing behind him except for dirt and shadows, and, far back in the tunnel, the glint of what might have been a blade.

'Cowards!' Florin jeered, realising it was hardly the smartest thing to do but doing it anyway.

There was no reply from the darkness beyond. Torn between relief and disappointment, Florin wiped the sweat from his brow, and gingerly touched the shallow cuts on his back. They left blood on his fingertips, but not much.

He waited for another minute before sheathing his sword. Only then did he turn, his skin crawling with the feeling of being watched, and limp back to his own quarters.

'Where have you been?' Lorenzo demanded as he pushed his way through the partition.

'Why?' Florin snapped back, his mood still jagged from the scrape he'd been in.

'Because we've found her.'

'Found who?'

'Who do you think?'

Florin, who'd been fumbling with his boots, stopped and looked up.

'You don't mean...?'

'The very same,' Lorenzo grinned. 'Katerina Hansebourg, our favourite heiress.'

'How sure are you? I mean, did you talk to her?'

'No, I didn't talk to her.'

'Then how do you know it's her?'

Lorenzo frowned as if suddenly uncertain.

'Hmm, you're right,' he said, scratching the bristles on his chin. 'Perhaps there's another eighteen year-old girl living with one of these ogre families. An eighteen year-old girl with a Bretonnian accent. And bright red hair.'

'No need to be sarcastic. I just wondered if you'd spoken to her.'

'Thought I'd leave that to you. Somehow girls seem to be weak-minded enough to prefer your company to mine.'

'Who wouldn't?' Florin asked as he finished tying his cut laces back together.

Lorenzo sucked on one of his three remaining teeth and regarded the younger man.

'Lost your pistol, I see.'

'Never mind that now...'

'It was a waste of money anyway.'

'You nag worse than a wife.'

'Still, a fool and his money are easily parted.'

Florin glared at his partner, who fell silent.

'Where's Sergei, anyway? I left him here.'

'Haven't seen him.'

The two men exchanged a thoughtful glance.

'Well, I'm sure he can look out for himself,' Florin decided, a little doubtfully. 'I think we should concentrate on securing the wench. That done we can decide how to get out of here.'

'Now that,' Lorenzo nodded, 'is a damned good idea.'

THE PAIR OF guards were huge, even for ogres. They dwarfed the supplicants who filed between them, heads bowed, to face whatever howling horror lay in the cavern beyond.

Their stink was just as impressive as their size. An eye-watering swelter of unwashed skin and rotten cloth, it was strong enough to be smelled even above the heavy fug that swamped the rest of the complex. But although their mountainous bodies reeked of ancient filth their weapons were clean, the edges shining with a scalpel sharpness in the torchlight.

Sergei studied them, and they studied him back, watching with the disinterest of tigers who see a mouse too small to be worth eating. Behind them the tunnel had been choked off, strangled by the crudely forged ironwork of a double door. The rivets that held it together wept orange tears of rust, as though saddened by the constant throbbing howl that came from behind them.

As the strigany watched, another ogre, stooped and white-haired, clumped past him and pushed his way through the doors. Sergei craned his neck for a glimpse of what lay beyond, but saw only a patch of flame-lit stone before the doors swung shut.

Encouraged by the fact that the guards had barely glanced at the ogre, let alone challenged him, Sergei straightened his back and strode confidently forward.

'No,' one of the ogres intoned, his voice as heavy as the gates he guarded.

Sergei looked into the depths of the ogre's eyes, and felt his confidence ebb.

'I wish to pass,' he said anyway.

'No. No gnoblars.'

'But I'm a human.'

The ogre looked at him closely.

'No. No who-mans'

As if to underline the words the noise from behind the door rose in pitch, twisting into a blood-curdling whine before dropping back down to a steady sob. Sergei licked his lips nervously, torn between curiosity and the sense of dread which was dampening his palms.

'All right, then, I won't pass,' he told the guard, as if he had any choice in the matter. 'But would you at least tell me what is behind there?'

The guard who had spoken remained as silent as the slab-built walls, and as expressionless. He had already lost interest in the small creature that stood squeaking before him. Despite the oddly well-built look of the thing, one gnoblar was much the same as another. They were always up to some mischief.

Sergei thought about repeating the question, then gave up. Sighing with what sounded suspiciously like relief, he turned away.

The sound from beyond the door seemed to turn to mocking laughter.

As it did so a sudden, wild idea seized the strigany. He would dodge the guards, rush through the doors, find his way to whatever was calling him from beyond and, and…

With a snap of common sense he rejected this madness. His breath grew faster as he looked at the door, suddenly afraid. That feeling was back, that feeling of unnatural vertigo that threatened to drop him falling through the iron doors and towards whatever lay beyond.

Shaking himself like a wet dog, the strigany decided that he'd had enough of the terrible siren song that had brought him here. If it was only for ogres then fine, it was only for ogres. He should count himself lucky and go, back to the levels where it was only a whisper.

But before he could turn to go the iron doors squeaked open and an ogre trudged out.

Beneath the play of the torchlight his skin was grey and drawn, and he held one bleeding hand in the other. There was a stump where his little finger had been. Blood still flowed from the fresh wound, and a grimace of pain exposed teeth that glittered like diamonds.

It was Krom.

For some reason, as he watched the ogre, Sergei felt suddenly ashamed. It was as though he'd somehow caught Krom in the midst of some private ritual. In fact, the feeling was so uncomfortable that the strigany was edging back along the wall when Krom looked up and saw him.

'You,' the ogre exclaimed, stomping towards him. 'Good. Come, and I will show you where the female is.'

So saying he swept past, leaving Sergei follow his retreating back and the trail of dark crimson droplets he left behind him.

AFTER HIS VICTORY, Jarmoosh returned to his tribe's quarters and collapsed into his ironwood throne. Raised up on an earthen platform, it dominated the cave, a comfortable eyrie from which the tyrant looked down upon his tribe as benignly as the sun upon a field of wheat.

It had grown strong since he had taken it over, this tribe. Jarmoosh felt a twinge of pride as he observed the dozen healthy bulls that lolled about in imitation of his own posture, and the youths who fought playfully amongst their shadows. Good ogres, all of them. Strong of gut and hard of limb.

There were no weaklings here. No softness. That was something no decent tyrant would stand for and Jarmoosh was no exception. Just as a smith uses a stone to sharpen a blade so he had used the northern mountains to hone his followers. Alone they had taken down the cave beasts they called shoggoths, even snow mammoths. And as a tribe they had hunted even greater prey in the form of their own kind.

When the season had been upon them they had warred against other tribes for mates and territory, joyfully testing their strength against those best able to match it. Jarmoosh had lost several of his charges in these struggles. He'd also lost his left eye.

Still, no matter, he thought, scratching his back with a half-picked bone. That was the way of the world. The strong thrived and the weak perished.

With a feeling of smug contentment the tyrant thought about the brood of females that his own strength had won. A gaggle of them awaited his pleasure beyond their screen. Even more valuable were the herd of rhinoxen that rested in the safety of the communal stables above.

Jarmoosh felt a low rumble of pleasure deep within his gut as he considered his riches. From his vagabond beginnings he had become one of the wealthiest of all the tyrants here. A first amongst equals.

He knew why, too.

It was because of his luck, his treasure. Despite the temptation to eat her during those first hunted days together, something had stayed his appetite. In a human that something would have been called affection. Jarmoosh preferred to think of it as instinct.

Now, he'd never dream of harming her. She was his talisman, and he treasured her accordingly.

The ogre let his eyes close, resting as his old muscles reknitted themselves sinew by painful sinew. Today's fight had been a good one. With any luck he'd recover fast enough for another before the Great Feast marked the end of his tribe's stay at Skabrand.

'Boss. A visitor.'

Jarmoosh grunted back into wakefulness to find Morgrut standing respectfully before him. Morgrut was as broad in the shoulders as he was deep in the gut. He was a strong fighter, respected by the tribe. That was one of the reasons why he was fast becoming Jarmoosh's heir apparent.

That's why he's always so respectful, the tyrant thought, pretending to be less awake than he was. *He knows I'll use any excuse to break him before he gets too strong.*

Good lad.

Jarmoosh waited for the younger ogre to drop his eyes before replying.

'Who?' he asked, laconic as always.

'His name is Krom. He comes from a western tribe.'

'What does he want?'

'Trade.'

Jarmoosh fell silent.

Considered.

Decided.

'Good. Bring him.'

Morgrut nodded and strode away to fetch the newcomer. Jarmoosh pretended not to notice the way the other bulls moved out of his way, as submissive as if he were already tyrant. Morgrut will challenge me soon, he thought, and the observation filled him with the patient happiness of a gourmet anticipating a fine meal.

His attention snapped back to the task in hand when Krom strode into the cavern. As well built as any of his lads, this one had the look of the vagabond about him, the smell of a wanderer. It made the old tyrant feel quite nostalgic.

'Greetings,' he said as his guest approached. 'My name is Jarmoosh.'

'I am Krom.'

The two ogres studied each other, weighing each other up with blank-faced curiosity. Then Jarmoosh glanced past his guest to the pet gnoblar that waited in his shadow, and his breath caught in his throat as he realised it wasn't a gnoblar after all. It was a human. A male human, judging by the stubble which covered its chin. Not a bad specimen, either, for one of the lesser races. It even had the strength to return the tyrant's gaze.

With a twinge of unease, Jarmoosh found himself thinking about Katerina. He wondered where she was, and whether or not she knew that there was another human here.

Maybe he should confine her to the females' area.

'I have come to make a trade,' Krom said, breaking his reverie. Dragging his attention away from the paling human, Jarmoosh turned to his guest.

'What have you to trade with?'

'My loyalty,' Krom told him. 'I will fight with you against the Tyrant Bashar Zog.'

Jarmoosh felt his unease grow at the mention of the name. The eastern tyrant was still no more than a cloud on the horizon, a rumour of a battle yet to be won. He was also a problem that Jarmoosh hadn't wanted to worry about until the joys of Skabrand were over with.

'How do you know that I wish to fight this tyrant?' he rumbled, eyeing this particularly disturbing vagabond with displeasure.

'The Maw,' Krom explained, and held up his mutilated hand. Jarmoosh looked at the slow trickle of blood that still ebbed from the wound. 'I fed it and it spoke to me.'

Jarmoosh considered this.

'The Maw is always right,' he admitted. 'Bashar is an offence against the ogres' true way.'

A rumble of agreement greeted these words, and Krom turned to see the watching bulls. Mention of war had animated them, and they'd gathered around eagerly.

'You have a strong tribe,' Krom observed, truthfully. 'But it would be well to ally with others.'

Jarmoosh grunted noncommittally.

'I will think about your offer,' he decided. 'What do you want me to offer you?'

'One thing only,' Krom told him. 'And that is the female human you keep. Her own tribe have sent a patrol to bring her home.'

Silence, broken only by the hiss of torches, blossomed in the cavern.

'No.' The tyrant shook his head. 'No, that one is not...'

'Jarmoosh?'

He turned to see that Katerina had slunk up behind him, and grunted with surprise. It wasn't her sudden appearance that struck him as strange but her voice. He could barely recognise it.

Usually it was sharp, and as certain as fire or ice. At other times, particularly when she was marshalling the tribe's gnoblars, it could be as sibilantly threatening as an adder's hiss. The tyrant had even heard it become as sweet as honey, usually when she had gotten exactly what she wanted.

But now she sounded uncertain. Even a little afraid.

'Jarmoosh, is that a man?' she asked, tugging at his elbow and staring, wide-eyed, at the human.

'Yes,' he replied, and all eyes turned on Sergei. He glared back defiantly. Even though he'd been forced to leave his sword at the gate, and even though the brutal creatures that towered above him looked capable of anything, he

wouldn't drop his eyes. He was a strigany, after all. And a
strigany feared nothing.

Then he saw Katerina and his jaw dropped.

Without really thinking about it he'd expected her to be
the usual merchant's daughter. She'd be plump and pasty,
he'd supposed, and trussed up in enough material to
clothe an entire family.

But the girl who looked back at him, his own amazement mirrored in her emerald eyes, was none of these
things. The crudely stitched patchwork of her clothing
revealed a body that was as hard and lean as any caravan
girl's. No anaemic dumpling this one; her skin glowed with
rude health between the patches of dirt that covered it.

Nor was her hair twisted up into the bizarre shapes fashion demanded. Instead the sleek tangle of it spilled down
onto her shoulders, falling as naturally as a waterfall and
shining with the deep red of a fire's embers.

Sergei, forgetting all about the ogres, wondered if it
would feel as smooth as it looked. Or as warm.

Yet all of these details were as nothing compared to the
single truth about this girl, and that was that she was beautiful. Even the pale line of scar tissue that traced one of her
cheekbones couldn't detract from that fact. Rather, it accen-
tuated it, made it more real.

Sergei realised that his mouth was open, and closed it
with a snap. Katerina, meanwhile, couldn't seem to stop
playing with her hair. Scowling with confusion she pulled
her hand away from her head. Then she licked her lips.

Palms dampening with an anxiety that no mere ogres
had managed to evoke, Sergei realised that he should say
something. He opened his mouth, took a step forward,
and squeaked.

Flames of embarrassment burned in his cheeks as he
coughed and tried again.

'Pleased to meet you,' he said, miserably. 'I'm Sergei
Chervez.'

Katerina goggled at him, as if amazed that he could
speak.

Sergei swallowed. He was so desperate for guidance he actually looked to Krom, but the ogre remained content to watch him suffer. Then the strigany looked back at Katerina, who seemed to be glaring at him.

'Can I ask what is your name please?' he pleaded.

''s Katerina,' Katerina mumbled. By now her brows had furrowed into what seemed to be an expression of pure rage.

'Oh,' said Sergei, and cast about for some way to keep the conversation going. What did girls like to talk about anyway? Real girls, that was, not ones like his cousins.

'I like your hair,' he offered. Katerina's hands flew up to her head, as if anxious to hide it.

But Jarmoosh had seen enough. Ogre he might be, but he knew a mating ritual when he saw one.

'Katerina,' he rumbled. 'Go and wait in the females' quarter.'

'What!' she snapped, her embarrassment finding expression in outrage. 'The females' quarter! No, I won't. I'm not some stupid breeder.'

A low rumble of disapproval, as threatening as the sound of distant thunder, reverberated amongst the watching bulls. Jarmoosh drew himself up, looming up over his humaness.

'Go to the females' quarter,' he repeated in the same, flat tone.

'No,' Katerina said, and stamped her foot down.

This defiance was too much for the tyrant to bear, especially in front of a stranger. With a strangled roar of rage he leapt to his feet, snatched the humaness up by her hips, and hurled her across the cave.

Before she had even landed, Sergei had sprung to her defence. His own battle cry was drowned by the ogre's own, but that didn't matter. All that mattered was that he was within striking distance of the beast who'd tried to murder his beloved.

Although unarmed, the strigany showed no hesitation. After all, he knew that the best weapons in the world were

speed and surprise, and they were weapons that he was
well trained in. Before the tyrant was even aware that he
was under attack Sergei had stamped his foot forward, the
heel connecting with the edge of the ogre's kneecap in a
blow that should have been crippling.

Jarmoosh looked down with mild interest as the attacker
struck him again. With a snarl Sergei drove his fist into
what, in a human, would have been a solar plexus. In an
ogre, all the attack reached was a band of hard, rubbery
muscle.

Recoiling from the failure, Sergei feinted left, then right.
Then he struck upwards, his fingers bunched into a hook
that was aimed at the ogre's throat.

But Jarmoosh had had enough of this foolishness. With
barely a flicker of movement he caught the human's fore-
arm and swept him through the air, banging him down
onto hard-packed earth as carelessly as a peasant swinging
a mattock.

Stars exploded in Sergei's head, bright against the sudden darkness of the world. He leapt to his feet, then
collapsed back onto the ground as his legs gave way. Struggling to hold onto consciousness he saw hands reaching
down for him, and tried to roll away, to escape.

He didn't stand a chance. Even as he slid into a deep,
peaceful well of unconsciousness Katerina had wrapped
her arms around him, and cradled his head against the
softness of her breasts.

'You're so brave,' she cooed as her hero's eyelids flickered
shut.

But he didn't hear her. He was already far, far away, dancing with angels who all had tangled red hair and thin scars
across their perfectly drawn cheekbones.

'WHAT DO YOU mean I can't see her?' Florin demanded. The
countless hours of fruitless searching for Katerina had
worn his temper thin. Returning to their mildewed quarters to find that Sergei had succeeded where he'd failed had
worn it even thinner.

It was so irritating that he hadn't even thought to ask the strigany where he'd received his beating. Bruises coloured half of his face so that it resembled a rotten apple, blue-grey injuries that would have knocked the fire out of most men.

They hadn't knocked the fire out of the strigany, though. Far from it.

'What do you think I mean?' he demanded back, drooling slightly from the corner of his mouth that was still numb.

The two men glared at each other until Lorenzo, with the theatrical sigh of a man used to separating fools from their folly, intervened.

'Why don't you let Sergei tell us what happened?' he suggested to Florin, who muttered and turned away. 'As well as Katerina, I'm wondering about who gave him such a hiding.'

'It's nothing,' Sergei lied, and touched the side of his face gingerly.

'It doesn't look like nothing.'

'Let's just say,' Sergei tried to smile, and winced instead, 'that it's not a good idea to box with an ogre.'

'You certainly know how to get into trouble,' Florin said, not without a touch of approval.

Lorenzo barked with laughter.

'Look who's talking. If you hadn't insulted that idiot Volavant so much that he burnt our tavern down, and if you hadn't decided to play the hero and lose your skin, and if…'

'Yes, yes, yes,' Florin hurriedly waved the observations away. 'Never mind that now. Look, Sergei, sorry if I was a little terse. But how did you find Katerina? We looked everywhere, and not a sniff.'

So Sergei told them all about their first meeting. He told them about her tribe, and Jarmoosh, and the bargain that Krom had offered for her return. Then he started to tell them about how beautiful she was. Oblivious to the rolling eyes of his companions he rambled on, illuminating their gloomy quarters with the clumsy poetry of the smitten.

'Easy on the eye then, is she?' Lorenzo said, cutting into a five-minute monologue about the colour of the wench's hair.

'Gorgeous,' said Sergei, simply, and looked up into the half-pitying and half-mocking faces of his companions. Their expressions were enough to finally subdue his rhapsody. Clearing his throat with embarrassment, Sergei decided to change the subject.

'Anyway, the thing is, the tyrant of her tribe has her confined to quarters until the Hungering. That's some sort of eating contest, I think. Krom reckons that by then nobody will be interested in anything else apart from this contest, and which tribe will win it. We can meet up with her then.'

'Wait a minute, wait a minute. Why wouldn't this tyrant let her come and see us now? Didn't you say Krom made a bargain for her?'

'No, he made an offer. The tyrant who owns her is still thinking about it.'

'Damn,' Florin said. The visions he'd had of walking in, wiping away the girl's tears of gratitude, then marching easily back to the caravan road were beginning to disappear, evaporating as quickly as alehouse plans the morning after.

'I wonder where Krom is,' Lorenzo murmured, his wrinkles deepening with thought. Sergei just shrugged.

'Don't know. After he brought me back here he went off again.'

Florin sucked at his teeth, and wondered about whether or not to go and see this Jarmoosh himself. Maybe he could make an offer, although he wasn't sure what with. He had a feeling that their small store of gold wouldn't be enough, and he doubted if the beast was likely to accept a letter of credit.

'When's this eating contest?' he asked.

'Tomorrow,' Sergei told him, his own thoughts already wandering back to the moment when Katerina had cradled his head against her breasts. If only he hadn't fallen unconscious just then.

'Then we'll do as Krom suggests,' Florin decided. 'And while we're waiting to see Sergei's new lover, we can find out where our horses are being kept. It might be wise to prepare for a quick getaway.'

The strigany was suddenly grateful for the bruising he'd taken. The throbbing numbness was a small price to pay for the way the discolouration hid his blushes.

THE PIT WAS so deep that the audience could see little of the waiting ogres apart from their scalps and shoulders. Whorls of blood already patched their skin, the patterns as black as pitch in the torchlight. One of them, leaning back against the rough stone lining of the pit, hardly seemed able to stand. The other four struggled to conceal torn muscles and fractured bones.

All of them had some sort of injury. The road that had brought them to this hallowed site had been long and violent, and blocked by the ambitions of a hundred other bulls. Between them the victors who stood here tonight had beaten every single one of them. It was that which had taken such a toll.

Still, injured or not, pride kept the five ogres standing straight backed and square jawed. The ambitions of their entire tribes rested on them, and the fact that their hands were chained did nothing to dispel their confidence.

This was the way of the Hungering, after all. And the Hungering was the surest route to glory an ogre could take. Even if they died, which they probably would, their place on the tribe's totem was assured, their welcome into the Great Maw guaranteed.

In marked contrast to their patience the crowd shifted restlessly. The edge of the pit had been walled off, the rim lined with blocks of granite strong enough to withstand the eager press of so many bodies. Occasionally, amongst all the shoving, fights almost flared up. But every time the belligerents would draw back, unwilling to risk missing the spectacle that was about to unfold below.

From behind the iron-plated door that led into the arena, something bellowed. The crowd hushed, listening eagerly. The beast bellowed again and, as loud as indigestion within a tyrant's gut, the rumble of approaching hooves drummed through the arena.

Only three of the audience remained unmoved by the rising tension. They were too busy watching the crowd, just as intently as the ogres were watching the pit. They had a good position, too, these men. The narrow ledge had been carved out of the walls to form a crude balcony, too light for an ogre's weight but sufficient for humans or gnoblars. It was even sufficient to support men as heavily laden as these; they seemed the size of small bears beneath the equipment that they dared not leave unguarded.

'See her yet?' Florin asked Sergei, who shook his head.

Lorenzo scratched thoughtfully.

'I'm surprised that you both think she'll come here. I mean, she might do, but I doubt it. Whatever these boys think of as entertainment, I doubt if it will appeal to a woman's tastes.'

'She'll come because she'll guess that we're here,' Sergei told him. 'I bet she wants to find us as much as we want to find her.'

'Ah, young love,' Florin muttered.

Luckily Sergei was too intent on the crowd below to be embarrassed. It was formed up like the concentric circles of an archer's target; the dark hole of the pit was the bulls-eye, the ring of ogres that surrounded it the first ring, and the circle of gnoblars that surrounded them the second.

The strigany watched the diminutive greenskins with professional interest as they milled around, light-fingered and sharp-eyed. Even as he watched, one of them ducked forward and, with a flash of steel, cut something from an ogre's belt. The victim of the crime remained oblivious. He was too busy trying to elbow his way into a better position.

'Maybe we should have sent someone to watch Katerina's quarters,' Florin said, half to himself.

But before he could reconsider a huge, echoing boom signalled that something had reached the pit door. A thrill of excitement ran through the onlookers, as though the noise had been the world's biggest dinner gong.

Barefooted in the sand of the pit, the five champions readied themselves. Moving with a surprising coordination for strangers they spread out, forming a crescent which faced the door. Florin forgot all about redeploying his gang as he craned forward, all of his attention drawn by the scene that was unfolding below.

Another impact boomed out. This time he could see the way that it rattled the iron plates on the door, shaking them as easily as a storm shakes tiles.

By now even the gnoblars had fallen silent. The anticipation that greased the air had grown thick enough to hold even them in its spell.

There was a second of absolute silence before, with a final crash, the door was smashed open and the beast charged into the ring.

Florin had seen its like before. Despite the flickering torchlight he recognised the shaggy pelt, the great yellowed horns, the powerful flex of its shoulders. He even recognised the rumbling bellow of its distress. This was the same breed of creature that the ogre hunter had bested.

This one seemed bigger, though. A lot bigger. It towered over the waiting champions like an ox over a gang of street urchins, and the tangle of its horns seemed to fill the pit.

But despite its size the waiting ogres didn't hesitate. Silent but for the jingling of their manacled hands they hurled themselves forward, their faces twisted with a wild fanaticism. The glittering crescents of their teeth almost looked like smiles as they leapt onto the rhinox.

Applause thundered like artillery as the first of them fastened his jaws into its hide. A moment later and the rest of the ogres had followed him, faces buried in the rhinox's bloodied pelt as they gnawed into its flesh.

'Ranald's balls,' Florin whispered as, with a bellow of rage, the beast flung itself against the side of the pit. The first of its attackers was pinned beneath its bulk, and the rhinox drove its weight against him. Although sandwiched between the animal and the stonework the ogre held on, jaws locked with a grim determination. It was only the snap of his spine which loosened them.

As he died the rhinox spun around, letting the crushed ogre fall like a rag doll onto the bloodied sand of the pit. One of the dead ogre's comrades felt the strip of skin he had fastened his teeth into tear free, and he was sent rocketing through the air. The ogre hit the wall head first, and was blinded by the resultant sheet of blood as he tried to struggle back to his feet.

He never made it.

Before he'd even had a chance to blink the blood from his eyes the rhinoxen was upon him, its head lowered to punch a horn through the ogre's gut.

A groan of sympathetic pain rose up from the audience as the beast skewered its victim. Then, the muscles of its neck bunching like a giant's fist, it hoisted him high into the air. An ivory tip erupted from the ogre's back, pushing even farther through his torso as the beast shook him like a captured battle flag.

Even as he struggled, the ogre's body began to tear apart. His entrails noosed down around the rhinox's head, terrible streamers for this grotesque carnival. They slipped down around its hooves as the rhinox continued to worry the body, lashing it about to spatter the baying audience with a misting of blood.

Sensing the stilling of its victim's heart, the beast threw the vanquished ogre to one side and turned its back on him contemptuously.

Yet even in the midst of these victories the rhinox was suffering. All the while the three survivors had been tearing great mouthfuls of its flesh away, their teeth slicing through living muscle as easily as spades through soil. Bleeding from a dozen wounds the rhinox lurched to one side, trying to find a wall against which to guard its back.

One of its tormentors leapt at its neck, but it turned quickly enough to catch his shoulder on its tusk. The ogre pulled itself off the spike and rolled back out of the way, already looking for another opening as another of its fellows closed in.

This one, not above using a gnoblar's trick, ducked under the beast's belly and fastened its jaws around a fetlock.

Eyes rolling with panic, the beast danced sideways in a clumsy jig. Its hooves stamped down onto the attacker, heavy blows that sounded like nails being driven into his coffin.

Ribs splintered. Organs ruptured. Blood gouted from the ogre's nose. But still he held on, grinding through the animal's tendons until, with a scream of pain, it fell. Only then did the ogre let his ruined body relax into oblivion.

One part of the crowd, the tribe brothers of the dying hero, roared their approval as the last of his life gurgled away. The stamp of their feet echoed around the cavern like a savage heartbeat, and, as the rhinox struggled back to its feet, the rest of the audience joined in.

The two remaining contenders, rhinox blood drooling down from their mouths, closed warily in on the beast. One of them, his leg dragging uselessly behind him, stopped, called something out to the other.

Then, as carelessly as if the maddened rhinox was no more than a cornered sheep, the ogre limped straight towards it.

Had it not been for the rage and the pain that burned within its tiny brain the beast might have smelt a trap in this slow advance. As it was, it just saw an opportunity, a chance to annihilate another of its attackers. With a enraged squeal it hurled itself towards the enemy, wounded leg trailing as it threw the battering ram of its skull towards him.

The ogre made no effort to dodge. Instead he spread his arms wide and took the full impact of the charge on his gut. His gut collapsed beneath the rhinox's attack, crushed as easily as an eggshell, and a groan of sorrow rose up from the onlookers.

But even as he died the crippled ogre's hands closed in on each side of the rhinox's head, his thumbs aimed at the tiny, maddened eyes. With the last flicker of consciousness he pressed his thumbs into those deep sockets and gouged.

The scream of pain was incredibly shrill for such a large animal and as piercing as an arrow point. Its wounds seemed to be forgotten as, completely blind, the stricken rhinox thrashed around the pit in a desperate frenzy.

But even as it lunged at invisible enemies the remaining ogre was seizing his chance. Waiting until the beast turned away he leapt onto its neck, wrapped his legs around the great slab of muscle, and swung around to close his jaws around the beast's throat.

The rhinox's cries were silenced. Blundering about, grinding the fallen ogres into a bloody mulch beneath its hooves, it could do no more than hiss as breathing became harder and harder. Lacking the strength to bite through the animal's windpipe, the last ogre had contented itself with pinching it shut, inflicting upon his prey the agonising inch by inch death of suffocation.

It took perhaps an hour for the beast to finally die. When it did, its last heartbeat fluttering away like a bat into the night, the ogre rolled away from its fallen body and staggered to his feet.

Applause thundered around the cavern. Feet stamped, hands clapped, and the very stones of the pit shook beneath the rolling chorus of praise and encouragement.

'It's exciting, isn't it?' said a voice from behind the three watching men. They turned as one. And, as one, they saw Katerina.

Sergei's face lit up with such joy that it became almost handsome.

Florin blinked with surprise. Then with desire. Then he smiled his most charming smile and took her hand.

'Enchanted,' he said and kissed it, his eyes lingering on hers for as long as his lips lingered on her hand.

Katerina giggled, but Sergei didn't see the joke. Instead, still tongue-tied, he glared at Florin with something approaching real hatred. Florin caught the expression. In response he looked back to Katerina and nodded towards Sergei, a comical expression twisting his face.

She laughed again as Sergei flushed a bright crimson.

Lorenzo looked from one face to the next. His own battered features crumpled with dismay at what he saw.

'Gods save us,' he muttered miserably as Florin, then Sergei, both offered Katerina their arms.

Behind them the crowd of ogres erupted into a fresh frenzy of applause as their champion carved the rhinox's heart out. The humans didn't notice.

Their own worlds had suddenly become much more intense than any blood sport.

CHAPTER EIGHT

ALL GODS ARE hungry. It is a fact that makes a mockery of their claims to be omnipotent (even though there are few willing to do the mocking).

After all, how can our celestial rulers truly be called divine when they are bound by the same chains of greed that ensnare the weakest of mortals? In fact, the gods are trapped even more completely than we are. Unlike our wishes, theirs are seldom tamed by the realities of mortal life. Instead they are left to grow wild and unchecked, as rife as weeds in an untended garden.

Yes, just like us, the gods are enslaved by what they want. And just like us they are dragged hither and thither by those parts of themselves that they will not, or cannot, control. The hooks of lust and desire pull them down to these baser realms of ours. The desire for adulation. The desire for power.

The desire for sacrifice.

Yet of all the gods, it is the ogres' which is perhaps the hungriest.

That's no surprise.

Hunger is all that it has.

There is no complex cosmology behind the ogres' worship of the Great Maw. No disputing priests or apocalyptic ambitions. There aren't even any statues, for ogres are too simple a folk to delude themselves with fantasies of anthropomorphism.

But although faceless, the Great Maw is never silent. Far from it. Whether it is symbolised by the deepest of caverns, or by a pit in the corner of the meanest of hovels, or at the bottom of a scrape hastily dug into the red soil of a battle-field, the Great Maw speaks to the faithful.

And usually what it says is: 'Feed Me'.

In Skabrand, though, there their Maw speaks of other things, of the truths and the secrets which haunt its worshippers' dreams. That was why generations past wrapped their festivals around its depths. That was also why a vast settlement had grown around this sacred representation of the Great Maw that was said to lie far off in the distant east.

In Skabrand, the Maw belches out knowledge to ogrekind as freely as a cormorant vomits up half-digested fish for her chicks.

Unfortunately, like the cormorant, the Maw first has to be fed itself. And so, a hundred feet beneath the howling blizzards which scoured the world above, the ogres solemnly filed into the great central chamber that contained it.

The victor led the procession. He carried the wet slab of the rhinox's heart pressed against his gut, leaving a spoor of blood behind him. Flies, thawed from winter slumber by the body heat and fires of this place, crawled across the ogre's darkly stained shoulders.

He took it as a compliment. Even the smallest creatures, it seemed, were intent on paying him tribute.

Ahead, the two ogres who guarded the portal swung both the doors wide open, revealing the cavern within. The air quickened as they did so, sucking past them to disappear into the void of their god.

Feeling the warm breath of the breeze on his back the victor followed it towards the emptiness of the Maw. Skabrand was whining with anticipation now, the insatiable nothingness of its form calling impatiently.

Straightening the boulders of his shoulders, the ogre paced around the crumbling stone of its lips. As always the pit filled him with the suicidal urge to leap, to jump into the final darkness of its belly just as eagerly as he had fought his way out of the darkness of his mother's womb.

He wouldn't jump, though. Not today. Not ever. He had too much pride to disgrace his tribe by succumbing to that lethal siren song.

The rest of the ogres followed him, fighting their own battles against the seductive whispers that scratched at the back of their minds. Silently, the good humour of the rhinox killing long gone beneath the temple atmosphere of the place, they gathered around the echoing blackness of the pit.

When they had all assembled the oldest butcher stepped forward. His weathered hide was creased with wrinkles as deep as wounds, the lines shattering the tattoos that coloured his skin. Not content with this vandalism, age had also stooped him, shrinking him so that he barely seemed taller than a man.

But for all of that, the ancient was still strong in the gut, and his voice was powerful enough to be heard above the Maw's keening. And so, patiently, giving the ritual the respect it deserved, he began to speak.

'Once more the equinox has come upon us,' he intoned, then paused as if to give the listening crowd the chance to disagree. None of them took it.

'Below us, the Maw grows hungry for sacrifice.'

Another pause as, with an eerie howl, the pit agreed.

'Many tribes have answered its call. And from that many, one ogre has been found. One who is worthy to make the sacrifice.'

All eyes turned to the blood-soaked victor, who stood still clutching his prize.

'His name,' the butcher intoned, 'is Veshnun. His tribe is that of Gord.'

'His name,' the assembled ogres repeated, the thunder of their voices momentarily silencing the calls of their god, 'is Veshnun. His tribe is that of Gord.'

The victor's gut swelled with pride to hear his name booming from the throats of his peers.

'Will he lead us in sacrifice?' the butcher asked.

The answer came back like a roll of thunder.

'Aye!' they cried, honouring the champion with the volume of their assent. 'He will lead us!'

'So be it.' The ancient took a step back and nodded to Veshnun. Slowly, savouring the moment, the ogre raised the dripping rhinox heart above his head. Then he hurled it down into the Maw of Skabrand.

No sooner had it slipped from view than the other ogres began to throw their own sacrifices into the pit. Choice cuts of meat were followed by casks of grog, or by torn-off trophies from the sports that had filled the preceding days. The bodies of the five unsuccessful challengers were thrust forward by their proud tribe brothers, and dropped into the darkness amongst a confetti rain of gore and meat.

The butcher watched approvingly, his eyes twinkling within the battered folds of his face. Only when the last of the tribes had deposited their gifts did he raise a hand, the withered fingers splayed over the pit in benediction.

'And now, it is time for all tribes' butchers to sit with us here and endure the visions to be seen within. And for the rest of you, it is time to feast, and make merry.'

A murmur of relief passed amongst the waiting bulls. Quickly, although not too quickly, they turned and filed out. Rare flashes of laughter burst out amongst them like strokes of lightning in a summer storm, explosive releases of a great tension.

Behind them a few remained. Gathering around the Great Maw the butchers prepared themselves. For the next three days they would battle their way through the madness of the visions that Skabrand would feed them, risking their souls and their sanity to retrieve foreknowledge of the year yet to come.

None of their brothers envied them. None of them even looked back.

The last of them had already left, hastening to the feasting halls.

Yitshak from the tribe of Jarmoosh looked after them, taking a last glance at the closing doors before squatting down and peering into the oracle of Skabrand's hungry depths.

LORENZO HAD NEVER learned the finer points of seduction. In fact, he'd never learned any of the points of seduction. When he wanted a woman he paid for her, just like everybody else. He left all the cooing and sighing and general foolishness to aristos.

Still, he was a man of wide experience and keen observation. Apart from gold, he had some idea of what opened a woman's heart (or more importantly, he considered, her legs). And he was pretty sure Florin had a lot more of it than Sergei.

Personally, Lorenzo liked the lad. But then, he wasn't put off by the fact that a lifetime spent as a human punch bag had done nothing to improve the strigany's looks. Now that he thought about it, Lorenzo doubted if Sergei's looks had been up to much in the first place. In many respects, he looked more like a skinny ogre than a elegible bachelor.

Things like that, he knew, bothered a girl. Especially when Florin's finely chiselled face was offered up as a direct alternative.

Then there was the whole talking to each other thing. Lorenzo was happy enough to say nothing when he was with his comrades and so was Sergei. Unfortunately, there being nothing to say never stopped a woman from saying it, and it was a fact that they usually expected their suitors to join in with this prattle.

Lorenzo felt an unusual stab of sympathy as he watched the trio that walked in front of him. After the ogres had

borne their champion away, Katerina had invited the men
back to see her own quarters. They'd agreed without a
moment's thought, and were now strolling through this
grimy underworld like aristos through a rose garden.

Florin, eloquent as always, was telling Katerina about a
dressmaker in his brother's employ, and about the sort of
dresses he would make for her. Listening with the rapt
attention of a cobra hearing a snake charmer's flute, Katerina hung on his every word as he told her about silks and
velvets and feathered hats.

Lorenzo couldn't see the strigany's face, but he could
guess what it would look like. Sullen embarrassment
jerked in every movement he made, which was hardly surprising. Whilst his beloved swooned over Florin, the lad
himself was being dragged along behind her like a dog on
a leash.

Poor boy, Lorenzo thought. At another time he would
have enjoyed the humour of the situation, despite his sympathy. But here and now it worried him. If ever a girl was
worth fighting over, it was this heiress. Not just for her
gold, either.

Although no romantic, Lorenzo had a peasant's appreci-
ation of good breeding stock, and Katerina Hansebourg
was certainly that. He watched the roll of her buttocks
beneath the soft leather of her leggings, and the healthy
sheen of her hair, and her straight back and firm body.

He was still miserably reflecting upon the wench's
charms when the curve of the central spiral brought them
to her tribe's quarters. Walking carefully past the ever-
sleeping guard she guided them into the dimly-lit stink of
the interior. It was empty, as abandoned as were all the
ogres' quarters during their ceremonies.

Florin stopped his spiel as they moved through the darkness, but despite the end of his story Katerina still hung on
to his arm as tightly as Sergei hung on to hers. When they
reached her quarters she made the men wait outside whilst
she, suddenly houseproud, went in to light her treasured
oil lamp and to roll up her bedding.

She also wanted to make sure that none of her gnoblars were loitering about, the grubby things. Contenting herself that they weren't, she took a final look around the cave that served as her boudoir and went to invite her guests inside.

As they ducked through the door Florin was already complimenting her on the cosiness of her apartment. But then he froze, the words dying on his lips as a predatory shape leapt out of the flickering darkness.

'Watch out!' he cried, pushing Katerina to one side and drawing his sword. The blade shone as bright as sin in the murk of the cavern, the stripe of it reflecting in the sabretusk's eyes like the bar of a cage.

'Don't hurt her!' Katerina snapped at Florin, her infatuation burnt away by a flash of alarm.

'What...?' Florin asked, his eyes never leaving the beast in front of him.

But Katerina had spent too long amongst the tribe to waste time on idle debate. Instead she answered with her hand, a stiff fingered blur that jabbed into the nerve above Florin's elbow. The blow sent his sword tumbling from his numbed fingers.

'Ow!' he cried, exclaiming with surprise more than pain.

'She's mine,' Katerina told him, and padded forward to smooth down the wary sabretusk's hackles. 'Don't hurt her.'

Woman and beast turned to glare at Florin. Somehow, their eyes were the same startling shade of green. They might almost have been sisters.

'I think she's very beautiful.'

To everybody's surprise, including his own, it had been Sergei who'd spoken.

'What?' Florin said, incredulously.

'That sabretusk. She's very beautiful.'

So saying he strolled over to the big animal and, as casually as if she'd been a stray moggy, tickled the white tuft of fur that jutted beneath the chin.

Green eyes narrowed with pleasure.

'She likes that,' Katerina told the strigany, smiling.

'Yes,' he nodded as the sabretusk's tongue rasped against the skin of his palm. 'When I was a boy we had a tiger in our caravan. I used to feed her.'

Katerina considered this.

'Good,' she decided, as emphatically as a judge passing a sentence.

Sergei stroked the sabretusk behind her ears with his thumbs. She purred, a low rumble that was almost a growl.

'What do you call her?' he asked, looking up into Katerina's face. For the first time since they'd met he sounded neither nervous or embarrassed.

'Tabby.'

Lorenzo snorted with laughter. Florin, beginning to realise that he might have lost some ground with the girl, cautiously picked up his sword and sheathed it.

'Yes, it's a fine beast,' he said, looking warily at the scimitars of the thing's teeth. They were as big as swords, outsized fangs even for such an outsized animal.

Florin manufactured a self-deprecating chuckle.

'She gave me quite a fright, just then,' he said, and took a step towards the animal. If his seduction of Katerina Hansebourg involved having to cuddle a tiger, he decided, then so be it.

But as he drew nearer Tabby's contented purr deepened, and her hackles rose.

Florin, trying not to look nervous, stopped in his tracks.

'I don't think she likes you,' Sergei said smugly.

Katerina just looked at him, face bland with cool appraisal.

Florin chewed his lip thoughtfully. He and the sabretusk exchanged a duellist's stare, a look of mutual antagonism and of grudging respect. But Florin couldn't back down now; Katerina's presence ensured that. So, with the tense preparedness of a man stepping out onto the thin ice of a freshly frozen lake, he took another step towards the cat.

She growled, the sound smooth despite the terrible warning it carried.

Florin took another step forward, the dampening palms of his hands held up in white flashes of surrender. The growl changed in pitch as he approached, becoming almost quizzical.

When he was an arm's length away Florin reached out his hand and, moving as slowly as treacle, reached out to touch the velveteen fur of the sabretusk's shoulder. The cat watched him silently, and Florin drew his hand back.

'Yes, she's very beautiful,' he said, locking eyes with Katerina.

She threw her head back and roared with sudden laughter.

'You thought that she was going to bite you, didn't you?' she howled. 'I've never seen anyone look so scared. Wasn't he funny, Sergei?'

'He certainly was.'

Seduction or not, a flash of pride burned in Florin's cheeks and he drew himself up.

'Well, anyway,' he grumbled as Katerina's laughter continued unabated. 'Now that we're here, I suppose that I should tell you why we've come.'

'Oh, I already know,' the girl said with a dismissive wave. 'The females told me all about it. My tribe wants me to return to the human world.'

'Yes, that's right,' Florin agreed eagerly. 'Your mother sent us to rescue you.'

'I know. She wasted your time, though.'

Florin and Sergei, suddenly both back on the same side, exchanged a quick look.

'Why do you say that?' Florin asked, and Katerina, who had gone to fetch her best clay drinking pots out of her chest, raised her eyebrows.

'Well, because of my animals, of course,' she said, laying the vessels out on the well-swept floor. 'They don't have anybody else to look after them. Here, sit down. I've got some fresh water, and dried meat.'

The three men did as they were bid, and she brought over a clay demijohn of cold water and a leaf-wrapped bundle of dried meat.

'Help yourselves,' she told them, a little awkwardly. This whole business of playing the hostess was quite new to her. The last time she had practised had been with scratch-built dolls during her last days with her father's caravan.

'Thanks,' said Florin, pouring a drink and taking a piece of venison. It looked like leather. It tasted like leather, too. He smiled anyway, and smacked his lips.

'Delicious,' he said, chewing hard.

'Thanks,' she said, and dropped her eyes. 'I made it myself.'

'The thing is,' Florin continued. 'You should come back with us to see your mother. She misses you dreadfully.'

'I'd like to,' Katerina mused, thoughtfully tearing a bite of meat off with strong, white teeth. 'But like I said, I can't. Tabby would be lonely without me.'

Florin glanced at the cat, half a ton of the most vicious predator in this vicious place, as it lolled behind her. He tried to picture what it would look like padding along one of Bordeleaux's streets. Or even through one of the Hansebourg mansions.

The image was strangely appealing.

'That's all right. You can bring her with you.'

Katerina scratched her head, absent-mindedly pinching off a flea and dropping it into the flame of the oil lamp.

'I suppose I could… but no. No. I couldn't leave the rhinox.'

'Couldn't they keep each other company?'

'It's not that. They need me to clean their wounds, and to stitch 'em up after they've been fighting. I have to protect them from the gnoblars, too. They can be quite nasty if they aren't disciplined.'

Florin thought back to the swarm of them he'd stumbled into, and had to agree.

'Are you sure?' he wondered, as if he didn't know the answer. 'Those rhinoxen… well, look what that one did today.'

Katerina smiled as though at some happy memory.

'Yes, it was a good creature. Very strong. I'm glad that it won its place in the Great Maw.'

'There you go, then.' Florin pressed his advantage. 'I reckon they'll soon learn to stick up for themselves once you're back in Bordeleaux.'

Katerina pursed her lips. Bordeleaux. The name sounded strange, and yet also familiar. It was like something she'd imagined or heard in a dream. For some reason it made her remember the smell of bread, and the taste of... of something nice. Something like roses.

She began to reply, but before she could, Sergei added his voice to the conversation.

'You don't have to go to Bordeleaux if you don't want to,' he told her, speaking through a mouthful. Florin glared at him as he swallowed, obviously enjoying the boot-leather texture of the meat.

'I know I don't have to,' she said, with the barest trace of irritation.

'I mean, if you go there and you don't like it, you can come back. I'll bring you back. If you wanted me to, I mean. I don't mind.'

Sergei's eloquence left him as easily as it had come. With an embarrassed shrug he helped himself to another piece of jerky, dropping his eyes as he chewed.

Katerina watched him eat.

'Why do you always act so afraid of me?' she asked, the question taking them all by surprise.

Sergei choked, coughed, swallowed.

'I don't,' he frowned in denial.

'Yes you do. I don't understand why. You're strong. You're brave. What do you think I'm going to do to you?'

Sergei shrugged, and pretended not to notice Lorenzo's leer.

'It's just that... well, I don't know how to speak to girls.'

'What do you mean? Why should you speak to me any differently than to them?'

The strigany looked from Lorenzo to Florin, eyes beseeching them for help.

None was forthcoming.

'Because... because I don't care if they like me or not.'

Katerina fell silent, and studied him with a still intensity. So did Tabby. Beneath the heat of this appraisal a bead of sweat formed on Sergei's forehead. Katerina watched it trickle down to his eyebrow with the absolute concentration of a hawk watching a mouse.

'So,' she said, eyebrows furrowed as she turned the thought over. 'You care what I think about you. Does that mean that you love me?'

The question was almost asked as casually as if they'd been discussing the weather. To Sergei it came like the worst sucker punch he'd ever taken. He opened his mouth to reply, but couldn't think of a single thing to say.

Despairingly, he snapped his mouth back shut and made a gesture that was halfway between a nod and a shrug.

Florin surprised himself by sympathising with his rival's discomfort. He also wanted to get back to the task in hand; he had a feeling that it was only a matter of time before Sergei, the big lug, frightened her off the idea of returning with them altogether.

'So, you'll come back with us, then?' he asked. 'I forgot to say but it'll be good for Tabby, too. You should see the beef we have. It's as sweet as honey and as soft as butter. She'll love it.'

'I'll think about it,' Katerina said, her eyes remaining on Sergei. 'In fact,' she continued, unconsciously assuming the imperious tone she used on her gnoblars, 'I want you and Lorenzo to leave me alone for a while. To let me think.'

A lifetime of bluff and negotiation told Florin that now was the time to graciously withdraw.

'Of course, we'll be happy to.' He bowed his head and got to his feet. 'Think it over, by all means. I'm sure your loving family wouldn't want us to pressure you. Come on lads, let's leave the lady to make her decision.'

Lorenzo pocketed a final piece of jerky, and let Sergei help him up.

'See you later,' the strigany said as he turned in hasty retreat.

'No,' Katerina said. 'I want you to stay here.'

Sergei's face fell. His expression was as mortified as Florin's, although for a completely different reason.

'Well, go and sit by the lady, lad,' Lorenzo encouraged, slapping him on the back. 'Me and Florin have got to go and look for the horses. Haven't we?'

Florin pulled himself together enough to mumble a 'yes' before his grinning comrade shoved him out of the door.

Behind him Sergei, iron-faced with the grim control of a man stepping onto a noose, went to sit by the prettiest girl for a thousand miles.

'I'm glad you love me,' Katerina told him as he settled down beside her. 'I think I love you too.'

'You do?'

'Oh yes,' she said, sliding closer to him. 'At least, I suppose I do. Every time I see you my heart starts to go faster and I feel… oh, I don't know. Something like hungry.'

As gently as if she were treating a wounded animal she reached out and brushed her fingertips across his bruised cheek. Then she slid them down, over his lips, along his jaw line, beneath the material of his shirt.

Sergei sat hypnotised beneath her touch. Then, scarcely believing that he had the nerve to do it, he leant towards her and seized a handful of her hair.

'You're very beautiful,' he breathed as he let it slide through his fingers. It felt as warm and soft as corn-silk beneath an autumn sun.

Katerina nodded at the comment absent-mindedly.

'I know,' she said, pressing herself against him. 'Your body is very hard. Harder than mine. Are all men like that?'

'No.' Sergei shook his head.

'Well.' With a lick of her lips Katerina pretended to reach the decision she'd made when she'd first saw him. 'I suppose that, as we're in love, we should mate.'

'What?' He squeaked. Then he cleared his throat and said it again.

'I said, we should mate.' Her eyes seemed darker as they fastened on his. 'I haven't done it before, but I've seen the rhinoxen do it often enough.'

'Oh yes?'

'Yes. They like it. I think I'd like it, too.'

Her fingers slipped lower down, gliding over his belly and tearing his breeches open with the pop of a lost button.

'I want to see what you look like before we mate, though,' she whispered, perhaps deciding that it was time to start playing hard to get. 'And you can see me.'

With this warning she pushed his shoulders to the floor, swung her thigh over his stomach as if to pin him there, and, with a single, well rehearsed movement, pulled her shapeless singlet of clothing up and over her head.

Sergei goggled. His mouth fell open. In fact, his astonishment was so obvious that Katerina felt a moment of panic.

'Is it... I mean, am I all right?'

Sergei nodded furiously, even managing to tear his eyes away from the wobble of her breasts for a second.

'Oh yes,' he said, the desperate conviction in his voice bringing a smile to her face. 'Very, very much.'

His eyes slid down her perfectly built, and perfectly naked, body. Lamp light shone like oil on her flawless skin, and as she adjusted her seat the soft contours of her curves were painted in highlights of gold.

Katerina's smile grew broader as she saw the approval in Sergei's eyes. Remembering something she'd seen a lifetime ago in the streets of Bordeleaux she leaned forward, the sway of her breasts having the same effect as a hypnotist's watch on her willing captive, and pressed her lips against his.

Sergei kissed her back, his hands automatically reaching up to squeeze the flex of her hips. Without breaking their kiss Katerina murmured with pleasure and began to rub herself against the ridged muscles of his belly.

Only when she'd become as flushed and breathless as a victorious athlete did she lift her head and look back down at him. The expression that curved her pouting lips was almost gloatingly possessive.

'Now you strip,' she ordered him.

So Sergei did.

As THE OGRES were completing their ceremonial feeding of the Great Maw, Florin and Lorenzo were having much less fun.

On the plus side they had at last found their horses, and their horses were well. Very well, in fact. In the long, subterranean chamber in which they'd been stabled they were warm and rested, and they'd also gorged themselves with good hay. It hung down from biers above their heads, and fresh water gurgled in a constant stream along the stone trough which ran the half-mile length of their quarters.

Florin was also very glad to see that the ivory they had salvaged was still attached to the horses' tack.

The only problem was that all of this excellent provision had been made for the gathered tribes' rhinoxen. The beasts, the musk of their shaggy hides as thick as soup in these closed quarters, watched the two men curiously as they fussed over their horses. The two travellers didn't return their stares, nor did they allow themselves to think of the damage just one of these things had done to five ogres.

Surprisingly, despite the fact that their cousins were big enough to make even Krom's ox look like a child's pony, their horses didn't seem at all alarmed to have been sequestered with them.

But then, Lorenzo reflected, what did horses know?

'Good girl,' Florin told one of the animals, letting her nuzzle a dried apple ring from out of his hand.

'If only all females were that easy to impress, eh boss?' Lorenzo goaded him. Anything to take his mind off the massive shapes that had gathered around, looming above them with the strained patience of troopers awaiting the order to attack.

'Don't know what you mean,' Florin scowled.

All three of Lorenzo's teeth flashed in the darkness.

'Unless you're referring to Mademoiselle Hansebourg, of course,' his friend continued, feeding another titbit to Krom's ox. It lowed with gratitude.

'And who else would I be referring to in this godsforsaken place?'

'Lorenzo,' Florin said, drawing himself up to cast a disapproving glance down at his old retainer. 'You're mistaken if you think that a man of honour, such as myself, would take advantage of our situation to seduce the object of our quest.'

'Is that so?'

Florin drew one eyebrow up haughtily. Then he winked.

'No, of course it isn't. Doesn't look as though I've got much choice, though, does it?'

'Nope.'

'Well then. If living with the ogres has addled the girl's brains to the extent that she prefers a callow strigany boxer to Florin d'Artaud, Hero of Lustria, then so be it.'

Lorenzo chuckled, then stopped as the sound drew the rhinoxen closer in.

'Anyway,' Florin said, feeding the last of the apple rings to another horse. 'Let's not talk about it. We've found our horses, now let's go and see Krom. Then we can try and find a way of getting drunk.'

'Spoken like a true romantic,' Lorenzo said, and started to edge his way out from between the rhinoxen.

KROM AND JARMOOSH sat side by side, their backs against the curved walls of Skabrand's central passageway. At their feet, laid out on low tables of crudely hewn logs, the feast stretched away. Glistening beneath the buzzing flies, the piled meat disappeared around the bend of the passageway like gristle within the curve of a horn.

The tables groaned beneath the weight of the food, and food there was aplenty. Before the bulls had paid their tribute to Skabrand's Maw, each tribe's butcher had ceremonially prepared a banquet.

This year the repast was even more sumptuous than usual. There were vast bowls of slick intestines, knotted into sausages that were still green with half digested grass. There were slabs of flash-scorched meat, and platters of tongues, and bowls of surprised-looking eyeballs. There were bones to gnaw on, and hooves that had been boiled into a jelly.

Best of all though was the bread. Great boulders of it lay on each table, the grey loaves as heavy as gravestones. Meal worms squirmed nervously through the crusts, much to the delight of the revellers. Ogre bread was never really done until the maggots gave it their seal of approval.

There was also ale, of course. At least, the ogres called it ale. It smelt more like rotten honey than hops, and although the sweetness was enough to draw the flies, it was deceptive. Beneath the sickly tang of it lay pure alcohol, and several ogres had already succumbed. Their bodies lay sprawled amongst the tables, snoring contentedly as they were robbed by gnoblars or trampled over by their fellows.

Jarmoosh regarded one of the fallen with something approaching jealousy. It had been a long time since he'd allowed himself such absolute abandon. Unfortunately, with power came responsibility.

Well, the responsibility not to let your underlings catch you incapacitated, anyway.

'This is very good,' Krom told him approvingly, speaking through a mouthful of raw tripe. 'Your hunters have provided as well as your butcher has cooked.'

'Yes,' Jarmoosh replied, and helped himself to a handful of eyeballs. They squelched between his teeth, and he relished the delicate flavour.

'Grot,' he called and, appearing as if by magic, a gnoblar appeared by his elbow. 'Bring more ale.'

'Yes, master,' it said, collecting their mugs and scurrying away. A moment later it appeared in the queue to the nearest cask, fighting its way through a knot of its fellows.

'I'm surprised you didn't bring your thinlings to serve you,' Jarmoosh said, selecting a bone and crunching it between his teeth as easily as a stick of celery.

Krom finished another mouthful of innards as he considered his reply.

'Those humans,' he said, smacking his lips loudly, 'aren't really like gnoblars. Some humans think themselves to be our betters.'

Jarmoosh barked with laughter.

'It's true,' Krom told him. 'It's a fact I've used to my advantage many times.'

'Yes.' Jarmoosh nodded, watching his gnoblar as it elbowed its way to the nearest ale cask. 'I worked for a human once. He was less foolish than most. He was also the sire of my humaness, Katerina.'

Both ogres considered the humaness, and her future. A few moments of silence passed.

'Some are as intelligent as us,' Krom considered, and selected a haunch of singed venison.

'Not many, though.'

'No. Not many,' Krom said with a loud bark of laughter.

At that moment, as if to underline the point, Florin and Lorenzo rounded the corner. Lorenzo was content to keep one eye on the path ahead, following his comrade as he gnawed on a slab of meat, so it was Florin who greeted Krom.

'Ho there,' he called, kicking a gnoblar out of the way and waving.

Krom returned the gesture clumsily.

The Bretonnian had expected to find their guide on his own, not surrounded by an entire tribe. As he approached it occurred to him that he had absolutely no idea of ogre etiquette. Back in the Old World the very concept would have been regarded as a joke. Here and now, though, Florin realised that it was a reality he should have tried to understand.

Ah well. Too late now.

'Can we join you?' he asked politely, and gestured to the patch of floor opposite the two ogres.

Krom looked at Jarmoosh, who grunted and waved the gnawed sceptre of his bone in invitation.

'Thanks,' said Florin. He sat down, crossed his legs and selected one of the less disgusting-looking morsels from the table.

'Mmmm,' he smiled, forcing down the sliver of uncooked flesh. 'It's very good.'

Jarmoosh, wondering if this human was going to be as entertaining as his feisty companion, leaned forward curiously.

'You like?' he asked, brows as big as biceps furrowed in ignorance.

'Yes,' Florin lied without hesitation. He even managed to lick his lips.

Jarmoosh and Krom exchanged a blank look.

'I thought that you humans fussed with food, slicing it and burning it.'

'Sometimes,' Florin admitted, unsure as to quite how much his hosts knew. 'But this is much better.'

'Yes, it is,' Jarmoosh rumbled. His tribe brothers, who had fallen silent as the conversation progressed, nudged each other appreciatively.

'And,' he decided, 'as you honour me, so I will honour you. You may have the best cut from our rhinox. Grot? Grot!'

The gnoblar rushed back, ale oozing over the rims of the tankards it carried. Jarmoosh took both and handed one to Krom before issuing his next order.

'Grot, go and bring our guests here the cabrones.'

The creature looked doubtfully at its master. Then it shrugged.

'Cooked?' it asked, but the ogre scowled at the very suggestion.

'No,' he said. 'Raw. Raw and whole. Just like our guests like 'em.'

The gnoblar scurried off and the rest of the tribe, as though losing interest, returned to their own conversations.

'Cabrones,' Florin repeated. 'I don't think I've ever had them before.'

'Well, you'll need them soon,' Krom mumbled. The ale, it seemed, had loosened his tongue. There was even something approaching a smile on the slab of his face.

'So, Sergei told me that you had come to some arrangement about Katerina?'

The ogres around them fell suddenly silent.

Florin swallowed uneasily.

'We do not talk of trade during the feast,' Krom explained, the smile wiped from his face.

'I'm sorry,' Florin said, cheeks reddening. 'I didn't know. It's different in my...'

'Here comes Grot,' Jarmoosh cut in, stopping any further unpleasantness, 'with your cabrones.'

Florin watched the gnoblar zigzagging back and forth beneath the weight of the vessel it carried. He told himself that it might be soup. The bowl was certainly deep enough.

Or it might be fish, served raw and vinegared in the Norscan fashion.

Or it might be a salad.

He told himself these things, but the attempt at humour did nothing to dispel his mounting sense of dread. The feeling reached a crescendo as the gnoblar banged the bowl down in front of him, shook the strain out of its wiry arms, and lifted the blood spattered cover.

'Here you are, my friend,' Jarmoosh told him, as blank-faced as his tribe brothers. 'The choicest cut. The cabrones.'

I can't do it, Florin told himself as he looked down into the bowl.

There's no way that I can do it.

It's impossible.

In the bottom of the pot, resting in a pool of gore, lay two fist-sized lumps of gnarled meat. They glistened back up at him, a challenge that had his gorge rising before he'd taken a single bite.

'Well, well, well,' Lorenzo said, looking over his shoulder. 'Aren't you the lucky one? They say, down in Araby, they're a great luxury. Course the Arabyans cook 'em first. But then, you and your new pals prefer things raw, don't you?'

The two men regarded the gristly-looking balls.

Florin hoped that they had been taken from a rhinox. The alternative was far too horrible to contemplate.

There's no way that I can eat them, he decided.

Not even one.

'Not hungry?' Krom asked him. The Bretonnian looked up, his face brightening with the hope of a drowning man who's been thrown a life line.

'No, I'm not really hungry now that you mention it,' Florin answered gratefully.

'Better eat 'em anyway,' Krom told him. 'It's our custom to be polite.'

Florin felt the lifeline turn to lead beneath his fingers. He took a last glance up at the ring of impassive ogres, each of whom was watching him like a hawk. Then, without giving himself the chance to think, he reached down and took one of the things.

It squelched beneath his fingers, the fibrous mess oozing liquids. Holding it up he examined it from all angles, and felt vaguely surprised at how heavy it was.

In the back of his mind he heard himself think, No, I can't do it.

But, just as he'd done when he'd rescued Nelly all those long months ago, he ignored that inner voice. Instead, moving with a trancelike calm, he pressed the thing into his mouth and bit down.

It wouldn't have been so bad if it hadn't been so tough. As it was, tearing off a mouthful was like trying to chew through leather. It took a full minute before he'd finally managed to swallow his first mouthful, the gob of cold flesh feeling as hard as a billiard ball as it slid down his throat. His gorge rose and he knew then that he wouldn't be able to take another mouthful.

He took one anyway.

This one was even worse. As well as grinding his teeth through the… no, don't think about it… as well as grinding his teeth he had to fight to keep the bloody mass he'd already swallowed down. Sweat ran down the pallid skin of his face as he chewed, and his whole stomach squirmed in protest.

Again he swallowed. Again his throat clenched and squeezed and tried to hurl the sticky mass back up.

One more bite, he told himself, blanking out the thought of the second... the second portion that remained in the puddle of congealed gore.

This time he didn't even bother to chew. Instead he just crushed the gristle between his molars a couple of times and swallowed, clenching his throat behind it as tightly as a fist.

With the same desperate concentration with which a tightrope walker refuses to think about the drop beneath his feet, Florin refused to think about what he'd just eaten. Instead he wiped his hand across the back of his mouth and smiled.

'Is it good?' Jarmoosh asked earnestly.

Florin, not trusting himself to speak, contented himself with a nod. His stomach clenched with nausea at even this small gesture, and he closed his eyes until it passed.

When he opened them the first thing he saw was the second ball laying in a sliming of blood. If that viscous liquid was just blood. Now that he thought about it there was no telling what else might be leaking from...

No.

No, don't think about it.

By now he was actually beginning to feel dizzy with disgust. It was as though the blood had drained from his head to join the rebellion in his stomach. Florin wiped the moisture from the cold skin of his brow, and decided to take refuge in bravado.

'These,' he said, picking the second cabrone up and carefully not looking at it, 'are very tasty.'

Jarmoosh's face remained impassive. He waited until the human had bitten down before replying.

'Yes,' the ogre rumbled. 'And we will bring you as many as you want.'

For a moment, a single moment, Florin appeared to be on the verge of exploding. His adam's apple shuffled up and down. Tears began to leak from the corner of his eyes, the sockets of which were as dark as a skull's against the dirty white of his face. Noises started to come from him.

But then, as though attempting suicide by strangulation, he squeezed his throat. The tactic seemed to work. After a moment he'd recovered enough to tear another bite off. Then another.

And then the cabrones were all gone.

'Would you like some more?' Jarmoosh asked politely. His guest, eyes bulging, merely ground his teeth together in reply.

'No,' he finally managed to choke the word out. The bowl still lay before him, sticky with a residue of pink goo. He looked away with a shudder.

'Now,' Jarmoosh asked the human. 'Tell me truly. Do you really prefer the way we prepare our food to your own?'

Florin was too distracted by the queasy roll of raw meat in his stomach to lie.

'No,' he admitted miserably. 'Not really.'

'I didn't think so.' Jarmoosh nodded. Then a wide smile split the shaved boulder of his head wide open and slowly, as if it was a gesture he was still learning, the tyrant winked.

'Now I must tell you the truth. The cabrones aren't the choicest cut. They aren't any cut at all. We usually give them to the gnoblars. It's not blood that you tasted oozing out of them, you understand. It's...'

But even as the ogres erupted into a bloodcurdling storm of laughter Florin was far, far away. Ashen-faced and slicked with a cold sweat, he was desperately thinking of gold, ships, statues.

Anything but for the revolting flesh that he'd just consumed.

Later, when the revellers had sucked their fingers clean and turned to the infinitely more serious matter of drinking, Krom leaned forward and whispered into Florin's ear.

'Well done,' he said, seeming not to notice the way the human flinched beneath his breath. 'You impressed him.'

'Oh good,' Florin grumbled, and wondered how long it would be until he'd be able to look at a butcher's block again.

* * *

IT TOOK A day for Florin's stomach to recover from its ordeal and to stop his guts from trying to force his meal back up. A day in which the ogres' feasting grew ever wilder and more violent.

Their capacity for food, it seemed, was matched only by their capacity for drink. Whereas a human drinking party would have long since ended in collapse, the passing days just seemed to make the ogres eager for more. The stuff which they drank actually seemed to be increasing their thirst, fuelling it rather than quenching it as though it were oil poured onto a fire.

The noise the celebrants made as they fought and argued and tried to sing was quite incredible. Occasionally a distant drumbeat would start up, the bone-jarring rhythm bringing the ogres to their feet in a wild dance that always ended in violence.

Even without the musicians, a constant brush fire of recreational bloodshed swept around the feasting hall. By now the cobbles were slicked with more gore than that which had dripped off the feasting tables.

It took twenty-four hours of being stuck in their quarters before the two Bretonnians were willing to risk such entertainments. Apart from the claustrophobia of their confinement, they decided that it was time to save Katerina from Sergei's company, and to finish the job of persuading her to come away with them.

The two friends scurried along the central corridor with their heads down, anxious to avoid the attention of their drunken hosts. Some of them lay sprawled across the cobbles, snoring as contentedly as if the stones were feather mattresses. Others, the misshapen lumps of their heads greased with sweat, called out to the humans, mistaking them for gnoblars in their drunkenness. Once a gnawed shoulder blade sliced through the air above their heads, the rough discus exploding against the far wall in a shower of splinters.

'These lads know how to party,' Lorenzo muttered as a pair of them rolled past, teeth buried in each other's shoulders.

Florin grunted his agreement as, just around the next corner, Jarmoosh's quarters came into view. As always, the guard on the door was sleeping. The two ducked past him and into the relative quiet inside.

Remembering their way past the cage door of the females' quarters they made their way to the central burrow, still deserted by the ogres. Taking their bearings from Jarmoosh's central dais they turned a corner and saw the hide covering of Katerina's quarters. The flap of leather was outlined by the light beyond, the yellow glow flickering as if in a strong wind.

As the two men approached they heard the noises that came from inside. The panting. The moaning. The occasional scream of joy.

For the second time in two days Florin felt his stomach roll, although this time it was with the bile of jealousy.

Lorenzo looked at him with something approaching sympathy.

'And to think,' Florin said, trying to shrug off his irritation, 'that I accepted this mission because I thought that Mademoiselle Hansebourg was a damsel in distress.'

From behind the leather curtain the damsel's voice twisted into a long, luxurious moan.

'Well, she sounds as though she's in distress,' Lorenzo offered.

Florin glared at him.

'Come on, let's go and wait by Jarmoosh's throne. I think I've heard about all I want to.'

There was some scurrying in the corners as the two men trooped back to the central chamber, and the glitter of wary green eyes. But the pair ignored Tabby as Tabby ignored them. With the ogres' feast accelerating towards even greater heights of exuberance outside, neither humans nor sabretusk begrudged each other the shelter they'd found.

Florin peered around the chamber moodily. Then, content that it was empty of anybody who would mind, he walked up to Jarmoosh's ironwood throne and sat himself down.

It felt good. Power always did.

'I'm going to get one of these when we build our next inn,' he decided, and swung his dangling feet.

'Why?' Lorenzo asked.

'So that I can oversee things in style. By the gods I'm looking forward to getting back. Seems like forever since we got here and I'm the only one not to be having any fun.'

'We could try some of that ogre ale,' Lorenzo suggested doubtfully, but Florin shook his head.

'I don't think so. Did you smell the stuff? I bet that if you put a match to it it'd burn like pitch.'

A piercing howl came from the direction of Katerina's quarters. For a moment both men pretended not to have heard it. Then their eyes met and they burst into laughter.

They were laughing so much that they almost didn't hear the ogres return. It was only the sudden scurrying of the gnoblars that alerted them. The patter of their fleeing feet was audible even though the careful pad of the ogres was not.

Florin jumped guiltily from Jarmoosh's chair as the two bulky shapes approached. He cast his eyes around for a hiding place and, Lorenzo following at his heels, he rolled into the shadows that lay behind the raised earth platform. It occurred to him that the best thing to do would be to go to Katerina's chamber, but a twinge of pride prevented him from doing so.

It was too late now, anyway. With a groan, one of the ogres lowered itself onto the throne. The other continued walking, pacing up and down in front of it like a tiger in a cage.

Uncomfortably aware of how easily they'd gone from being guests to being spies the two men lay still and unmoving. The sound of their own heartbeats seemed incredibly loud.

It was almost a relief when the rumble of the ogres' voices drowned the sound out.

'So the Maw has spoken,' Jarmoosh said, his voice as heavy as lead.

'Yes,' Yitshak momentarily paused in his pacing to reply.

A moment's silence passed, and even from his hiding place Florin could feel the tension that grew between the two. It reminded him of that which hung over a poker table, or perhaps between merchants who had yet to agree on a price.

It was Yitshak who broke the silence.

'The Maw has spoken as loudly now as it ever has. You know that I am but a pup compared to the other butchers, but even I was shown such visions… such visions…'

The voice trailed off. Whatever the Butcher Yitshak had seen, he seemed to be reliving it now. Then he shuddered, and the grisly ornaments which dangled from his belt rattled like a flagellant's bells.

'I saw visions,' he repeated, 'that were so bright they almost blinded me.'

Another silence stretched out between the two. This time it was Jarmoosh who broke it.

'What did you see?' he asked.

Yitshak drew in a deep, shuddering breath. Then he sighed, a sound as long and low as wind in a lychee tree's branches.

Florin, sweating in the darkness, realised that he'd never known an ogre to show such emotion. Not even Krom at the sight of his brother's crucifixion.

It was a strangely disturbing thought.

'I saw… that is, we saw… two paths. That was all. Only two paths.'

The butcher's footsteps continued to pad up and down beneath the throne. Despite his unogrish emotion Yitshak's voice had still remained as flat as slate. It made the naked excitement in Jarmoosh's voice even more surprising.

'Bashar Zog?' he asked, the name half statement and half question.

It was enough to bring Yitshak to a standstill.

'Yes,' he said. 'Bashar Zog.'

The ironwood of Jarmoosh's throne squeaked as he leaned eagerly forward.

'What are the two paths?'

'Annihilation,' Yitshak replied. 'Or victory.'

'Which is more likely?'

'Does it matter?'

Florin jumped as Jarmoosh roared with laughter.

'No,' he said, and the humans could hear the joy in his voice. It was strong and true, like the hum of a released bowstring or the thud of an axe into flesh.

'And the other butchers,' the ogre continued. 'They will be telling their tyrants the same thing, yes?'

'Yes. That is why we broke our fastness a day early. Preparations must be made. A strategy formed.'

'Excellent,' Jarmoosh said, and his throne creaked again as he settled back. The conversation ground to a halt, the two ogres content to remain alone with their own thoughts. Finally, just when it seemed to Florin that one of them was bound to hear the pulse that hammered in his throat, Yitshak broke the silence.

'There is one other thing. I think that I alone saw it.'

'Yes?'

'Your plan. With the gorgers. It might work.'

'Might?'

'Might.'

Jarmoosh grunted.

'And that is all I have to tell you,' Yitshak said, his voice suddenly weak with exhaustion. 'Now I will go and rest. Tomorrow we will hold council in the presence of the Maw. Before I return there I need... strength.'

'Yes, go,' Jarmoosh rumbled. 'Rest. And eat. You have brought pride to the tribe.'

'We'll see,' Yitshak grumbled, and his words were followed by the fading pad of his feet into the darkness. Jarmoosh remained behind to sit and to think.

Hours seemed to pass. Cramps bit into the hiding men's muscles with iron teeth, and their bladders swelled painfully. The urge to fidget became almost unbearable.

But only almost. As long as Jarmoosh sat just a couple of feet away, the Bretonnians bore their discomfort with a desperate stoicism. Willingly or not the two men had become spies in the tyrant's kingdom, and they could scarcely imagine what terrible punishments that might bring.

They tried not to think about it.

More time passed, as slow as drying paint. The only consolation, Florin decided, was that at least he didn't have to listen to Katerina's enthusiasm any more. She and Sergei, it seemed, had exhausted each other.

Florin tried not to think about that either.

Damn this place, he silently cursed. This is the last time I leave Bordeleaux. The world outside is nothing but trouble. If only that damned fire hadn't…

'You can come out now.'

The voice rumbled with an easy confidence that stopped the breath in the hiding men's throats. If they'd been lying still already, they positively froze now. The ogre's throne squeaked beneath his shifting weight, and their eyes widened in the darkness.

'Come out from there,' Jarmoosh repeated, voice deepening into a bone rattling growl. 'Stand before me.'

With a resigned look at Lorenzo, Florin stretched out and got to his feet. He carefully dusted off his clothes and smiled at Jarmoosh.

'Hello,' he said, with a polite nod. 'I'm sorry that I didn't greet you, but I was fast asleep. Is the feast over, then?'

Jarmoosh studied him with a face that would have shamed a poker player.

'It will be soon,' he answered.

'Oh. Well, then,' Florin desperately cast about for something to say. 'It was very impressive.'

'Yes,' Jarmoosh assented, then lapsed back into silent appraisal.

Florin gave up on the attempt at polite conversation. Instead he forced himself to return the ogre's steady gaze. His eyes looked as blank as those of a fish on a slab, and his face was as devoid of expression as a boxer's fist.

Eventually, he spoke.

'I like you,' he told Florin. 'And your companions.'

'Thanks.'

'You make me laugh.'

Jarmoosh leaned back and scratched the stubble that spiked his eyebrows.

'As you heard, we will soon be at war. I think it's a war we will lose.'

Florin briefly considered denying that he'd heard the conversation. He decided against it. If he'd ever thought of these bulky monsters as idiots that was one illusion that he no longer suffered from.

'The enemy we fight has no honour,' Jarmoosh mused, as if this was of no more concern than the colour of their hair. 'They are bloodthirsty in victory. They even eat their defeated tribe's gnoblars.'

Florin thought fast.

'It would be a shame,' he pointed out, 'if they ate Katerina.'

Jarmoosh grunted his agreement.

'Yes,' he said. 'That's why I want you to take her with you. Anyway, she's been coming into heat for the last six years, now. It's about time she found a mate.'

'Yes,' Florin said, trying to keep the emotion out of his voice. 'That's true.'

'Good. Then I will leave you to give her the news. I have other bones to gnaw.'

So saying, Jarmoosh got to his feet and stomped past Florin's bow. When he reached the door of the chamber he paused, turning back to call: 'Tell your friend that he can come out now. I won't eat him after all.'

The ogre was still chuckling at his own wit as he marched out into the passage way beyond.

'You heard the ogre,' Florin called. 'Seems they do have some dietary standards after all.'

Lorenzo scrambled to his feet, pressed his hands into the stoop of his back, and groaned.

'I'm getting too old for this,' he grumbled.

'Let's go and tell the lovebirds that it's time to go, then,' Florin grinned, then winked at his friend. 'This time next month we'll be clean, rich and drunk.'

Lorenzo grinned back.

'Lead on then, boss!' he said, with a low bow that was only half mocking.

CHAPTER NINE

AFTER THE STEWED air of Skabrand the air outside felt as sharp as an icicle. It felt clean, too, as clean as the blinding whiteness that stretched away on all sides. The wasteland glittered beneath the pure blue vastness of the sky above. Now that the wind had fallen silent the world had relapsed into a deathly silence, a quietude that was almost perfect.

Yet between the twin realms of white and blue there did move a single shape. Clasped between two immensities it looked tiny and defiant, its small life of no more consequence than the plumes of its breath or the fleas which crawled through its rhinox's fur.

Fortunately the ogre was unimpressed by thoughts of mortality. So was his rhinox. The low rumble of its complaints were due only to its having been singled out from its herd. Whilst its brothers remained in the warmth and plenitude of Skabrand it, poor beast, had been chosen to carry its master further north. It could already smell the bones of the mountains that lay ahead, and the heart of winter that prowled beyond them.

But despite his mount's complaints, Jarmoosh felt his spirits lift, soaring as high as the snow vultures that circled overhead. It felt good to be outside again. It felt even better to be heading to war. It had been three months since he'd last tested his tribe's strength against another's, and that had been three months too long.

Compared to the task which lay ahead, though, war was easy.

The battered lumps of his face shifted into a rare smile. He took a deep lungful of the bitingly cold air, and searched the far horizon expectantly.

Perhaps he would die there.

No, not perhaps.

Probably.

Jarmoosh's smile grew broader. Life was good.

'No. I won't.' Katerina didn't say it loud. Neither did she say it angrily. She didn't need to. She was so certain that loud or angry weren't necessary.

'But you have to. Jarmoosh said that you could. He said that he wanted you to,' Florin almost pleaded.

'If he thinks that I'm going to leave my tribe just as it's going into battle, he's crazy,' she told him, and leaned back into Sergei's lap. The strigany shifted beneath the pleasant weight and stroked a strand of hair back from her brow. Katerina turned to smile at him. Her green eyes narrowed and she looked as though she were about to start purring.

Florin scowled. He looked away and into the flames of the fire as if for inspiration.

'Your tribe is waiting for you at Bordeleaux.' He tried another appeal. 'More than your tribe, in fact. Your family. Think of how your mother must feel.'

'She'll be all right for a while longer,' Katerina told him with a lazy assurance.

The Bretonnian threw up his hands in despair. After Jarmoosh had given his permission for him to take the girl away, he'd thought that the worst part of this damned expedition was behind him. But somehow, since she'd been closeted with Sergei, she seemed to have gone off the idea of returning with them at all.

Damn that strigany, Florin thought, not trying to control his jealousy any longer. Why doesn't he help?

He glared at Sergei, who smiled back. By the gods, he was annoying. He'd changed since the last time Florin had seen him. The underlying aggression that had been so much of his character had drained away. In its place there remained a sort of grotesque playfulness.

Florin decided that he hated people who were in love.

'Sergei.' The Bretonnian bit back his irritation as he sought his help. 'You're obviously fond of Katerina. Tell her why she should come back with us.'

'She will,' the strigany said without the slightest trace of his usual rancour. 'Just as soon as her tribe have defeated their enemies.'

'Defeated their…' Florin gasped with exasperation. 'Their enemy is Bashar Zog. You saw what he did to Krom's brother and his mates. That's what they're going to do to this lot, too. Why do you think Jarmoosh wants us to take her away from here? It's for her own good, you must see that.'

'Oh, I don't know,' Sergei said happily, and tweaked his beloved's nose. She giggled and wriggled against him. 'I don't care, either. If Katerina says we stay, we stay.'

Florin winced as the strigany bent down to kiss her.

'Do you have to keep doing that?' he asked, sourly. Sergei nodded happily.

'Yes,' he said.

'For Shallya's sake,' Florin muttered, and poked morosely at the fire.

'Don't look so miserable,' Katerina chided him. 'You're in a bad mood because you don't have a mate, but there must be plenty of females waiting for you at home. You're not bad.'

Somehow Katerina's analysis did little to lift the Bretonnian's mood.

'Anyway, I've got something that'll cheer you up.'

Gently disentangling herself from her lover's embrace she padded over to the battered chest that held all of her possessions. After a moment's rummaging she pulled something from inside of it.

'Here you go,' she said, tossing the bundle to Florin. He caught it, the shape strangely familiar, and gingerly peeled back the dirty rags that swaddled it.

'My gun!' he exclaimed, happy in spite of himself. 'Where did you get it?'

'Oh, one of my gnoblars stole it for me when you first arrived. But now that I like you, you can have it back.'

Florin thought about that for a moment. Then he shrugged.

'Thank you,' he said, and meant it. It felt good to have the reassuring weight of the weapon again.

'You can use it when we fight Bashar,' Katerina told him as she stepped behind Sergei. She seemed to immediately forget Florin, all of her attention now focused on rubbing the muscles that ridged Sergei's boxer's shoulders.

'So I can,' Florin said, ruefully, and tested the firing spring.

Sergei made a low groan of pleasure and looked up at Katerina with wide cow eyes.

'We'll be going then,' Florin decided hastily, and got to his feet.

A moment later the two Bretonnians emerged into the tribe's main burrow. Most of the assembled bulls ignored them. Others regarded them with hungover belligerence, or appraised them with lazy hunger. Even as more of their tribe brothers trailed in, those already here had greased the air, thickening it with the stink of their bodies and the gaseous fruits of their digestion.

Never mind, Florin considered, despite the ways his eyes had started to water. Compared to the sight of Katerina and Sergei kissing and cuddling, these monsters were as beautiful as a line of chorus girls.

* * *

WHEN DUSK HAD fallen the mountains had been no more than a ragged edge on the horizon. But now, in the space of a single night, they had grown huge, their jagged spires casting cold shadows across the sloping plain below.

Jarmoosh paused, the mist of his rhinox's breath clouding around him as he squinted at the peaks and ridges ahead. He knew them well, these features, for his tribe had hunted here often. They'd become masters of ambush in the high passes, waiting patiently as autumn drove the herds down from the far north.

There had once been another reason to bring them to these mountains, or rather to the labyrinths that twisted beneath them. It was for that that Jarmoosh had come here, the anvil upon which his strategy would be forged or broken.

The sun grew higher, banishing the shadows from the terrain ahead, and the ogre grunted with satisfaction. He could see it now. The granite spires that marked the entry to the crevasse were as clear as the horns on his rhinox's head, twin markers that told him that his navigation had been almost perfect.

Jarmoosh grunted again, this time with satisfaction, and dug his heels into his mount's flank. It lumbered into a walk, its legs swinging in a slow, steady rhythm that devoured the miles with a deceptive speed.

He waited until his form was hidden by shadow before looking behind him. He saw nothing. Even the plumes of smoke from Skabrand's many chimneys were lost in the distance.

But although he couldn't see them he knew that they were there. Bashar's trackers had been following him from the start, the smell of them a pungent tang on the wind's cold breath.

Jarmoosh wondered if they'd follow him into the mountains. He hoped not. He hoped that they'd take him for no more than a lone hunter, eager to get a couple of day's march on his rivals.

Still, no point taking any chances. He waited until the axe stroke of the crevasse had swallowed him up, the sheer walls on either side seeming to rise up to the very heavens, before stopping. His rhinox lowed with uncertainty as he swung off its back, but a word from its rider reassured the beast. Then, with a slap on her rump that was hard enough to raise a cloud of dust from her pelt, Jarmoosh drove his mount into the narrowing passageway ahead.

Only when it had turned a corner did he haul himself up to the ledge he'd chosen. It was barely as broad as he was, and as sharp with geology as with ice. Jarmoosh didn't mind. Ignoring the discomfort he wriggled himself into position, then froze.

It was thus, lying as motionless as some dead thing in the snow, that the ogre waited to see if his pursuers pursued him still.

'Wait,' Krom told them. As the other ogres fought their way out of Jarmoosh's burrow he held a meaty arm in front of the humans, pressing them back into a cavity behind the doorway.

'Good idea,' Florin agreed, his nose wrinkling as he caught a whiff of the ogre's armpit. He hadn't had any intention of doing anything else but waiting here, anyway. The butchers had returned from their council barely an hour ago, and the decision they'd brought had tipped Skabrand into chaos. The arteries of its passageways now heaved with ogres. Their boisterous voices mingled with their servants' occasional shrieks of pain as the mob ground its way up towards the surface.

Katerina frowned.

'Maybe we should go and make sure your horses are all right,' she said. Sergei nodded his agreement, but before she could lead them out into the meat grinder of Skabrand's central hall Krom held up his hand.

'Our beasts will be safe. The truce is good until we are a day's march from Skabrand's Maw. Nobody will harm them.'

Florin was glad to hear it. Even as he watched he saw a young ogre use the crudely grafted iron claw that served him as a hand to hook a gnoblar out of his way and to throw it behind him. Before it could rise, another bull, quite unaware of the doom it brought, crushed the bleeding figure beneath his iron boots.

'They're certainly in a hurry,' Florin observed.

'Someone must have rung a dinner bell,' Lorenzo told him.

Krom regarded the older man, who pretended not to notice his scrutiny.

'A dinner bell,' the ogre repeated at length, his face serious. Then, as suddenly as the snap of a noose, he bellowed with laughter.

'Very funny!'

For a moment Lorenzo was afraid that the ogre was actually going to punch him on the arm, a good-natured gesture that would probably have snapped the bone. But Krom restrained himself. Instead of a slap he offered some advice.

'You humans,' he said, face blank once more. 'You should leave. Go south. Go home. Live a while longer.'

'No.' Katerina's reply was as sharp as a whip. 'I won't leave my tribe to fight alone.'

'In that case,' Krom told her with a shrug, 'we will fight together. Jarmoosh has given me leave to join his battle line. We will die together.'

'Won't that be cosy?' Lorenzo muttered. Florin sighed miserably.

Of the three adventurers only Sergei seemed not to mind. In fact, ever since Katerina had got her hands on him, the strigany hadn't seemed to mind anything. He now spent his whole life wearing an expression of exhausted contentment.

Lucky bastard, Florin thought.

He watched a pair of bulls march past. Without breaking their stride, or even looking at each other, the two were trading blows, taking turns to pummel each other in a competition they hadn't had time to finish.

Another half hour passed, and with it the last of the ogres. As soon as the way was clear a swarm of gnoblars

emerged to scurry after their masters like rats fleeing from
a burning barn. Occasionally one of them would cast a
covetous gaze at the horse tack and other equipment the
humans were carrying, which made Florin glad to be
armed and amongst friends. He doubted if these desperate
underlings shared even the crude forms of honour the
ogres clung to.

Krom let the last trickle of them limp away before leading his little party out into the deserted passageway. They
followed the spiralling length of the passageway, climbing
the steady rise of it up to the blinding white rectangle of
the main door.

After the long days spent underground the world above
was so bright that it was actually painfull. It was cold, too.
Colder even than Florin remembered. He stamped his feet
into the churned up snow and blew into his hands.

He blinked away the tears of cold and squinted, watching the great mass of livestock that were being driven from
another entrance. The beasts milled about, clouds of steam
rising off them as they emerged from the warmth of their
stables. Rhinoxen, bad tempered after being dragged up
here, bellowed and pushed against each other.

Florin peered through the shifting herd, trying to catch
sight of their horses. But before he did Sergei, put his
thumbs into his mouth and gave a shrill whistle, the sound
sharp enough to pierce the clean winter air like a needle
through cloth.

A moment later, trotting nervously through its towering
stable mates, Sergei's horse came trotting towards them, its
fellows following.

'Oh, you are clever,' Katerina cooed and hugged the strigany.

Florin thought that he was going to be sick. Instead, he
greeted his horse, letting Nelly nuzzle his hand before he
got down to strapping on her tack.

'Good girl,' he told her, and slid the saddle onto her
back. The belt that held it was tight; in the week they'd
been underground she'd managed to get fatter, regaining

the weight she'd lost on the way here. A moment later, Florin swung himself up onto her back.

I felt good to be in the saddle again. Good to be at eye level with the ogres, and to be able to study the distant horizons.

Nelly turned, and man and horse both gazed wistfully to the south. That way lay the caravan road. The path back to civilization, such as it was.

Florin wasted a moment on an idle daydream which involved tying Katerina up, throwing her over a horse, and taking her back there against her will.

He might have tried it, too, if it hadn't been for Sergei. The Bretonnian sighed, resigned to the fact that if he and Lorenzo left now, they would leave alone.

So, one more fight, he thought. So be it.

He'd be damned if there'd be any heroics from him, though. The quicker the ogres slaughtered each other, the happier he'd be. He'd keep an eye on the girl, of course, but that was it. When these savages got down to it there was no way he was going to get in between them. Not even to help Krom.

No way at all.

THE SCOUTS THAT had followed Jarmoosh hadn't hurried. They had no reason to. Their orders had been to make sure that he didn't return to aid his fellows, that was all. So, as long as the lone bull kept going, they weren't going to risk their skinny green necks by annoying him.

If there had been more of the wolf riders they might have thought differently. If nothing else, the ogre's rhinox looked fat and juicy, good eating in these hungry months.

But there were only four of the scouts, and even with the help of their wolves that wasn't enough to make for an easy fight. That was why they made it all the way to the mountains before the greenskins began to squabble.

The argument had been started by the two who had the least winter clothing. They had wanted to return to the main body of their army, there to wait amongst Bashar

Zog's ranks. That way they'd be on hand for their share in the spoils of victory.

Their comrades jeered at the stupidity of the suggestion. Why risk getting involved in the fighting? Their orders gave them the perfect excuse to stay safely away from the battle-field. There'd be plenty of time to collect loot afterwards.

Not the best of it, though, their comrades argued. The best of it would be taken by those with the nerve to follow the ogres closely.

But, the pair with fur cloaks argued, those that followed the ogres closely would be in no position to defend their acquisitions. Especially from those who'd had the sense to keep themselves safe and rested.

The argument would have lasted until dusk if the wolves hadn't grown weary of standing in the snow. Even as their riders bickered they'd followed the lead of the alpha male. Ignoring the squeak of the goblin that clung to its back it turned and loped into the dark fastness of the mountains ahead, the smell of prey rich in its nostrils.

The smell grew stronger as it threaded its way through the boulders and snow drifts that littered the narrowing crevasse. The wolf began to slaver, and picked up its pace.

That was when Jarmoosh pounced.

His attack was perfectly timed. Before his victims even knew that they were under attack the ogre's iron-shod heels had snapped the spine of the last wolf in the line, and his fists had decapitated its rider with a savage twist.

The three survivors squealed with terror as Jarmoosh, roaring like a tsunami, hurled the head at them. It flew through their ranks like a grisly comet, the dead goblin's terrified expression trailing a splatter of blood behind it.

The wolves panicked. Tucking their tails in between their legs like whipped dogs they turned and bolted, howling with dismay as they fled from the ogre and into the depths of the crevasse.

Jarmoosh licked the blood off of his hands and smiled after the fleeing shapes. There was no escape for them that way. Barely a mile ahead the stone walls closed in as tightly as a noose. It was there, when they were packed and crushed together, that he would slaughter them.

Reaching behind him, the ogre unslung his cleaver and paced after his prey.

It seemed he would have some gifts to bring to those he sought after all.

THE TRIBES WANDERED across the plain in a broken line. Every couple of hundred yards the line thickened into a knot of bulls that had gathered around their tribe's totems. For the most part, though, the exodus from Skabrand was a trailing, disintegrating thing, a chaotic mob of dawdling livestock and straggling females.

For all their talk of war, the ogres reminded Florin of nothing so much as a column of refugees. The hastily bundled possessions they'd strapped to their livestock; the intermingling of males, females and mewling infants; the determination to keep on going no matter what – these and a dozen other factors gave the families that had left Skabrand the appearance of a folk already beaten.

Florin wished they were. That way he might have been able to persuade Katerina to leave.

But despite their rambling advance these ogres weren't beaten. Far from it. Although none of his hosts had told Florin exactly what their strategy was, he assumed that they'd devised one. After all, it was anticipation rather than anxiety that glittered in their eyes.

Even the females seemed to be looking forward to the fight. Florin found himself watching one such specimen with a sort of horrified fascination. Despite the freezing climate she wore little more than the males, and her bare breasts sagged over her fattened midriff like empty saddlebags.

The hulking monstrosity caught Florin looking at her. The smashed contours of her face remaining as blank as ever until, horribly, she gave him an obscene wink.

Florin swallowed and hastily looked away.

Undeterred by his reaction, nor by the infant that clung to her back like an ape to a rock face, the female began to lumber towards the Bretonnian.

To his immense relief the enemy appeared at precisely that moment. A volley of warning calls bellowed out around them, and all eyes turned to study the far horizon.

'Shallya's mercy,' Lorenzo cursed as he saw them.

Florin said nothing. A moment ago there had been nothing to see against the soft lines of the snow-covered horizon apart from the shapes of mountains, looming up in the north. But now, on all sides, the plain was studded with a profusion of figures. At this distance they looked as tiny and numerous as ants, but he had no doubts as to who they were.

'Looks like we're not alone,' Florin mused. 'Reckon they're Bashar's lot?' he asked.

'Yes.'

The voice was deep enough to make the Bretonnians jump. They turned to find that Krom had joined them.

'Oh, hello,' Florin greeted him.

The ogre nodded.

'So, Krom,' the Bretonnian asked, determined not to be put off. 'We're outnumbered and surrounded. What strategy will we pursue?'

'We march,' the ogre answered.

'And what will happen when we stop marching?'

'We will fight.'

Despite the intimidating bulk of his strange comrade, Florin felt his temper starting to rise.

'Yes, but in what formation will we fight?' he demanded, determined to extract a useful answer for a change.

Krom turned the full blast of his crystalline grin on the human. Quartz and saliva glinted in the sunlight, the dazzling display marred only by the scraps of rotten meat that remained trapped between the teeth.

'We will fight by tribes,' the ogre told him. 'You will wait behind me, and I will fight beside Jarmoosh's tribe brothers.'

Florin opened his mouth to try again, but Krom held up his hand.

'Don't ask me any more,' he rumbled, the tone of his voice deepening as though in unspoken threat. 'You don't need to know any more.'

The Bretonnian shrugged, unsure as to whether he felt better or not. On the one hand, it did seem that the tribes had some idea of what they were doing. On the other, battles were terrifying enough when you were in command; being driven into them as blindly as a boar into a slaughterhouse was even worse.

He looked towards the distant shapes of the enemy again. Perhaps it was his imagination, but they already looked bigger.

Florin decided to risk Krom's wrath by asking one more question.

'When do you think we will fight?'

The ogre remained silent for a moment, turning the question over as thoroughly as a cow chewing the cud.

At length he decided to answer.

'At the mountains,' he said, nodding towards the jagged heights ahead. 'When we reach the mountains, they will close in on us, there to break us.'

Ranald's teeth, Florin thought, why did he have to tell me that?

THE MOUNTAINS GREW taller, as if nourished by the light of the afternoon sun. That, Florin decided, was probably a good thing. There was no longer any doubt that the two horns of the enemy were closing in on them. Flashes of armour gleamed from amongst their marching columns, mute threats made of accidental semaphore.

For the first time Florin began to wonder what facing ogres in combat would be like, and a burst of fear exploded within his stomach. Nervously, scarcely aware that he was doing it, he checked that his pistol was charged, then edged his horse closer to Lorenzo's.

'Remember Lustria?' he said, trying to bolster his confidence with the memory of past victories.

But Lorenzo was of a different frame of mind.

'I was trying not to think about it,' he grumbled. 'Why dwell on that bloodbath when we're about to walk into another one? Still, at least in the jungle it wasn't this damned cold. I haven't been able to feel my toes for an hour. And this wind is sharper than a wife's tongue.'

'Never mind,' Florin said. 'We're almost to the mountains now, so it won't be long before Bashar's boys put an end to all of our worries.'

Lorenzo sniggered at the gallows humour.

'Of course,' he said, and spat into the snow. 'Silly me. I don't know what I was worrying about. Must be getting senile.'

'It's been a long time coming,' Florin agreed. Lorenzo, for once at a loss for words, just nodded to the two figures who rode ahead of them.

'Sergei and his beloved don't seem overly worried, either,' he said.

And Florin had to admit, to himself at least, that they didn't. Riding together so close that their knees touched, they were actually holding hands. Holding hands! What's more, Sergei seemed as happy to be listening to Katerina as she was to be talking.

'What a pair,' the Bretonnian said, a hint of genuine admiration creeping into his voice.

He watched the stubbled lump of the strigany's crown as he leant over to kiss Katerina. To his surprise he felt not jealousy, but pity. A battle was no place to be with your woman.

Especially not one as dear as this wench was to Sergei.

For the thousandth time Florin tried to work out how to persuade Katerina to leave this mess and to flee south, but even as he plotted he knew that it was an idle exercise. They were trapped on all sides now, and the enemy was tightening his grip with a boa's determination. The best they could hope to do was to wait for the confusion of defeat, and then slip away.

Katerina giggled, the laughter as carefree as a child at play. Florin pursed his lips and looked again at the murderous hosts that were closing in on them. The ugly smears of their inhuman faces could just about be seen now, the brutal features of a brutal race.

They would be glad to hear Katerina's voice twisted into a scream of pain, he knew. Glad to see her smooth flesh torn apart, and crammed into their stinking maws as though it were worth no more than salt pork.

Filthy animals, he thought, and for the first time since the enemy had appeared he felt something apart from fear.

What he felt now was hatred.

He fed his rage as eagerly as a man feeds the flames of a fire on a cold night. The anxiety that had haunted him slipped away, and he glared across the mile or so of frozen wilderness that separated the two forces.

There weren't just ogres, he realised. There were goblins too. Just as the tribe's own greenskins trailed along behind them, so it was with Bashar's forces. Even as he watched a huge mob of the nasty things appeared from over a distant ridge, sticking as closely together as a cloud of locusts as they followed their allies to war.

Florin observed them with a cold disinterest. Only the hulking ogres concerned him now, and his trigger finger itched. A thin smile spread across his hardening features as he imagined what a bullet would do to their misshapen skulls, and he blessed his own wisdom in choosing this weapon.

With a pistol in his hand, the ogres' great size would become their greatest weakness.

The brightness bled out of the day, and Florin looked up to the mountains that had blotted out the sun. The two spires thrust upwards in an obscene salute. The Bretonnian wondered if they were an omen.

But before he could brood upon it too much a series of bellowed orders rolled back through their ranks and the column divided. Each tribe headed towards the sheer face of rock ahead, there to turn their backs towards the safety of its granite fastness.

As Jarmoosh's tribe, now led by Butcher Yitshak, marched to its station Florin noticed the crevasse that divided the two flanks of this makeshift army. It seemed a waste to ignore such a narrow defile; if they fought there Bashar's superior numbers wouldn't count for much.

'Krom,' He told the ogre as he led them to Jarmoosh's standard. 'I have an idea.'

'What is it?'

So Florin told him.

When the ogre started to laugh Florin's rage became so great that he almost began to look forward to the battle.

By the gods, he thought as the tribe ranked up, I hate ogres.

JARMOOSH HAD MADE short work of the wolves. Ignoring the sting of their teeth he'd slashed their legs from beneath them, crippling all three with a single blow. Then he'd gone back, crushing the skull of each with a workmanlike deliberation. Whilst he'd been doing that, the goblins had tried to escape.

They hadn't tried hard enough.

Within a hundred paces Jarmoosh had caught the slowest. It was trying to climb the sheer face of the crevasse, its claws scraping uselessly against the basalt, and the ogre plucked its scrabbling form off of the rock face like a toadstool from a cave wall. His instinct, and his intention, had been to snap its neck there and then. But even as he had felt for the knuckles of its twisting spine inspiration had struck.

Of course, he thought! Why didn't I see it earlier?

Jarmoosh was so awed by his sudden stroke of genius that he almost dropped the goblin. With a grunt he brought his attention back to its squirming body and, ignoring the shrieking, he knotted a noose of rawhide around its bony ankles. Then he slung it across his shoulder like a stolen lamb and raced away after the others.

It was a matter of seconds before he'd caught the next greenskin. Letting it sink its needle teeth into the meat of his hand Jarmoosh quickly tied it up, barely tightening the knot before thundering off after the final scout.

The final goblin urinated in pure terror as it turned to find the ogre bearing down on it. Panicking, it rolled into a gap in the rock and tried to squirm through. But Jarmoosh was too quick. A dozen heartbeats later he'd dragged its struggling form out from under the rock, so that now he had three goblins twisting and whining behind him.

Jarmoosh checked the bonds that held their feet, and decided to fasten their hands too. He worked carefully, taking a surgeon's care not to damage them as he knotted more strips of rawhide around their wrists.

Finally he stood back, content with his work. He watched them for a while as they writhed around on the icy floor of the crevasse, and when he was sure the bonds would hold he dragged them back to the ruined bodies of their mounts.

Beyond the furry carcasses the crevasse seemed to end in a sheer rock wall. Black ice smoothed its surface, giving the old basalt a smooth lustre, although the stone beneath looked strangely tortured. It seemed to be dented, knocked out of shape like the bottom of an old copper pot.

Jarmoosh eyed it warily as he tidied his victims into two heaps. He made one of the dead, the wolves' bodies already stiffening into rigor mortis, and another of the living, who were already arguing. Then he stepped forward, pulled an iron bound club from his belt, and struck the ice-covered rock.

Although the ogre threw all of his massive weight into the attack, the result was disappointing. No more than a few splinters of ice and rock sheared away from the cliff face, and the shrapnel flecked Jarmoosh's skin with pinpricks of blood. Undeterred by this the ogre swung the club back and tried again. And again.

The goblins cringed with fresh terror at this evidence of their captor's insanity. It seemed that he was intent on making war against the very mountain, a war which he would surely lose. That wouldn't have mattered, but they knew from bitter experience how ogres took defeat.

Or rather, who they took it out on.

Jarmoosh continued banging against the stone with the frenzied energy of a wasp banging against a pane of glass. There was nothing half-hearted about the effort. Despite the chill of the air sweat oiled his rolling muscles, and the veins bulged beneath his skin like hawsers.

The onslaught continued for a dozen blows. Exactly a dozen. After the last of them had rung out, Jarmoosh stood back, wiped the back of his hand across his damp fore-head, and waited.

There was a single breathless moment, just long enough for him to worry that he might have been mistaken. But then the mountain began to crack.

It was like watching the surface of a frozen lake when the mirage of its marble solidity is shattered, when a cantering hoof or a falling branch shows that its iron hide can be fractured as easily as an eggshell.

The sheer face of stone broke just as easily now. Tiny lines, none of them wider than a single hair, raced across it in sudden tattoos.

Unlike a thawing lake, though, this fragmentation was no accident of nature. There was no messy, jigsaw disinte-gration here. Instead the basalt cracked open with the geometrical precision of clockwork, the rock opening rather than a shattering.

The process was over almost as soon as it had begun. Behind it left the outline of a vast, featureless door.

Jarmoosh took a long, shuddering breath. He looked at his club, hefting it in his hand before reluctantly placing it on the ground. His cleaver followed, and the steel spike he carried within his boot.

The ogre regarded his weapons, his face blank with thought. Then he sighed unhappily, and reached around to the small of his back to untie his gut plate. Checking that the bundle of rags he carried in his belt hadn't been dis-lodged he gave the vast steel bowl a last wistful look, then propped it up besides his weapons. His paunch was pale compared to the rest of his skin, although impressively heavy.

With a silent prayer that it would be impressive enough, Jarmoosh grabbed hold of the wolves' tails and pushed against the centre of the door.

It swung open, the movement as smoothly silent as a cat in the night. Jarmoosh gazed into the pitch blackness beyond. Then he took another deep breath, thrust out his gut, and strode into the abyss that awaited.

For the first few feet his way was lit by the light that spilled in from the doorway. But as he advanced it faded away, diluted to nothing by the immensity of the darkness here.

The ogre closed his eyes and listened to the ring of his footsteps. They echoed off distant cavern walls, the only sound to be heard apart from the slither of the carrion he'd brought with him. Even the wind had fallen silent, as though it had been unwilling to follow him into this sunless pit.

Jarmoosh marched on, only stopping when the silver rectangle of the doorway had shrunk to the size of his outstretched hand. From somewhere to his left he thought he'd heard the first whispers of movement. His nose wrinkled as he sniffed the air, recognising the musty smell that thickened it. It reminded him of sickness. The worst kind of sickness.

Good.

That was what he had come here for.

From the darkness there came another rustle of movement, barely louder than the hiss of blood in his ears. This time there was no mistaking it for what it was, though, and Jarmoosh was pleased. If he could hear one, he knew that there must be more. A dozen, a score... who knew how many of the things survived down here? For all Jarmoosh knew there could be a thousand of them, their twisted forms circling around him like rats around a babe. Behind him, a lank shape lurched across the light from the doorway.

Jarmoosh rolled his head to ease the tension out of his shoulders, then carried on walking. He moved slowly, confidently. He moved as though this evil-smelling realm was his own, and as though, of all the monsters within, he was the greatest.

Behind him the wolves bounced, their blood smearing the stone of the cavern floor. The smell of it wafted through the darkness, the copper tang sharp enough to rouse things that had been starving all their lives.

Jarmoosh waited until he heard the first of them lapping the trail clean before he called out.

'Brothers!' his voice boomed out once, then many times, the echoes of it volleying off distant walls and unseen heights. When the last ghosts of it finally died he listened.

The silence had returned.

'Brothers,' the ogre repeated, deepening his voice to aid the boom of the echoes. 'I have come for you!'

Again the cannonade of his declaration was followed by silence.

'Come. Taste a little of what waits for you above!'

And with that the ogre chose one the wolves and hurled it into the darkness. The thud of its stiffening form sounded in the distance, and Jarmoosh selected another. This one he threw in the opposite direction, but it didn't thud. It didn't land at all.

As he hurled the third away he heard the unmistakable squelch of flesh being torn, and the eager slurping of cold blood. There was a sudden rush of movement in the darkness as others scuttled forward to join the feast.

'Brothers, I come to take you to a feeding ground that would make the Great Maw belch.'

There was no reply to this boast. Nor was there any pause in the sounds of bones being splintered and chewed.

Jarmoosh reached to the bundle of rags he'd brought with him, each of them large enough to wrap around his head. He squinted into the darkness, and wondered if the pale blobs he could see were real or just a trick of the darkness.

The sound of the wolves being devoured died away. It was replaced by an ominous shuffling as those who'd eaten, and those who'd missed out, closed in around Jarmoosh. He opened his arms wide and lifted his jaw so that his throat was exposed.

'Smell my honesty,' he bid them and, sensing that he was blind and unarmed in the darkness, they accepted his offer.

Noses as damp as rotten tomatoes snuffled along the warmth of his veins. Slimy tongues licked the sweat from his skin. Occasionally a pair of claws would pinch, feeling the hard sinews of his muscle.

Eventually the first tentative bite came, teeth closing around one of his fingers.

Jarmoosh's response was unthinking and immediate. Despite his vulnerability he growled, the threat rumbling through those around him with the fearless belligerence of a thunderstorm.

They paused. Then they drew back.

Jarmoosh tried to ignore the rush of relief that flooded through him. His work wasn't done yet.

'So, my brothers,' he rumbled as the teeth were removed from his finger. 'Who will be the first?'

Although they were so close that he could feel the heat of their bodies on his skin, they were still no more than blurs in the darkness. The only features Jarmoosh could see were their eyes.

It wasn't just that they were black. It was more than that. Somehow their sightless orbs seemed incapable of reflecting any light, even the hint that lit this nightmare world. Instead of eyes they might have been holes cut through the fabric of this universe into some other, more terrible place.

Maybe, Jarmoosh though, they are.

'I welcome you, brother,' he said, and as gently as a midwife swaddles a newborn he wrapped a length of cloth around that hellish gaze and fastened it into a blindfold.

The monster hissed its gratitude even as it was pushed to one side by another, eager for its own preparation.

'I welcome you, brother,' Jarmoosh intoned again. It was a phrase he was to use over and over again, the sound soon becoming meaningless with repetition as he prepared these horrors for the feast that awaited them.

KATERINA SHOULD HAVE been excited, she supposed. It wasn't that she hadn't fought alongside her tribe brothers before. She had. Many was the time that Jarmoosh had sent her slinking ahead to spy on the enemy, or let her lead the tribe's gnoblars on thieving expeditions.

But this wasn't just some raid, it was a battle. A full-on, head-first contest of tribal strength that she'd hitherto only been able to dream about.

Yes, she should have been excited. But somehow all she could think about was Sergei and how wonderful he was.

She looked at him now, peering over the heads of the gnoblars that had gathered around her for safety. One of them, its eyes fixed innocently on the distant horizon, was trying to pick the strigany's pocket. Katerina decided to shout a warning, but before she could Sergei felt the thief's fingers. Without a second's hesitation he swung around, throwing all of his weight behind the punch to the thief's head.

Katerina giggled as it rolled backwards, and Tabby looked up at her quizzically.

'Poor thing,' Katerina told the sabretusk, and rubbed her behind her ears. 'You don't know what it's like to be in love, do you?'

The cat purred and rubbed against her, jealously soaking up the attention while it could.

Katerina remembered the battle and dragged her attention to the manoeuvres that were unfolding beyond their line.

They weren't very impressive. There seemed to be none of the cunning and reckless daring that made raiding such an exhilarating pursuit. Instead the tribes of Skabrand just waited, standing as patiently as megaliths beneath the shadows of the mountains.

Meanwhile the enemy approached in a long, unbroken line. The hulking shapes of their tyrants prowled amongst them, regulating their advance with threats and occasional eruptions of violence. Some of Bashar's army had already suffered their first wounds, bleeding from the clouts that their tyrants had inflicted on them from rushing forward too eagerly.

Katerina squinted at the enemy, making out individual faces amongst their massed ranks. The ogres were pierced and mutilated and tattooed, their skin decorated in the same fashions of her own tribe. Their gnoblars, the little villains indistinguishable from her own, darted between their feet or slunk along behind them with natural cowardice.

As Bashar's ogres drew nearer she could see that some of them were missing digits or limbs; they'd been given up as honourable payments, she supposed, for honourable defeats.

The enemy's warriors, she decided, could have been her own tribe brothers.

Except, of course, for the fact that they slaughtered the herds of their defeated foes, feeding them to the Great Maw in ostentatious sacrifice.

Katerina's hand dropped once more to stroke Tabby's golden fur, and for no particular reason she remembered the day that she'd found her, a kitten hiding beneath the corpse of its slain mother.

Her fingers tightened and she hugged the sabretusk to her. If Bashar won today then he'd send Tabby to the bottom of a hastily dug Great Maw. Sergei too.

'No,' she decided, as if the very fact of her will was enough to determine the outcome of the battle. 'We will win.'

Tabby squirmed away from a grip that had become uncomfortably hard, and Katerina turned to study those who waited with her. There were the gnoblars, of course, a milling crowd of them. Then there was Tabby, whose tail had begun to twitch nervously. Then there were the four men, including Florin with his gun.

A ragged enough squad, but so be it.

As the horde approached, Katerina begin to think of the best way to use her little regiment.

CHAPTER TEN

THE BATTLE BEGAN almost formally, as though it was no more than some great game. The abrupt rise of the basalt cliffs was the only advantage the ground offered, and as the tribes of Skabrand had already taken it their foes were content to line up before them. Their units remained as neatly ranked as the pieces on a chessboard as they advanced, and even this they did without any apparent urgency. Slowly, the thump of their feet as deliberate as a funeral march, they advanced.

They only stopped when their shadows had been swallowed up by the greater shadows of the mountains beyond. When the two forces had come within shouting distance Bashar Zog, Over Tyrant of the North, Mouthpiece of the Great Maw, and Destroyer of the Plains, stepped forward.

Even without the iron skin of his armour, he was a giant for his kind. The top of his metalled head rose higher than the largest bull, and his shoulders were almost as wide as a rhinox.

But most impressive of all was his gut was huge, a hemisphere of muscle and fat that thrust out before him like the ram of a war galley. Maybe it was that which gave him the courage to step forward alone. Leaving his army behind him he walked into easy bowshot and, with a slow deliberation, lifted off the steel cauldron of his helmet.

All eyes turned to the face that was revealed within. Somehow, it didn't seem right. This wasn't the face of some all-conquering tyrant. It was just the battered mug of an average bull. He looked like the sort of ogre who could have been any of Katerina's tribe brothers.

But when he spoke his voice was huge, a bellow that seemed to come from the very ground beneath his feet.

'Clans of the west,' he addressed them. 'Join me now, and live. Oppose me, and die.'

It was a simple message. And after barely a moment's hesitation it received a simple reply.

'No!' the first of the western tyrants roared. The call was taken up by his brothers, and then raced through the other tribes, lifting their voices up into joyous belligerence.

'No!'

The voices grew louder, and a stamping of feet began to shake the very earth upon which they stood. Here and there bulls overcome by bloodlust lurched forward towards Bashar. But somehow, despite the volcanic roar of their fellows' encouragement, all it took was a single glance from the over tyrant to stop them in their tracks.

Bashar waited for the first crescendo of defiance to die down before raising his hands, calling for silence as though his foes were his to command.

It was a ridiculous gesture, they told themselves... as they fell silent.

'I have your answer,' the over tyrant's voice boomed out again. 'And I promise you all a swift end.'

With that, his motions unhurried despite the proximity of his enemies, Bashar shoved his helmet back down over the bland lump of his head and strolled back to his lines.

As he turned his back the tribes of Skabrand began to chant again, the stamp of their feet shaking the frozen crust of the earth as if it were the skin of a drum. Their butchers moved amongst them, holding them in line just as the butchers on the other side were doing.

But seconds later there was no need.

IT OCCURRED TO Florin later that the attack must have been triggered by a pre-arranged signal. As soon as Bashar had stepped out of the shadow of the mountains and into the sunlight beyond, his horde had charged. They came in a single, disciplined rush, and as they attacked the sound of the tribes' defiance was drowned beneath the roar of their own battle-cry.

It was a single word, a name, a charm that had carried them to a hundred bloody victories.

'Bashar!' they bellowed, as if he were a god himself.

'Bashar!'

With the force of a herd of rhinoxen, his followers hurled themselves towards their outnumbered foe. Their onslaught seemed as elemental as the seasons, and as unstoppable as the rising tide of the sea.

Although when this tide hit the rock of the defence it was with a spray of blood, not foam.

The noise of the impact was deafening. To the roar of battle and the thunder of charging feet was added the lightning crack of steel upon steel, and the deep thunk of weapons into flesh. The stricken roared like wounded bears, whilst their comrades cheered or cursed, or laughed as the joy of bloodshed overcame them.

Incredibly, the defenders' line held. Even though Bashar's horde outnumbered them five to one, the westerners had their backs to the mountains and their flanks to their brothers.

Even so they were pushed back towards the towering rock behind them, and the hobbled rhinoxen that huddled beneath its heights. As they were pressed back they left the bloody chaff of their fallen comrades behind them, the bodies mangled under the advancing boots or set upon by packs of gnoblars.

Barely a quarter of an hour after the battle had been joined, the outcome was obvious. Inch by bloody inch Bashar's horde was grinding the tribes of Skabrand against the mountains as remorselessly as a miller grinds corn.

JARMOOSH HAD RUN out of rags with which to bind their eyes long before his task was finished. Loath to waste any who would follow him, he tore off his breeches and fashioned fresh blindfolds from the greasy cloth. When that was gone he took off his belt, carefully biting through the stitching to bind the eyes of the last few.

Only then did he shoulder his way through their slavering forms and lead them towards the chill brightness of the world beyond. Despite their size, and the quickening madness of their hunger, some hesitated when they smelt the clean breath of the air outside. After countless years spent in the stale darkness, the world above was a strange and disturbing place, even with their eyes bandaged.

But then they caught a whiff of the warm-blooded creatures that struggled in the snow beyond, and their doubts vanished.

Jarmoosh felt them surge behind him and picked up his step, hurrying out of the cavern door to seize the gnoblars that awaited him. He left one in the snow, a taster for the monstrosities that he had summoned, but he cut the bonds that held the ankles of the other two.

'Watch,' he told them unnecessarily as the depths vomited out their foul inhabitants.

The bound gnoblar was perhaps the luckiest. It saw its fate for only a moment before, their noses wrinkling and their tongues thrust out to taste the air, the monsters fell upon his screeching body and devoured it.

'Taste the blood, my brothers,' Jarmoosh said, and held up the two survivors. They writhed and struggled in his hands and, as soon as the front rank of horrors caught a whiff of them, the ogre dropped them.

They bolted back down the crevasse like rats down a sewer. Behind them the shambling horde of predators stumbled into eager pursuit.

Jarmoosh stood back as they surged past him. Despite their blindness they moved quickly, the lank stoop of their bony forms bending almost double as they loped after the fleeing gnoblars. Their limbs were spider-thin, although they had sinews of steel, and their sun-starved hides were as pale as the skin of a drowned corpse.

They stank, too, even compared to ogres. Their twisted bodies were slimed with some foul excrescence that was probably a part of their disease. It grimed the jagged ivory of their claws, mingling with the other filth that coated them to create poisons that Jarmoosh could only imagine.

Worst of all was the one unforgivable deformity that had consigned these degenerates to a life of blindness and cannibalism.

Although they had been born to ogre females, none of them had the slightest trace of a gut.

Jarmoosh watched their hideous enthusiasm as they rushed passed him, blood and ropes of saliva drooling from their gaping mouths. He felt disgust for them, yes. Every ogre did. But he also felt pity.

There but for the blessing of the Great Maw go I, he thought, and turned to follow his cursed brethren out to the battle.

SANDWICHED BETWEEN THE thinning ranks of Jarmoosh's bulls and the shifting herd of females and rhinoxen behind them, Katerina searched the carnage in front of her with a keen eye. Her blood was pounding now, bringing a flush to her cheeks that reminded Sergei of a new dawn, and the excitement lent her a diamond clarity of thought.

Although Yitshak had ordered her to stay behind their lines she wanted to fight. And in order to fight she needed an opening. A chink in the scrum that she could slip through before returning to the attack.

From beside her, the report sharp enough to cut through the pandemonium of battle, Florin's pistol fired. There was a brief whiff of acrid smoke, and a thump as one of the enemy fell backwards.

'Yes!' the Bretonnian exulted, and Katerina flashed him a brilliant smile. She knew that she'd been right to like him at their first meeting. Not that he was anywhere near as handsome as Sergei, of course.

As if reading her mind Florin turned, the terrified joy of battle burnishing his eyes. He blew her a kiss and took a deep bow.

Then he jumped back as, just in front of him, a pair of Jarmoosh's strongest bruisers were felled. The ogres that had been hacked down fell as heavily as oak trees, and the gap they left was wide enough to drive a cart through.

But before Katerina could duck through the gap Krom leapt into it. Trampling his fallen comrades bodies underfoot he swung his axe forward, exacting a bone-crunching revenge for their deaths.

Yet even as he fought, their line was pushed back further. The tribe's gnoblars, now scrabbling amongst the bodies of the rhinoxen or desperately trying to scale the rock upon which they were being crushed, began to squeal with panic.

'Don't worry!' Katerina commanded them, her voice a whip snap of savage determination. Most of the greenskins fell silent, more afraid of her than of the enemy.

Florin and Sergei exchanged a terrified grin, and the Bretonnian reloaded.

'Quite a girlfriend you've got there,' Florin yelled to Sergei, who tried not to look smug.

'Thanks.'

'We have to get her away from here,' Florin shouted even louder, raising his voice over what sounded like the boom of a distant cannon. 'When the line breaks, we'll go through. Straight through. We'll carry on out the other side and we won't stop until we reach the caravan road.'

Sergei shook his head.

'She wants to stay and fight.'

Florin opened his mouth to reply. Then he laughed bitterly.

'Fine,' he cried, outrage at the woman's unreasonableness lending him a wild courage. 'Fine. We'll stay and fight.'

Lorenzo, who'd been listening to the exchange, cursed.

'Most wenches,' he complained, as something which looked like a gnoblar flew screaming over their heads, 'want jewellery, or frocks, or new cooking pots; but not Katerina de bloody Hansebourg. Oooooooo no. She has to have glory.'

The old man spat after he said the word, as if to clean his mouth.

'She's an honourable person,' Sergei told him, but Lorenzo just rolled his eyes.

Katerina, who'd been busy comforting the rhinoxen, strode over to them. Hands on her hips, she issued her orders.

'We will wait,' she told them, 'until Krom opens up a gap in the line. Any gap. When we see it, we'll push through it, turn, and attack the enemy from the rear. Do you understand?'

Florin wasn't sure if he was amused or insulted by her arrogance. To think that a strip of a girl like this would dare to try to order him, Florin d'Artaud, hero of Lustria, into an action that was… was…

Well, it wasn't actually a bad idea.

But before he could either quarrel or agree he noticed that the noise of the battle seemed to be dying down. Not completely; the air was still tortured by the constant chorus of combat. The vanquished still bellowed, and the victors still roared. Behind them, though, a hush had fallen over the other ranks.

And into that hush came the sound of Jarmoosh's monsters.

UNLIKE NORMAL OGRES, their cursed brethren didn't roar as they charged into battle. Rather they moaned, a low whine that was as hungry and constant as the north wind. Some of them chewed on their own limbs in an effort to bite back the sound; decades of stealthy cannibalism had taught them the value of silence. For most, though, the excitement was too much.

After lives spent hunting skinny vermin and bony young-sters through the subterranean labyrinths of their prison, the smell of so much fresh blood was a promise of paradise.

They poured out of the crevasse in a stampede of slaver-ing desire. The dwindling specks of the two fleeing gnoblars were forgotten as, whimpering with hunger, they turned to the feast that had appeared beneath their noses.

With neither fanfare nor challenge the cannibals hurried to gorge themselves on the back ranks of Bashar's line.

The lull that had fallen over the battlefield was shattered by a thousand warning cries. The attackers' line, which moments before had been rolling forward to certain vic-tory, now found itself caught between the hammer of blood-crazed monstrosities and the anvil of the Western tribes.

Crushed between two foes, they did what any ogres would do.

They fought on.

It was a mistake. To their front, their surviving enemies had neither the desire nor the opportunity to give way. To the rear, their enemies were even more implacable.

It seemed that the gaunt, insect-like forms of the canni-bals were made of steel. Blades bounced over rubbery sinews or bones that shone through their emaciated hides. Even when the weapons of Bashar's followers did bite deep they were often dragged out of their owners hands, trapped by wounds that acted like grasping maws.

Worse, no matter what damage they took, these vora-cious horrors seemed not to mind. All they minded was eating, tearing great mouthfuls out of their enemies, or rending them with filth-encrusted claws.

The Easterners' line swayed between these two fronts, writhing like a serpent's spine between an ogre's fists. Then, barely a quarter of an hour after the mountains had disgorged their foul inhabitants, the army of Bashar Zog snapped.

It started on the edges, where the running was the easiest, and within moments the whole horde was in retreat. Leaving their dead trampled into the snow, and the living to suffer the appetites of their hellish brethren, the Easterners bolted. Where once there had been an army there now remained only a hundred decimated tribes, each fleeing into the icy wastes beyond.

The ogres of Skabrand jeered as their enemies fled, hurling insults at their retreating backs.

The true victors of the battle didn't call out at all, though. They just chewed and slobbered and gulped down their spoils, the fruits of their dismemberments steaming in the cold winter air.

One of them, the blue-veined marble of its skin pink beneath a smearing of gore, pulled its head from the hollowed out stomach of its victim. It lifted its blind head, sniffed, then turned and lurched towards Jarmoosh's tribe.

Florin raised his pistol, aiming between the forms of the ogres in front of him.

'Don't,' a voice snapped, and Katerina pushed the gun down.

Florin watched the gangling cannibal lurch forward quizzically, drooling blood as it opened mouth to taste the air.

'Why not?'

'Because it's cruel!'

And for the first time since he'd seen her, Florin was no longer disappointed that Katerina de Hansebourg had chosen Sergei over him.

Beautiful or not, he decided, she was obviously insane.

CHAPTER ELEVEN

'AH, MY BOY, you have made me a very proud man.'

Mordicio opened his arms, the gesture revealing the sweat which patched his tunic, and embraced Florin. The younger man tried to evade him by stepping back into the carriage which had brought them from the docks, but it was too late. The coachman had already closed the door behind him with a heavy thunk and a flash of gold from the Hansebourg crest.

'Thanks, Mordicio,' Florin wriggled from the embrace. 'It's certainly good to be back in Bordeleaux.'

'Did you enjoy the boat ride?' the money lender asked, for all the world as though he was interested.

'Not bad,' Florin said. In fact the passage between Marienburg and Bordeleaux had been a vomit-inducing roller coaster of storms and gales. But then, any voyage which didn't end in disease and wreckage was good enough for a merchant's son like him.

And at least it hadn't been as bad as their journey back from the ogres' lands to the 'civilisation' of the Empire.

'And this,' Mordicio's smile grew wider, 'must be Katerina de Hansebourg.'

Katerina, her eyes widening with amazement as she studied the palace that surrounded the courtyard, glanced at the old man. Deciding that he looked more gnoblar than human she grunted dismissively, and turned to Sergei as he clambered out of the carriage behind her.

'It's huge,' she told him. 'Look at how high the buildings are. Big enough for rhinoxen, even. I bet Tabby will like it, when we let her out of that silly cage.'

'It's a shame that the captain insisted,' Sergei said, and Katerina nodded as she pushed rudely past Mordicio to inspect the carriage horses.

'If only she hadn't hurt that fool of a sailor quite so much. Although it was his own fault for teasing her.'

Mordicio looked quizzically at Florin, who nodded.

'This is indeed Katerina de Hansebourg.'

Both men watched the heiress as she wrestled the horse's back leg up, pulled a dagger from beneath her ill-fitting petticoats, and dug a stone out of its hoof.

'That's better,' she said, patting the animal on the rump and tossing the stone away. Everybody pretended not to hear the sound of breaking glass as it smashed through a window.

'Well my boy, what do you think?' Mordicio asked, and for a moment Florin thought that he was addressing him. But then, for the first time, he noticed the character that had been skulking behind the moneylender. It might have been his shadow, or perhaps a mirror image frozen in time. The gaunt body, the sharp features, the acquisitive gleam in the eye – although the man was perhaps half a century younger than Mordicio he looked almost his double.

Poor bugger, Florin thought.

'I like her well enough,' the apparition said, bulbous eyes fastened on the flash of bare skin that showed between Katerina's laces.

'Of course you do,' Mordicio grinned. 'Oh, by the way, Florin, have you met my son, Rabin?'

His son, Florin thought. That explains it.

'It's an honour to meet you, sir,' he said and held out his hand. Rabin looked at it nervously then shook, his grip as damp and bony as a gutted fish.

'Likewise,' Rabin mumbled

'And Florin, you must come to the wedding,' Mordicio added.

'The wedding?'

'Yes, the wedding. Didn't you know? It's all been arranged. Rabin and Katerina have been affianced. I agreed it with the comtesse, before you left. It's a very good match. With my brains and her money… well, you see that Katerina's a very lucky girl.'

Florin heard Lorenzo make a small, choking noise behind him. He felt like making a small, choking sound himself.

'Rabin and Katerina want to get married?' he asked, swallowing heavily.

'Want, will, what's the difference?' the moneylender asked with a carefree shrug.

'And you and the comtesse have already agreed on it?'

Mordicio, who seldom missed a trick, looked at Florin.

'Ah, I see. Got ideas yourself have you, my boy? Ideas of grateful heiresses? I don't blame you, on my life I don't, but you'd better forget them. Katerina will marry Rabin. It was a condition of my funding the expedition.'

They watched Katerina lead Sergei over to study the stone dragon that towered up in one corner of the courtyard. She jumped onto the pedestal, her skirts falling open to reveal the creamy skin of her inner thigh.

Rabin made a small moaning sound.

'Well, if you'll pay us we'll be on our way,' Florin decided hastily.

'So soon!' Mordicio cried. 'But the comtesse will be down in a moment to thank you. She's just preparing her make-up.'

'No, no, no,' Florin said hastily. 'Tell her not to mention it. Anyway, I'm sure I'll see her later. But now I want to go and see my… my brother.'

'As you wish, as you wish.' Mordicio shrugged and pulled a small canvas bag from the pouch he wore on his belt. 'Here's the rest of your money. Count it, my boy. Make sure it's right.'

Florin contented himself with a quick glance before bidding Mordicio farewell and turning to leave.

'Katerina,' he said, snatching her hand for a quick kiss on his way to the gate. 'I'll come and see you in a day or two.'

'All right,' she nodded, and for the first time a rare shadow of doubt flickered across her face.

'Don't worry,' Lorenzo told her, squeezing her shoulder. 'Sergei will look after you.'

Her uncertainty vanished beneath a bright smile and, oblivious to Rabin's hiss of indrawn breath, she seized the strigany's hand.

'Yes, he will,' she said.

A moment later and Florin and Lorenzo had escaped from the Hansebourg's mansion. Below them, Bordeleaux rolled down towards the sea, the worst of its squalor hidden by the shadows of the setting sun. Breathing deeply of the city's familiar air the two men set off at a brisk walk.

'So,' Lorenzo said as they ducked down the first alleyway that they came to. 'Katerina and young Rabin are engaged to be married.'

'Yes,' Florin nodded.

'He seems like a nice lad.'

'No need to be sarcastic.'

They lapsed into a companionable silence as the alley emerged onto a cobbled thoroughfare. The breeze here carried with it the smell of roast pork and garlic, and they followed their noses to a tavern.

It wasn't until the serving wench had been dispatched with their orders for very, very well cooked meat that the conversation resumed.

'Not such a bad trip after all was it?' Florin winked at Lorenzo. 'With the money we got for that ivory in Grummand, combined with the rest of our payment from Mordicio, we should be able to rebuild the Lizard's Head and have it up and running in no time!'

'Why don't you call it the Ogre's Head this time?' Lorenzo said.

Silence descended as the men considered.

'About Katerina,' Lorenzo wondered. 'Do you think that we should have told Mordicio that the ship's captain has already married her off to Sergei?'

Florin pretended to think for a moment before shaking his head.

'No,' he said. 'Why spoil the surprise?'

And, unable to contain themselves any longer, the two of them began to howl with laughter.

EPILOGUE

On the plains below, summer had arrived, but up here that made little difference. Up here the ice remained as hard as the spires it sheathed, and the eternal snow filled the crevasses with a deathly silence.

For a long time the only movement in this high domain had come from the rush of the wind or the grind of the mountain's bones against each other. Recently, though, other things had ascended into the thin air of these barren peaks. Shivering and huddled they dragged themselves through the everlasting winter, their every step betraying their exhaustion.

Only one of them seemed immune to the biting elements. He was the largest amongst them, even after he had abandoned his armour, and led the bedraggled column into the mountains. With barely a shiver he elbowed his way through the snow drifts that barred their path, or dared the razor sharp ridges over which it led.

Bashar Zog now wore only the furs of a hunter. His axe he still carried, and his helmet swung at his belt as a

promise of better times to come. Even now, when all that
remained of his empire were these few followers, he knew
that this exile would be short-lived.

He knew because the Great Maw had told him. It had
spoken to him in his dreams, and told him that his fate
would be nothing so mundane as freezing or falling.

No, the god had whispered. The fate of Bashar Zog and
his followers would be much greater. It would be a thing of
legends, a tale that would live around the fires of his race
for a thousand years.

The ice that sheened his face cracked as the over tyrant
smiled, and he strode forward with renewed energy. What
feats would he perform to become part of such a legend, he
wondered. What traps and stratagems would he employ?

Only time would tell, he decided, and put the thought to
one side. For now, all he had to do was to find a new territory and start rebuilding.

EVEN AS BASHAR Zog contemplated the mystery of the spectacular fate that awaited him, one of his followers had met
his own. The bite mark that had been inflicted on him during the battle had never quite healed, and for the past
week, heat had been bleeding from the wound as well as
suffering from gangrene.

When the stricken bruiser lay down in the snow to die he
did it with relief, accepting the comfort of death almost as
soon as the crystals crunched beneath him.

By the time the footprints of his comrades had been
scoured away by the wind, he was as lifeless as any of the
other frozen sculptures that shaped this world. He would
have rested for centuries if another bundled shape hadn't
stumbled across him.

This was another ogre, his form unmistakable even
within the mess of furs he wore. His face blank beneath a
shapeless fur hood he examined the corpse for a moment,
then kicked it over and squatted down besides it.

There was a flash of steel, a spill of guts and the figure
began to feed. For a while the slurp and crunch of raw meat

rivalled the hungry whine of the wind. Then, with an avalanche of a belch, the ogre finished its repast.

It struggled back to its feet and licked the blood from its lips, the gesture revealing quartz teeth stained pink with blood. Even more cheering than the meal was the thought that, if his prey were willing to leave good meat in their wake, then they didn't know that they were being followed.

Good.

The bloodstained ogre didn't yet know how he was going to inflict his vengeance on Zog's tribe. He just knew that he would inflict it, and that it would be terrible.

With this happy thought Krom turned his face into the quickening blizzard and, with a final burp, set off after his prey.

ABOUT THE AUTHOR

Robert Earl graduated from Keele University in 1994, after which he started a career in sales. Three years later though, he'd had more than enough of that and since then he has been working, living and travelling in the Balkans and the Middle East.

Robert is currently back in the UK with his Romanian wife (who is still giving him hell for using her brothers' names in the *Inferno!* story 'The Vampire Hunters'). His first Warhammer novel was *The Burning Shore*. *Wild Kingdoms* is his second novel.